One Hot Murder

Center Point
Large Print

Also by Lorraine Bartlett and available from
Center Point Large Print:

A Crafty Killing
The Walled Flower

**This Large Print Book carries the
Seal of Approval of N.A.V.H.**

One Hot Murder

LORRAINE BARTLETT

CENTER POINT LARGE PRINT
THORNDIKE, MAINE

This Center Point Large Print edition
is published in the year 2013 by arrangement with
The Berkley Publishing Group,
a member of Penguin Group (USA) Inc.

The text of this Large Print edition is unabridged.
In other aspects, this book may vary
from the original edition.
Printed in the United States of America
on permanent paper.
Set in 16-point Times New Roman type.

ISBN: 978-1-61173-677-9

Library of Congress Cataloging-in-Publication Data

Bartlett, L. L. (Lorraine L.)
One hot murder / Lorraine Bartlett. — Center Point Large Print edition.
pages cm
ISBN 978-1-61173-677-9 (Library binding : alk. paper)
1. Summer—Fiction. 2. Fire investigation—Fiction.
3. Murder—Investigation—Fiction. 4. Large type books. I. Title.
PS3602.A83955O54 2013
813′.6—dc23
                                                        2012046426

For my "niece" Sophie Stanley

Acknowledgments

Whenever I come to a snag in my writing, I always seem to know someone with the appropriate expertise. My thanks go to my favorite landlady, Liz Eng, for sharing her knowledge of rental properties. I consulted author Kathryn Shay for information on firefighters. Krista Davis and Wendy Lyn Watson gave me legal advice, and Pamela James came up with the title. Steve Betlem of John Betlem Heating and Cooling shared his knowledge of HVAC systems and let me know what I could and could not do with them.

Thanks also go to my wonderful editor, Tom Colgan, and the world's best agent, Jessica Faust.

Most of all, I'd like to thank my husband, Frank, who supports me in everything I do.

To learn more about the Victoria Square Mysteries, and find more of Katie's recipes, I hope you'll visit my website, www.Lorraine Bartlett.com, and consider signing up for my periodically e-mailed newsletter.

One

When the idea came to Katie Bonner to live over her boyfriend's pizza parlor, it seemed like a great one. And it was. In April and May—and even early June. The heat radiating from the pizza ovens kept her tiny apartment warm and cozy.

And then came July and things got sticky. Literally.

I'll get a window air conditioner, Katie thought to herself, and then discovered that while the pizzeria could handle the electrical load from a large AC unit out back, the circuit panel in her apartment could not.

Did her landlord/boyfriend, Andy Rust, want to upgrade it?

Um . . . no.

Had that caused friction between them?

Definitely.

It was a sultry Saturday evening and twilight was about to fall as Katie gazed out the apartment's front window overlooking Victoria Square. The air was stifling in her tiny apartment. So much so that she'd only picked at the cold salad she'd bought at the local grocery store, since she hadn't felt like cooking. The oscillating fan on a stand circulated the air around her, but did nothing to actually lower the room's oppressive temperature. Her two cats, Della and Mason, didn't seem to mind the heat at all, or at least they didn't show it—except for the inordinate amount of hair they seemed to shed on the rugs and every piece of upholstered furniture. Katie was glad she had a vacuum cleaner with a hose attachment. The cats would sack out on the cool ceramic tile in the bathroom and purr contentedly when she went in to check on them.

She sighed as she stared at the old Webster mansion on the opposite end of Victoria Square, the quaint shopping district within the village of McKinlay Mill, New York. For years she'd had her eye on buying the old house in hopes of turning it into The English Ivy Inn. Instead, her late husband had taken everything they had saved to buy the building and invested it in Artisans Alley, a going concern that was quickly going downhill. Chad had died in a car accident less than a year later. Ezra Hilton, the Alley's manager, had followed him in death some seven months after that. Katie had inherited a majority interest in the artisans arcade and became its rather reluctant manager.

She sighed once more as she studied the old Victorian home. For years she'd pictured it restored to its former glory, from the outside color scheme to the redecoration of every room within. Years ago the house had been split into apartments, so it had six bathrooms that would make perfect on-suites. She even hung on to a storage unit filled with antique furniture and collectibles meant to fill each room, despite the pain of writing a check every month to pay for it.

Katie had had big plans for The English Ivy Inn. Not only would she host sumptuous breakfasts for her guests, but also put on teas in the afternoon—for wedding and baby showers, as well as birthday and anniversary teas. And she wouldn't have been in competition with the Square's tea shop, as she intended them to be for special groups or her guests, and not open to the public at large.

At least, that had been her intent—something she hadn't been able to give up on. After all, what was life worth without hopes and dreams?

For now, she'd just have to be content hosting Artisans Alley's Christmas in July potluck dinner. During the holiday season, everyone was too busy working or celebrating with their own families, so it was decided that the Alley's vendors would party after the Fourth of July holiday. It was to be an after-hours cookout in the Square's parking lot. A record heat wave had hit the area and didn't want to dissipate. She could pray for a little of the snow western New York is so famous for, but she didn't think it would happen.

Her gaze traveled back to the old Webster

mansion. *You're a fool, my girl. You'll never get the inn, even if it is up for sale once again.* Yet no one seemed in a hurry to buy the old place, and that suited Katie just fine.

She pulled at the sweaty collar of her yellow Artisans Alley T-shirt, wondering if she should take a walk to the strip mall and the seasonal ice cream stand there. Hot as it was, it had to be cooler outside than in. And one triple vanilla cone rolled in slivered almonds would make her feel a lot cooler—at least for the five or so minutes it would take to eat it.

She glanced out the window one last time. Though it needed so much work before it could become habitable once again, gazing at the old Webster mansion never bored her. But this time it wasn't the mansion that caught her attention. The south side of Victoria Square seemed to glow in the gathering twilight, and it wasn't from the warm feelings she felt for the lovely shopping district.

"Good Lord!" Katie cried and jumped to her feet. "The Square's on fire!"

Grabbing her cell phone, she ran for the stairs, flew down them, but paused at the front of the pizzeria and yanked open the door. Andy stood in front of one of the ovens with a long-handled wooden paddle in hand loaded with a large pizza.

"Andy—the Square's on fire—the Square's on fire!" she hollered and turned, letting go of the door. She punched in 911 and started running east toward the end of the Square, where a trail of smoke rose from the back of one of the shops—Wood U.

The dispatcher came on the line.

"There's a fire on Victoria Square—send the fire department fast!"

"Address, please?"

Katie's mind whirled. "I don't know. Number five—or six—or maybe seven Victoria Square in McKinlay Mill. Please, send someone fast!"

She halted in front of Wood U—a shop specializing in wooden gifts and small furniture—and took in the sight. From this vantage point, there seemed to be more smoke than actual fire. Maybe the fire department could save it, or at least contain the blaze before it spread to the other shops—or worse, to the old, tinder-dry Webster mansion, which was its closest neighbor.

Luckily the fire department wasn't more than a couple of blocks from Victoria Square, and soon Katie heard the piercing wail of sirens as two fire trucks and a rescue squad pulled into Victoria Square. With all the shops closed for the day, there was plenty of room for them to spread out. Eight firefighters spilled from the trucks, grabbed hoses, and hooked them to two of the hydrants in the Square, while their chief and another fire-fighter ascertained where best to approach the blaze.

"Can you save it? Can you save it?" Katie called, but the men were too intent on their work to answer her.

A Sheriff's Office cruiser pulled up about the same time as the first of the rubberneckers arrived to watch the show. One of them called and waved a hand to capture Katie's attention.

"Good heavens," Gilda Ringwald-Stratton called, her face flushed from running from her store, Gilda's Gourmet Baskets. Trust Gilda to still be working at this hour. "Is Dennis inside?" she asked, her eyes flashing with worry.

Dennis Wheeler owned Wood U. During the school year, his wife, Abby, took care of the store when he was at work as the industrial arts teacher at McKinlay Mill High School. He took care of it during the summers—or at least that had been their arrangement. Now that Dennis had retired from teaching, he wasn't sure what they were doing. Like most of the businesses on Victoria Square, the store should have been closed at this time of the evening—with no one inside. At least, Katie hoped so.

"Maybe one of us should call their house to make sure," Gilda suggested. "I've got the Merchants Association member list in my store."

"You do that. I'm sure they'll be heartsick to learn there's been a fire. But at least if it's one of the merchants who tells them, it might come as less of a shock."

12

Gilda nodded. "I'll be back in a few minutes," she said, and scooted back toward her store, leaving Katie to worry alone.

The smoke billowed from the back of the shop as the firefighters manned their hoses, spraying it down. Another fire truck arrived from nearby Parma. These firefighters set up a pump beside McKinlay Creek, and soon they, too, were dousing the building. Within a minute or so, they shut down their hoses and began the work of investigating what had started the fire.

"That wasn't too bad," she heard the fire chief tell one of his men.

The Square's gas lamps seemed to grow brighter as the sky darkened, and Katie moved back from the structure, hoping to get away from the stench of burned wood. Her mind was awhirl. How could this have happened? What would it mean for the Square? And what would Dennis say when he learned about the condition of his store?

Cell phone still in hand, Gilda hurried across the parking lot. She was nearly breathless when she reached Katie. "I called Abby. She's on her way."

"Was Dennis at home?"

Gilda shook her head. "She's pretty frantic. She said Dennis was working late in the shop tonight. She hadn't heard from him since he closed about six."

A little more than three hours before.

Katie bit her lip, wishing the darkness had brought a cooling breeze with it.

Gilda craned her neck to try to see what the firefighters were doing out back. "Have they come up with a cause yet?"

Katie shook her head. "I'm going to take a walk around the Square's back parking lot to see if Dennis's car is back there."

"Do you want me to come with you?" Gilda offered.

"You'd better wait here for Abby. She might need a familiar face—and maybe a shoulder to cry on."

"Hurry back," Gilda called.

The crowd of onlookers had grown considerably, and Katie had to thread her way through them. She jogged around the side of The Perfect Grape, the Square's wine shop, until she could see the back parking lot. Sure enough, Dennis Wheeler's aging green minivan was parked not far from the back of his shop, which was still crawling with firefighters.

With a heavy heart, Katie headed back to the front lot.

She had almost made it back to Gilda when a familiar gray Sebring—its horn honking frantically—made its way through the throng of onlookers. Finally the driver shoved the gearshift into Park and pulled the keys from the ignition.

She yanked open her door, jumped out, and started running toward Wood U.

Abby Wheeler's face was already red and puffy from crying. Katie picked up speed to intercept her just as she joined Gilda.

"Was Dennis inside?" Abby called, her eyes wild.

"We don't know," Gilda said.

"I'm afraid his car is still parked out back," Katie said, hating to be the bearer of bad news, but Abby would have learned the truth soon enough.

"I'm so sorry," Gilda said, patting Abby's arm.

"Just because the car is parked out back doesn't have to mean Dennis was inside," Katie said, trying to sound encouraging, although she felt anything but.

There didn't seem to be much else to say. A trembling Abby stared at the scorched building as silent tears continued to cascade down her cheeks.

Eventually the sooty fire chief exited the building and removed his face mask. "Better send for the meat wagon," he told the deputy. "We found a body inside."

Abby closed her eyes and began to sob.

"Come on, Abby. Come and sit down over here," Gilda said, and managed to turn Abby away from the building, leading her back to her car.

"Do you think it was smoke inhalation?" the deputy asked.

The chief shook his head. "Not unless he could breathe through a hole in the middle of his face."

"Murder?" Katie whispered and was instantly sorry, hoping Abby was well out of earshot.

The deputy turned to face her, his expression grim and angry. "Don't you say a word about this," he commanded.

"It'll be common knowledge by tomorrow," she said.

"Yes, but let the Sheriff's Office be the one to announce it to the world—not you."

She nodded and stepped away from the deputy.

A clatter behind her caused Katie to look up. Andy had arrived with a couple of his teenaged employees and begun to set up a folding table. Once it was up, the boys set out four large pizzas and a case of pop for the firefighters. "Just a little thank-you for saving the Square," he said, handing out napkins to the first of the guys in the helmets, heavy fireproof jackets, and boots.

Katie wandered up to stand beside Andy. "That was thoughtful of you to bring food for the firefighters."

"I'm damn grateful they put out the fire before the whole Square could go up—including my shop. And I figure it'll be a trial run for the party next Saturday." The Merchants Association members—those who owned the businesses that made up Victoria Square—had been invited to the potluck as well.

Too bad Andy wasn't as thoughtful about making Katie comfortable in her apartment and upgrading the wiring. If she used the air conditioner—which she wouldn't—*it* might start a fire. But then, he hadn't wanted to rent her the place to begin with, although she had—in her unbiased opinion—already proven to be an outstanding tenant. She swallowed down a pang of guilt. Okay, she was feeling just a little testy—but it was more directed at the heat and humidity, not at Andy.

"What's the extent of the damage?" he asked, with a nod toward the building.

"I'm not sure. From the front, it looks like mostly smoke. But they did break down the back door."

"Then there's a chance the Wheelers could reopen soon?" he asked, his tone neutral.

"That's debatable. Insurance companies are notoriously slow about paying claims. Worse than that, they found a body in there."

"Was it Dennis?" Andy asked, shocked.

"His car is parked out back, but I'm hoping it wasn't him. Maybe someone broke in and set the place afire and then couldn't get out." But not with a bullet through the brain. So far she was the only one on the Square who knew that little fact, and though she'd already decided to share

17

it with Andy, this wasn't the time or the place.

"That's not as ridiculous a theory as you might think," the chief said as he reached for a slice of pizza. "There's evidence the back door had been tampered with."

Oh no! Had Dennis surprised an armed robber who'd expected the premises to be easy pickings on a Saturday night?

Andy's brow furrowed. He bit his bottom lip and he shot a concerned glance back toward his shop. Was he thinking about missing calls from customers? Katie shrugged it off. "How long will you and your men stick around?" she asked the chief.

"We'll wait for the medical examiner and hang around long enough for the emergency closure crew to board up the place. We've already got a call in to them. They should be here at any time now."

"We'll stay out of your hair," Andy said, and snagged Katie's arm. They moved out of the way and watched as some more of the firemen arrived to scarf down pizza, while the others continued their cleanup.

Andy nodded toward Abby and Gilda still leaning against the side of Abby's car. "What about her?"

Gilda had wrapped an arm around Abby's shoulder, which still shook with wrenching sobs. "I don't know her well, so I hope maybe Gilda or another of the merchants can call a relative. I don't think she should be alone tonight."

"Are they sure the dead guy was Wheeler?" Andy asked again. There was something odd in his tone.

"No one's said. I mean, no one asked for any of us to identify the body. Maybe they make a relative do that at the morgue." Katie didn't like to think about it. She looked back at Abby and wasn't sure the poor woman could handle it.

A large truck pulled into the lot. The emergency enclosure firm. That was fast. A couple of brawny guys spilled from the cab and spoke with one of the firefighters before they went around back and started unloading plywood.

"Looks like the party is about to end," Andy said. He was right. All the pizza boxes he and his employees had brought over were now empty, and all the pop cans were gone. "I'm going to pack up my stuff and go back to the shop. I've already spent far too much time away from there."

"Are we still on for dinner on Tuesday?" Katie asked.

"Sure. Despite the fact Jim's on vacation"— the assistant manager Andy had hired after embarking on his new venture selling cinnamon buns—"I've already arranged for coverage from the guys. We'll have a nice uninterrupted dinner."

For all of an hour. But then, she'd known Andy was married to his pizza business when they started going out. Still, she'd gotten spoiled during the past few months when they'd actually gone out on some real dates—to restaurants and the occasional movie. For the most part, their relationship had worked out. And she had an ulterior motive for inviting him. Maybe if he experienced just how hot it could get in the apartment . . .

Andy leaned in and gave her a quick kiss. "Stop on by later if you get hungry."

"I will," she said, giving him a parting smile. She watched him as he rounded up his workers and gathered up his table and the remnants of the makeshift dinner he'd given the firefighters.

Katie turned back to watch the emergency enclosure crew assemble their gear, waiting for the fire chief to give them the okay to board up the smoke-stained building. Surely that couldn't happen until the medical examiner had removed the body.

Poor Dennis Wheeler. What had he done to deserve a bullet through the head?

And who had pulled the trigger?

Two

Katie had grown up in a drafty old house. Like Scarlett O'Hara vowing never to be hungry again, she'd vowed never to be cold again. After another sweltering night in the sauna disguised as her apartment, she'd be pleased to eat those words. How she longed to wear a skin of goose-flesh instead of a constant sheen of perspiration. Thank goodness the apartment's plumbing was in better shape than its electrical system. She was getting her money's worth out of the rain showerhead she'd had put in.

She knew from experience that if she didn't get to Artisans Alley early and crank up the old air-conditioning, the strain from the midday heat would kill the thing. It was practically on life support as it was. Sadly, the old building was just too big for the unit the former owner/manager, Ezra Hilton, had installed. And he must have had a shortage of funds when it came to adding the ductwork, too. Some parts of the old applesauce warehouse were cold as a freezer, while others were warm enough to bake bread—or at least several of the vendors had described it that way.

Worse yet, Katie's office was one of the areas that hadn't been graced with ductwork. She relied

21

on a junky old fan under her desk to keep her from melting into a puddle on the floor. Funny how the disgruntled vendors didn't notice that when they came to her to complain about the temperatures in their booths.

The doors to the Alley had been opened for vendor setup for less than five minutes when Katie's favorite vendor arrived for the day, appearing at her open door with a clipboard in hand.

"I was so upset when I heard the news about the fire at Wood U. Have they identified the body yet?" Rose Nash asked before she even said good morning. Thanks to the extended period of dry weather, the elderly woman hadn't worn her signature plastic headscarf for months.

Katie shook her head. "There's supposed to be a news conference later today. I suppose someone in authority will make the announcement then."

Rose shook her head. "Do you think it's Dennis?"

"As far as I know, no one has seen him since he closed the shop yesterday evening, so there's a strong possibility."

Rose shook her head again and frowned. "What will the Merchants Association do?"

Katie shrugged. "Send flowers to his widow. That's about all we *can* do."

A loud rap on the door frame caused both women to turn. "Katie, you've got to do *some-*

thing about the air-conditioning! It's stifling hot up in the loft."

Katie sighed. She'd known *that* was coming—and had guessed right about who would be the first to complain that day. Godfrey Foster had been a thorn in her side since she'd rented a booth to him some two months before. The overweight, fussy, nervous barrel of a man always seemed to be wringing his hands and sweating, even when the temperature wasn't in the nineties as it already was that day. Rings of perspiration darkened the underarms of the green golf shirt that clung to his padded torso, and his forehead was beaded with sweat. And his so-called "art" really pushed the limit of the term. Faux renditions of the masters' classic paintings made with—of all things—colored dryer lint.

He wasn't finished complaining. "I'm surprised our customers that actually make it up the stairs aren't fainting in droves. You might want to put the fire-rescue number on speed dial just in case."

Not only was Godfrey standing in the vendors' lounge, but so was Ida-with-the-giant-wart-on-her-face Mitchell. Ida was the Alley's most eccentric vendor and took care of the Alley's tag room, taping down the vendors' sales tags so they could compare them with their printed inventory of sales they received with their checks on Tuesdays. She didn't seem to be doing any-thing—just standing there, which wasn't unusual.

When she wasn't fussing over the sales tags, she could often be found just standing around, staring into space.

Katie turned her attention directly to Godfrey. "I'm sorry, but the repairman was here on Friday."

"Well, he didn't fix it."

"And he can't. The simple truth is the building is far too big for the unit we've got and there's no more money in the budget to add another unit—at least not this season."

Godfrey planted his hands on his hips. "Why not?"

Katie sighed. She was surprised he didn't stamp his foot, too. And how many times did she have to remind the vendors that she was keeping the place open under dire financial duress?

"Oh, don't be such a bore, Godfrey," Rose chided. "Unless you've got ten grand to sink into the HVAC, just shut up."

Katie, Godfrey, and Ida were all startled by Rose's outburst, although Katie was also secretly pleased. She'd been dying to tell Godfrey off for the past eight weeks.

Godfrey stood there with his mouth open, breathing in short, appalled breaths. Finally he closed it and glared at Katie. "Are you going to let this old woman speak to me like that?" he demanded.

"Rose," Katie said with a bit of a scolding lilt,

although it was difficult to keep a smile from creeping onto her lips. Rose was starting to sound a lot like her best friend, Edie Silver.

"I'm not that much older than you, Godfrey, so watch your mouth," Rose retorted.

Godfrey's mouth dropped open again, and he stood there for a good ten seconds before Rose started in on him once more. She consulted her clipboard. "I see you've signed up to come to the holiday party on Saturday night, but you neglected to add what you were bringing."

"Bringing?" Godfrey asked.

"It *is* a potluck dinner. Everyone who comes has to bring something."

"I can't cook," Godfrey said, appalled.

"Does your wife cook?" Rose pressed.

"Yes, but she's out of town."

Rose consulted her list again. "Then how about napkins? No one has signed up to bring napkins."

"I—I—"

"Napkins it is," Rose said, marking it down.

Godfrey didn't say anything more. Instead, he turned and stalked off.

Ida remained standing in the vendors' lounge, her expression still rather startled. "Can I help you with anything, Ida?" Katie asked rather pointedly. Ida was not her favorite vendor.

Ida shook her head, pivoted, and scurried away—ratlike.

Katie turned back to Rose.

"Sorry about blowing up at Godfrey like that, Katie. But that man never stops complaining," Rose said. "And we *do* need napkins for the potluck."

"I must admit I've almost lost my temper with him on a number of occasions. There always seems to be one or two vendors who refuse to be placated."

"I'm as sorry as he is to hear that the air-conditioning problem can't be easily solved," Rose said and sighed.

"No more than me. It's as hot as hell in my office. Between here and my apartment, I'm going to have to start buying antiperspirant by the case."

"Just wait a few years until you start having hot flashes," Rose warned.

"*Many* years from now, I hope."

"While you're back here cooking, it's so cold up front I have to wear a sweater when I'm working on the register. But at least it's easier to wear more clothes than to feel like you need to peel some off," Rose said. "Can't they do something about the ductwork? Rearrange it or something to disperse the cool air?"

Katie shook her head. "Not without that ten-plus grand you just mentioned. But I'm putting it on the top of my wish list for the Alley."

Rose nodded. "While you do that, I'll put the coffee on. Those of us working in arctic conditions will appreciate it. Can I bring you some?"

"I'm going to pour myself a big glass of cold water," Katie said, and hoped that the ice trays in the vendors' lounge refrigerator were still full.

Rose nodded. "I've got my work cut out for me today. I'm going to try to track down the rest of the slackers on my list and finalize the menu for the potluck. I'll get back to you on that later today. And Edie said she'd talk to you about the logistics, too."

"Great. I haven't seen her in at least a week. Where's she been hiding?"

"She's had family stuff to contend with. She'll be in either tomorrow or the next day. Oh, and she's worried about the weather on Saturday."

"So am I. If this heat wave doesn't break, we may have to cram everyone into the lobby instead of holding the picnic outside."

"At least the lobby's cool."

"But it won't be if we have to squeeze in sixty or eighty people."

"I hadn't thought of that." Rose shrugged. "I'll get the coffee going and then I need to get moving on my list before customers start arriving." She gave Katie a nod and headed for the coffeemaker.

Since Katie had left herself a long to-do list the day before, she figured she had better get started, too. She found that if she didn't make a list, tasks that needed to be completed were seldom addressed, thanks to the many distractions and interruptions she constantly contended with . . . such as Godfrey's visit.

She read through the items and had begun to prioritize the tasks when she became aware of another's presence. She looked up to find Detective Ray Davenport standing in her doorway.

"I wasn't expecting to see you—especially this early in the morning—and on a Sunday, too," Katie said. The detective had worked on two homicide cases in McKinlay Mill since Katie had taken over as manager of Artisans Alley. That she'd been involved on both occasions hadn't endeared her to the detective. "To what do I owe the pleasure?" she asked.

The detective offered a toothy grin that gave Katie the willies. "I was hoping we could talk about the murder on the Square last night. As the head of the Merchants Association, I thought you might have some insights that could help me with my investigation."

Katie blinked. A smile and now he was being . . . dare she even think it: nice! And he was asking for *her* opinions. That was a first.

"I'd be happy to help in any way I can, Detective. She gestured to her solitary guest chair. "Come in and sit down. Would you like a cup of coffee? It should be ready by now."

"That sounds nice," he said, taking the chair.

Katie stood. "How do you like it?"

"Just cream, milk, whitener—whatever you've got on hand."

She nodded. "I'll be right back."

Katie found a clean cup hanging on the rack, poured the coffee, and was doctoring it when Rose reentered the vendors' lounge to grab a cup for herself. She nodded toward Davenport, who seemed to be inspecting the ceiling in Katie's office. "What's he doing here?" she hissed.

"He wants me to help him with his case."

Rose blinked in astonishment. Davenport hadn't seemed eager to welcome Rose's or Katie's help when Rose's niece's remains had been discovered several months before. "Is he feeling all right?" She looked around Katie to stare at the detective. Davenport smiled and wiggled his fingers in a wave.

Rose quickly straightened, her mouth hanging open in surprise. Katie wondered if her own expression mirrored Rose's. Then Rose seemed to shake herself. "Do you think he could have had a ministroke or something? Maybe we should call an ambulance."

"I'll get to the bottom of all this niceness," Katie said, then finished stirring the detective's coffee, set the spoon down on the counter, and started back for her office.

Katie handed Davenport the cup, and turned to

close her office door. She turned on the fan under her desk and set it on low so they could still hear each other speak. "Sorry it's so hot in here, but our AC is on the fritz. Or rather, it never seems to filter through to my office, but I figured you probably wouldn't want any of the vendors to overhear our conversation."

"Thank you."

There he was being *nice* again. It seemed so out of character.

He took a sip of his coffee and sobered. "Before we get started, I wanted to let you know that this will be my last official case for the Sheriff's Office. I'm due to retire at the end of the week."

"Oh." Well, that explained it. "Congratulations. How many years have you been a deputy?"

"Thirty."

Ten years longer than she'd thought. "What will you do next?"

He smiled again, showing his rather yellow teeth. "A little of this, a little of that. I'm only sorry that my wife isn't here to enjoy the next few years with me. We'd made plans, and . . . well, in her honor, I'm going to carry on with them. My girls want that for me, too."

Ah, yes. Hadn't Deputy Schuler once told Katie the detective had daughters?

"That's great. I'm sure your wife would be pleased."

He nodded and looked away, misty-eyed. Katie

fought the urge to touch his arm. They weren't really friends, but it was obvious he wasn't over the loss, and once again she felt a pang of regret at losing Chad. They came at such odd moments and she wondered if she'd ever really get used to it.

She broke the quiet. "How can I help you, Detective?"

Davenport took another sip of coffee and then cleared his throat. "The autopsy on the Wood U fire's victim was set for this morning. I should have the prelim on my desk when I return to the office, but it's pretty clear this was murder."

She nodded. "I heard the fire chief say the victim had been shot in the head."

"While we believe the deceased to be the owner of the shop, Dennis Wheeler, the damage to the victim's face was too great for a visual ID."

Katie's breath caught in her throat. The fire chief had made the wound sound almost incidental. "Does that mean—"

"He was shot in the back of the head with a large-caliber gun. Probably a Magnum. The exit wound obliterated almost all the facial features, and took most of the teeth with them, so dental ID is going to be just about impossible, too."

"It sounds like whoever did it didn't want the victim to be identified at all."

"You got that right. We'll be doing DNA testing, but that could take months. Our governor was serious when he said he wanted to balance the state budget. The crime lab took a hit along with just about every other agency in the state."

"Does that mean you won't solve the case before you leave the department?"

"I'm determined to solve it, but we might not have a positive ID on the victim for some time."

"Where do you start?"

"By talking to the merchants on Victoria Square. I assume you can give me a list of everyone."

"I'd be glad to." She reached into her desk drawer, took out a folder, and withdrew a sheet of paper. She turned in her chair to place it on the platen of her all-in-one copier/printer. Seconds later she handed Davenport the copy.

"This will be a big help. Thank you." He folded the sheet and put it into the inside breast pocket of his jacket. He had to be boiling in that suit coat. With the door closed, Katie had started to sweat as well. She switched the fan's speed to its medium setting.

"Now, tell me what you know about Dennis Wheeler," Davenport said quietly.

Katie sighed. "Truthfully, I didn't know him well. He seemed perfectly nice. He always participated in our Association meetings, making good suggestions. Until recently he worked full-time at the McKinlay Mill High School as an industrial arts teacher."

"Did your late husband know him?"

Katie shrugged. "If he did, he never said so. These past few years Chad was more interested in talking about his friends here at Artisans Alley than those at school." She looked around the shabby office and again felt a pang of regret that she was stuck here instead of refurbishing the old Webster mansion. And though she felt more charitable toward the place of late, that Chad had invested their life savings in this money pit—without her knowledge or consent—still galled her.

"I'll be talking with the school principal later today to see if Wheeler had any trouble with his students."

Katie's eyes widened and she remembered Andy's expression the night before when they'd spoken about Dennis with the fire chief. He'd looked concerned. He employed boys from the high school who were considered at-risk, mentoring them to keep them out of trouble. Did he suspect one of his employees had something to do with the fire at Wood U? Surely none of those boys was capable of murder.

"Is something wrong, Mrs. Bonner?"

Katie laughed nervously. "Not at all. Just thinking."

"Was Wheeler well liked by the other merchants?" Davenport went on.

"He seemed to be."

"Was he a good businessman?"

Katie frowned. "As far as I know. Like many of the other merchants, his business seemed to pick up since . . ." To say since she took over managing Artisans Alley and became the Merchants Association president sounded self-congratulating, no matter that it was true. "Since the rebirth of Victoria Square."

Davenport nodded. "What about his wife? Do you know her?"

"Just to say hello. She rarely came to our meetings, but she seemed perfectly nice, too."

"Could they have had marital problems?"

Katie started, then realized cops always asked that question. "Not as far as I know." Abby had been awfully upset the night before. Katie couldn't imagine she'd been putting on an act.

"I'm sorry, Detective. I don't seem to be much help to you this time. I guess I'm still in shock. The other deaths I've dealt with here on Victoria Square were of people I wasn't well acquainted with. I know I just told you I didn't really know Dennis, but—he was one of *my* people. As president of the Merchants Association, I feel a certain responsibility for keeping everyone here on the Square safe. Somehow, I feel I've failed."

"Mrs. Bonner, you've always been a help. A pain in my—side . . ." Katie had the distinct impression he'd been about to mention a portion of his lower anatomy. "But always a help."

Was it cynical to wonder why he was being so

34

pleasant? Katie watched as Davenport sipped his coffee. The man must be made of strong stuff to drink hot coffee in such a small, airless room on a blistering hot day. "One last question, and then I'll stop bothering you. As far as you know, did Wheeler have any enemies?"

Katie shook her head, but her thoughts went back to Andy's employees. Her husband had a few troublemakers in his classes over the years. One of them had been vindictive after Chad had failed him for the year, slashing the tires on his car. Insurance had covered it, but the boy was unrepentant, and though he admitted he'd done the deed, Chad had no tangible proof and they had both taken care where they parked their vehicles after the incident. Could Dennis have had a similar experience?

Davenport drained his cup and stood. "Thank you for speaking with me today, Mrs. Bonner."

Katie stood as well. "You're welcome." He was still being nice, and she felt obliged to return the favor. "When will you be speaking with the rest of the merchants?"

"That's next on my list of things to do."

"Since The Perfect Grape is the closest shop to Artisans Alley, I'd be glad to introduce you to Conrad Stratton, or have you already met him?"

"I don't believe I have. And thank you, I'd appreciate it."

"I'll walk you over," she said and opened her office door, startled to find Godfrey Foster bent over, as though he'd been listening to their conversation. "Can I help you?" Katie asked rather sharply.

"Uh . . . I just came from the washroom and noticed my shoe was untied," Godfrey said and laughed nervously. Katie looked down. Sure enough, the laces of his left shoe had come undone. He shuffled away from the door, put his foot on one of the chairs around the table in the vendors' lounge, and tied it.

Katie and Davenport cut through the lounge and, ignoring the lint art vendor, started for the side door. Artisans Alley wouldn't be opening for at least another hour, and neither would the other shops and boutiques that ringed Victoria Square, but Katie was pretty sure Conrad would already be at The Perfect Grape. He liked to dust the wine bottles and make sure everything was shipshape before opening each day.

She and Davenport walked across the already hot tarmac in amiable silence. The lights were on in the wine shop, although the sign that hung in the window said CLOSED. Katie knocked on the glass. Conrad looked up from the paperwork spread across his sales counter, smiled, and hurried to the door. "Can I help you Katie?" he greeted her.

"Conrad, this is Detective Davenport with the

Sheriff's Office. He'd like to ask you some questions about Dennis Wheeler."

Conrad shook his head and tsked. "Poor man, poor man." He offered his hand and Davenport shook it. "Please, come in. Will you be staying, too, Katie?"

Katie noticed movement at the end of the Square, recognizing the car that had just pulled into the lot. "No. I have some other business to attend to. Nice seeing you. And if you have any other questions, Detective, feel free to call me."

"I will," he said, and allowed Conrad to usher him into The Perfect Grape.

Katie knew she shouldn't pay attention to what was happening at the other end of Victoria Square. She should just mind her own business and get back to work. But instead of heading back to her office, Katie turned north toward the old Webster mansion. Something was up, and she was determined to find out just what.

Three

With hammer in hand, Fred Cunningham, of Cunningham Realty, climbed out from behind the wheel of his Cadillac. That could only mean one thing: The FOR SALE sign would be coming down. Someone had bought the old Webster mansion. Again.

Katie hightailed it across the parking lot. By the time she arrived at the old Victorian mansion, Fred was already removing the nails from the sign that had hung on the porch column for the past three months.

Katie slowed down and walked the last twenty feet. Once again her dream of owning the old place had evaporated. "Who bought it this time?" she asked, fighting the urge to cry. "Anyone I know?"

Fred turned. He'd left his sports jacket and tie in the car. Despite the hour, his white, short-sleeved dress shirt looked wrinkled and damp— just like she felt. "I figured I'd see you today. You have an uncanny knack for showing up whenever I come to take down this sign. And no, I don't think you know the new owners."

"When will they be taking possession of the old place?"

"Tomorrow."

"So soon?" she asked.

Fred nodded. "A couple of gentlemen from Boston. Or at least one of them is originally from Boston. The other is a McKinlay Mill native, Nick Farrell. He and his partner are relocating to the area so they can take care of an ailing relative."

"And they just happened to want to buy *my* inn."

"Katie," Fred admonished, "I know you love

this old place and you wish it was *you* taking stewardship, but the fact is you—"

"Can't afford it and never will," she finished for him.

Fred shook his head sadly. She didn't want his pity. She wanted that house!

"You'd better tell me everything. I'd rather know what's coming than waste time guessing and brooding about it," she admitted.

Fred's lips quirked into a smile. "They've had an architect go through the place, and they've hired a contractor who'll start work the day after closing."

"That quick?"

"They're motivated to open the place by Thanksgiving. They want to take advantage of Victoria Square's Dickens Festival. They've already booked a wedding for New Year's Eve."

"What?" she cried. How could they book a wedding when they didn't even legally own the place?

Fred's smile widened. "Apparently it's the daughter of a friend. They plan to do a lot of weddings—and even have plans for a wedding suite up on the top floor."

"Swell," Katie groused. She'd planned the very same thing.

Fred turned back to the sign and yanked out another nail. "That's not the only change coming to Victoria Square."

Katie wasn't sure she could take any more good (or was it bad?) news and felt like leaning against the weatherworn picket fence, but knew it would probably topple over, taking her with it. "What do you mean?"

"I closed the deal on another property just last month . . . well before the fire."

Katie blinked. "On Wood U? I didn't even know it had been up for sale. Just the building or the business, too?"

"Both." He shook his head and frowned. "I feel bad for the new owner."

"Who bought it?"

"I've been asked not to divulge that information."

Hmm. Just because he wouldn't say didn't mean she couldn't find out. The deed would be filed with the county clerk . . . eventually. She'd have to schedule a trip to the local tax assessor's office. It would certainly be on file there, too. Then again, did she really care all that much? Not personally, but . . . since she was the head of the Merchants Association, it behooved her to find out.

"How long had it been up for sale?"

"It wasn't. The new owner approached me to intercede. I asked Dennis if he'd consider selling and he jumped at the chance."

Katie frowned. "I thought he was happy in his work."

Fred shrugged.

"Did you know about the fire?" Katie asked.

Fred glanced at the boarded-up building. Yellow crime tape hung limply from its front façade. "Oh, yeah, I heard."

"So what happens to the business? I mean, I saw Dennis working there yesterday, still acting like he owned the place."

"The new owner wasn't prepared to take over the business for a while. He hired Dennis to stay on and run it, at least until the end of summer."

"And now Dennis has been murdered."

"Another reason the new owner doesn't want a lot of bad publicity. As it is, he's got to wait for his insurance company to assess the damage so he can make a claim. He wants to reopen before—"

"Yeah, yeah," Katie cut him off. "Thanksgiving, so he can take advantage of the increased traffic during the Square's Dickens Festival."

Fred wrenched the last nail from the sign and pulled it down. "What's good for the Square is good for Artisans Alley," he reminded her. "And how are things going?"

"They'd be better if the old place didn't double as an oven."

"How long will it be before you can improve your HVAC systems?"

"Forever."

"Now, Katie," Fred chided.

"I could take out another loan, but I really don't want to. I'd like to pay myself a decent salary one day, and maybe put aside a few dollars for retirement." She shook her head.

"Correct me if I'm wrong, but you've already bought out your partner and paid off a big chunk of the debt on the old place."

She grudgingly nodded.

"How many empty vendor spaces do you have?"

"Four."

"Which means you've got sixteen more vendors than you had when you took over. You've rented out two of the four empty shops in the front of the building, and I've got some people I may want to bring through later this week to look at the remaining space. I'd say you've made terrific progress in only nine months."

When he put it that way, she had to reluctantly agree. It only seemed like the business's problems were insurmountable when she had to deal with juggling the accounts and placating cranky vendors on a day-to-day basis.

Fred came down the stairs, carefully closed the rickety gate, and joined her. They both looked up at the old home, she admiringly and he with what looked like a sense of relief.

"Speaking of the empty rental space within Artisans Alley, I've had a nibble on a short-term rental on one of them—for a party. What do you think about collecting two hundred dollars for one night?"

"And your fee?"

"All taken care of."

"It's fine with me. It'll pay for the service call for the air-conditioning guy who visited Friday."

"Great. They'd like to come in the day before the event to clean and decorate and they promised to come back the day after to make sure everything's shipshape."

"Even better."

"I'll get a check to you in the next couple of days."

"Thank you." They both turned to take in the Webster mansion once more. "It didn't take much time to find a buyer for the old place this time," Katie commented sadly.

"The Ryans were lucky to unload it so quickly. It sat empty for years before they bought it."

Before I would have bought it, Katie told herself.

"It was a huge financial burden for them," he continued.

"They seemed like nice people. I'm glad they won't have to worry about it anymore."

"I'll tell you what. After they close the deal, I'll bring the mansion's new owners around to see you. I have a feeling the three of you are going to become good friends. That way, you'll be able to see that they're going to take good care of the house—maybe do everything you'd planned on doing. You *do* want what's best for the house, don't you?"

Yes, she reluctantly admitted to herself, she did. It had torn her apart to see it languish in disrepair for all these years. Now . . . maybe the best thing *would* be for someone else to take care of it . . . until the next time it went up for sale. Of course, then it would cost a lot *more* money, but the structural flaws would be repaired, and it would sport a new roof. All she'd have to do was decorate it to her heart's content and start reeling in guests by the houseful.

She sighed. It was such a lovely fantasy.

Fred hefted the sign and Katie walked him back to his car. "Thank you."

"For what?" he asked as he opened his trunk and tossed the sign inside.

"For making me accept the reality of my situation."

"I haven't given up on you yet," Fred said with a smile. "You're determined. You're going to have your English Ivy Inn someday. It might not be here, but it *will* be beautiful and you *will* be a successful innkeeper."

"From your lips . . ." She let the sentence trail off.

Fred got into his car, waved, and then drove away.

As Katie walked back toward Artisans Alley, she thought about what Fred had said. Wood U had been sold for at least a month, and yet Dennis had come to the last Victoria Square Merchants Association meeting and voted on measures as he always had. Wasn't there something in the charter that said only the actual owners of a member business could vote? She'd have to check the minutes to see if there'd been a tie-breaking vote. If so, they might need to revisit some old business. And did the new owner have to rejoin or did Dennis's membership pass to him like the keys to the building had?

Katie sighed as she trudged on. She'd have to pull out the Association's rules and regulations and figure out what to do about it before Wednesday night's monthly meeting.

And she'd have to tell Detective Davenport what Fred had told her. She shook her head.

Dennis . . . what were you thinking? And why weren't you honest with us?

Katie had a feeling that there was a lot more to this whole fiasco than a fire and a suspicious death. A whole lot more.

Swell.

Rather than interrupt Davenport's conversation with Conrad, Katie pulled the cell phone from her jeans pocket and left him a voice mail message and gave him Fred Cunningham's phone number.

He could better answer whatever questions the detective would have.

She entered the Alley through the front door, greeted several of her vendors and customers, and headed back toward the vendors' lounge.

Gwen Hardy, the Alley's resident weaver, sat at the vintage chrome and Formica table in the lounge, reading the morning paper and nursing a sweating can of pop. A box fan roared behind her. She looked up as Katie entered. "Good morning."

"Not so far," Katie grumbled. She didn't elaborate and went to pour herself that tall glass of cold water she'd promised herself earlier. She opened the fridge. Not only did she find the water bottle empty, but the ice cube trays in the freezer were in the same condition. Cursing under her breath, she refilled both before downing a cup of lukewarm water from the tap. She'd have to wait several hours for her cooling refreshment.

Once back in her office, she sat down in her chair and noticed a pile of old papers sitting on what had been her formerly tidy desk. They hadn't been there when she and the detective had left some twenty minutes before. Katie bent down to set the stack of papers on the small square heater under her desk and–*whoosh!*—they fell to the floor in an untidy mess. "What the heck?" She bent down and immediately saw the problem: Her heater was missing.

Muttering a few more curses under her breath,

she bent down to collect the papers, tidied the stack, and set it on her desk before leaving her office.

"Uh-oh. You don't look happy," Gwen said, polishing off the last of her pop.

"It appears that someone has taken the little heater from my office."

Gwen blinked, startled. "Who needs heat in the middle of July? The place is as hot as a blast furnace."

"I've had a few vendors complain that their booths are too cold. They think it keeps customers from buying their crafts."

"If any of them want to change booths, they're welcome to mine. The devil himself could be comfortable in the chaise lounge I'm using to show off my rugs."

"I think I'll take a walk around to see if I can find the guilty culprit."

"And what will happen if you find him or her?" Gwen asked, trying to keep from smiling.

"All hell really *will* break loose."

"Before you go, I was wondering if you could put another sign up on the fridge. I left a six-pack of pop in it the other day and it's all gone. I labeled them and everything."

Every few weeks, lunches, pop, and any other food item not nailed down would disappear from the fridge. All the vendors came and went and Katie never really paid attention to who was putting things in or taking things out of the community refrigerator—and nobody would admit to liberating items that did not belong to them either.

"I'd like to know who keeps ripping down my signs," Katie said with a rueful shake of her head. "I'll do it as soon as I get back."

Gwen toasted her with her empty pop can. "Thanks."

Katie took a few steps forward and then paused. "Are you coming to the potluck dinner on Saturday night?"

"Wouldn't miss it."

"What are you bringing?"

"Since this is supposed to be a Christmas party, I thought I'd bring some fudge. Goodness knows I haven't had any since the holidays."

"Oh, sinful!" Katie said and laughed. She liked Gwen. Unlike now, maybe at the much-delayed Christmas party she might actually have time to have a real conversation with the woman.

Katie made a quick circuit around the back of the Alley, straining to listen for the familiar sound of the heater's rather noisy fan. She'd gotten so she looked forward to hearing it on a cold day in winter. It would be several more months before she thought she'd hear it again. The only problem was—she didn't hear it running. Did that mean someone had taken it from her office and removed it from the building? Could whoever took it be the same person who'd been raiding the fridge?

Maybe she had a bigger problem than the missing soda cans.

Rose Nash knew just about everything that went on in Artisans Alley. Katie decided to check in with her before she made what she anticipated was another fruitless course around the first floor.

Rose was at her register with what had to be the first customer of the day, and her wrapper hadn't yet arrived. Katie stepped up behind her and began to wrap several beautiful pottery plates with a peacock motif and an iridescent glaze.

Rose finished the transaction, bade the customer good-bye, and turned to face Katie. "Thanks for stepping in."

"I can't stay long."

"That's okay, Liz just went to help a customer. She should be right back. What's up?"

"The heater in my office is missing. I was wondering if you knew anything about it."

Rose smiled. "I didn't take it, if that's what you mean."

"I didn't."

Rose's gaze traveled over Katie's shoulder and suddenly Katie knew just where to find her personal heater.

"Looks like it's time to visit the tag room," she said. Rose handed her the chipped coffee mug containing the sales tags she had just taken off the merchandise. "Here. As long as you're going in there, put Ida to work."

Katie accepted the mug and headed for the tag room, hoping she would be able to keep her temper in check. Dealing with Ida was always an ordeal. The woman suffered from obsessive-compulsive disorder. She had to do everything in exacting order all the time. She seemed incapable of breaking her set routine, and understanding the social norms that most people took for granted. Ezra Hilton had felt sorry for Ida and allowed her to keep her booth rent-free for a number of years. That had to change when Katie became manager—she'd needed to pull Artisans Alley out of the red, and fast. However, she wasn't without compassion and had allowed Ida to display her handmade lace on a shelf in one of the display cases out back in exchange for her work in the tag room—something Ida seemed content to consider as her life's work.

Katie stood at the tag room's door and peered inside. Ida sat on one of the folding chairs, hunched over the long table, inspecting one of the vendor's tags, then turned to the correct stack of papers, shuffled through them, and carefully reached for her Scotch tape, grabbed a piece, and attached the tag to the paper. Then she carefully stacked the papers and began the process once again.

Katie sighed. No wonder it took the woman so long to do the task. Why didn't she just sort all the tags into piles corresponding to the numbered sheets of paper and *then* attach them?

It wouldn't do any good to argue with Ida. In fact, just saying hello could turn into a difficult conversation. And sure enough, Katie's small square heater was cranking away behind Ida, who probably had a very warm butt to show for it. Oddly enough, she was dressed in a sleeveless top, shorts that showed her ample cellulite, and sandals. No wonder she was cold sitting under an air-conditioning duct.

"Ahem," Katie said.

Ida continued to examine the sales tags before her.

Katie cleared her throat even louder.

Ida did not look up.

Annoyed, Katie stepped into the room. "Ida?"

The older woman grabbed another piece of tape and placed it on a sales tag and put them both on another of the paper sheets before her.

"Ida!" Katie tried again, much louder.

Still no reaction. Did the woman need a hearing aid?

Katie marched over to her heater and hit the off switch. The fan continued to run for at least another thirty seconds as Katie stood there, glaring at Ida. When the fan finally quit, Ida's head jerked up, as though she'd just awakened from a doze. She saw Katie standing over her and squealed in surprise.

"Goodness! Were you trying to scare me?" she accused.

"I've been trying to get your attention for more than a minute," Katie said.

"Well, you might have called me by name," Ida admonished.

"I did—and more than once."

"Oh . . . well." Ida shrugged and returned her attention to her work.

"Ida, why did you take this heater from my office?" Katie asked.

Ida didn't look up. "I was cold."

"I don't appreciate people taking my things."

Ida grabbed another piece of tape and stuck down another tag.

Katie unplugged the heater and picked it up. It wasn't exactly heavy, but it wasn't featherlight either. Suddenly Ida seemed to come back to the here and now.

"You can't take that away."

"It's *mine,*" Katie reminded her.

"Yes, but *I'm* using it."

"Without my permission," Katie reminded her.

"Why would I need permission to use it?" Ida asked.

"Because it doesn't belong to you."

"But without it, I'll be cold."

"Then I suggest you dress more appropriately in the future."

"How?"

Katie sighed. "If you know you'll be cold working here in the tag room, then you should wear slacks and long sleeves—or bring a sweater when you come here."

Ida waved a hand in annoyance. "That's really stupid. I'd be much too hot when I drive here and then when I go back home at closing time."

"Does your car have air-conditioning?" Katie asked.

"Yes, but I never use it. The car uses more gas when you turn on the AC. Everybody knows that, and I'm on a tight budget."

"Believe it or not, so is Artisans Alley," Katie said. The bulky heater was getting heavy, making her arms ache.

"How does that affect me?" Ida asked, clueless.

"You are not to use this heater. Tomorrow I want you to bring a sweater," Katie reiterated.

"But then my legs and feet will be cold."

"Bring some sweatpants and socks."

"I can't wear socks with sandals," Ida said.

"Why not?"

"Because that just looks *dumb,*" she asserted.

Katie sighed. There was no use arguing with the woman. She turned and stalked out of the room.

"Hey, bring that heater back," Ida called, but Katie ignored her and headed out the door.

Rose had been waiting for Katie to return to the main showroom. "You got your heater," she said in amazement.

"Of course I did. It's mine."

"But without it, Ida will be cold."

Rose was beginning to sound just like Ida. "She only has to work another seven hours and then she can go bake in her car on the drive home."

Rose looked appalled. "But Ida's old."

"And . . ." Katie had to stop and remind herself that Ida was . . . special. Therefore, she did not holler "aggravating." Instead, she headed back to her office. "And I have to get back to work," she said in exasperation.

It was going to be a very long day.

The phone was ringing when Katie got back to her office. She put the heater down and was about to answer it when it went silent. Rose must have answered it up front.

Katie sat down at her desk and started straightening the papers that had been living on the heater for the past few weeks when she heard a loud *boop* over the intercom. "Katie, call for you on line one," came Rose's voice.

Katie lifted the phone's receiver and pressed the blinking hold button. "Katie Bonner."

"Katie, my love, what are you doing for lunch?"

Katie smiled. She and her lawyer, Seth Landers, had been lunching together at least once a week since the first week she'd taken over Artisans

Alley. "I hope I'm having it with you. But why are you calling on a Sunday?"

"There's a chance I'll be tied up in court all week. And I didn't want to miss out on your company."

"You make me blush."

"It's very becoming."

She actually did blush. "Okay, where shall we meet?"

"How about *our* place?"

Katie shook her head. Their place was Del's Diner. Seth had a particular fondness for their meatloaf platter. "Meet you there at noon?"

"How about ten after."

"You've got a date."

"See you there," he said and rang off.

Katie settled the phone back on its cradle. Andy had never been jealous of the time she spent with Seth, who was gay—no need to feel threatened at all, although Katie would have enjoyed seeing Andy just the slightest bit jealous . . . at least once.

But Katie was looking forward to this lunch date for more than just the egg salad on rye she was likely to order. Seth was the only lawyer in town and had once specialized in real estate law. Chances were the new owners of the Webster mansion had employed his services to seal the deal, and if so, she fully intended to pick his brain about them.

Before Katie could start work again, the phone rang. Hopefully it was something Rose could handle, so she turned her attention to her computer. It was time to start hounding those who were late with their rent. She opened her spreadsheet and heard the *boop* of the intercom. "Katie, call for you on line one."

It was a wonder Katie ever got anything done. She picked up the receiver. "Katie Bonner here."

"Katie? It's Vonne Barnett."

For a moment, Katie drew a blank on the name.

"From Afternoon Tea?" Vonne reminded her.

Ah yes. The new co-owner of the recently reopened tea shop on the Square.

"What can I do for you, Vonne?"

"It's that Fiske woman again."

Katie closed her eyes and let her head droop. *Swell.* Just before the tea shop reopened, Nona Fiske, owner of The Quiet Quilter, had put out signs giving her shop designated parking—in direct violation of the Merchants Association's charter, and directly infringing on the area around the tea shop. She'd been told to take them down, had at first refused, and then grudgingly done so, but apparently they were back up again.

"It's bad enough this heat wave has kept people from visiting the shop . . ." Who wanted to drink hot tea when it was ninety-plus degrees outside? "But now she's kept the few that do show up from parking in front of our shop."

"I will speak to her again. And I will make a point to bring it up at the Merchants Association meeting on Wednesday. Will you be there?"

"I wouldn't miss it. My mom has been out of town, but she heard about the murder at Wood U. She's very upset. Will you be addressing that, too?"

"I'm sure the topic will come up."

"We heard about the other killings on the Square, but we thought that was over. I'm not sure we would have opened here if we'd known there were going to be more killings."

"I understand your concerns. These things usually happen in a fit of passion, and there seems to be a lot of passion here on the Square."

"I just hope it's the heat and not this latest death that's keeping my customers away," Vonne said.

Katie sighed. "Me, too."

"I'd better get back to work. I suppose there's a chance somebody might show up for brunch," Vonne said.

"Good-bye," Katie said and hung up the phone.

Fine. Another problem. She'd had no idea when she was suckered into taking the job how much time being president of the Merchants Association would be.

Sweat rolled down her neck as Katie twirled the knob on her Rolodex, and then called The Quiet Quilter. It rang several times before an answering machine picked up, telling Katie that the store was closed Sundays. She'd expected as much and hung up the phone. Now she'd have to trudge across the lot and remove the cement-filled wheels that held the signs. She'd roll them to the back of The Quiet Quilter, which would make it more difficult for sixty-something Nona, who was rather petite, to haul them back out. But first she'd draft a note and attach it to the front and back doors of the shop so Nona would find it first thing Monday morning—no matter which entrance she came in.

She put a sheet of Merchants Association letterhead in the printer, typed up a note, and hit the print button. Next up, to build an even greater sweat hauling those heavy signs out of the parking lot.

Some days Katie absolutely loathed the sight of Victoria Square.

Four

Lunchtime approached, and Ida was on the warpath. She stood outside the tag room, rubbing her arms as though she were shivering, and telling anyone who would listen—vendors *and* customers—what a terrible, mean witch (although she told them they should substitute the *w* with a *b*) Katie was.

Katie ignored her as she sailed out the front door and headed for the strip mall a few blocks away that housed a number of businesses—including Del's Diner. Although the temperature was in the mid-nineties, her car was sure to be over one hundred and twenty degrees, and it wasn't worth frying to travel such a short distance. She'd be just as hot and sweaty in the car as walking, and anyway, she needed a break from sitting at the desk in her stuffy office.

Katie had nearly reached the melting point when she stepped inside Del's, which felt like a refrigerator compared to the great outdoors. She looked across the booths, which were divided by a central aisle, and saw Seth in the back, waving for her to join him.

Seth sipped his iced tea as Katie slipped into the booth seat opposite him. "Hot day," he said. Most days he was dressed in a suit coat, but today he sat there in a golf shirt, looking relaxed. "I thought I'd melt on the drive over here. My AC never got a chance to really kick in."

"That's why I walked. I feel cooked, too."

Seth signaled to Sandy, the waitress who worked the lunchtime trade, for another glass of tea for Katie. While Katie perused the menu she knew by heart, Sandy filled a tumbler from a sweating pitcher of tea, then refilled Seth's glass.

"I'll have the Cobb salad with raspberry

vinaigrette on the side," Seth said. "And what do you want, Katie?"

She sighed and set the menu aside. "Egg salad on rye, with extra pickles on the side, please."

Sandy gave them both a wink. "You got it." She took back Katie's menu and headed toward the kitchen.

"No meatloaf?" Katie asked.

"I refuse to be predictable," Seth said. "So, what's the gossip about Wood U burning?"

"I spoke to Detective Davenport this morning. At that time they hadn't identified the body."

Seth pursed his lips and shook his head. "I heard Wheeler's car was out back. It's likely it *was* him."

"I'm afraid so," Katie agreed. "Did you know Dennis had sold Wood U?"

Seth squirmed in his seat and wouldn't meet her gaze. "Um . . . I—I . . ."

"You represented him at the closing, didn't you?"

"No, I didn't," he said, picking up his tumbler and swallowing a big gulp of tea.

"Does that mean you represented the buyer?"

"Maybe," he said.

"Fred Cunningham wouldn't tell me who bought the business."

Seth still wouldn't look at her.

"And you aren't going to either, are you?"

He shook his head. "I've been asked not to. The

new owner doesn't yet feel comfortable enough to be revealed."

Katie frowned. "Oh, come on. We're not talking about the Pope or Santa himself owning the joint. It's just a little gift shop on Victoria Square."

Seth held up a hand to stave off any more complaints. "I know, I know. But I promised. And unlike some of my colleagues, I keep my word."

Katie's frown deepened. "Do I look like a blabbermouth?"

Seth shook his head and reached for her hand, holding on to it in brotherly fashion. "No, you don't. I'd trust you with my life."

"You would?" she asked, surprised.

He nodded. "But like I wouldn't break a promise to you, I won't break one to the new owner either."

Katie sighed. "Well, if you put it that way." Still, she wasn't about to completely let him off the hook.

He patted her hand and reached for his glass once again. Sandy arrived with their orders. "Can I get you anything else?" They both shook their heads. "Eat hearty!" she said, and headed to the next booth to check on her other patrons.

Seth dived into his salad, while Katie nudged a pickle slice around on her plate. "Did you know the old Webster mansion had been sold again?" Katie asked.

Seth stopped chewing, frowned, and again seemed to squirm inside his shirt.

"You *did* know," she said with consternation. "Was that a secret, too?"

He swallowed, shook his head, and took another gulp of tea. "As it turns out, I know the new owners."

"Just a couple of guys from Boston, eh?" Katie asked and picked up a sandwich half.

"I went to their wedding back in February," he admitted.

She vaguely remembered him telling her that. "Then you've known them for a long time?"

"Well, one of them anyway. Nick and I have been friends since high school."

"Then he really *is* a local lad? Fred said one of the guys was coming back to help take care of an ailing relative."

"He's a good nephew. And his husband is a great guy, too."

Then it occurred to Katie just what Seth was not saying. "*You* told them about the Webster mansion, didn't you?"

"Nick called me in early May. He remembered that I used to specialize in real estate law and asked me if I knew of a property that would make a great inn. Of course I told him about the Webster mansion."

"But you knew that I had my heart set on it," Katie said. Well, whined.

"Your heart maybe, but your wallet was in no position to acquire it. Not now—and maybe not ever."

"Do you have to put it so bluntly?"

Seth sighed. "Katie, why do you torture yourself over that place so much? It's not the only potential inn in McKinlay Mill."

"But it *is* the only property that would make a good inn on Victoria Square."

"We've been over this before," he said, stabbing a grape tomato with his fork. "When you *are* in a position to buy a property, your best bet is to acquire something down by the new marina. That way you'd have guests for the entire summer—not just for four weeks at Christmas. And you could rent rooms to fishermen all year."

"Even in winter?"

"Have you ever heard of ice fishing?"

She nodded, but still felt hurt—maybe even a little betrayed—that he was responsible for the latest sale of the Webster mansion.

"What are they going to call it?" she asked.

"Sassy Sally's—after Nick's aunt."

Katie cringed. "That name is all wrong for the property."

Seth shrugged. "Oh, I don't know. It fits her to a T. She wouldn't be alive today if she wasn't full of piss and vinegar. She's a pistol. Literally." He turned his full attention to his salad.

"What?" Katie asked, confused.

Seth didn't bother to look up from his food. "She used to run the skeet range at the country club. She's a hell of a shot."

Katie ate a couple of bites of her sandwich before she spoke again. "Fred said I'd probably become good friends with the new owners. Nick and . . . who else?"

"Don Parsons. Great guys. You *will* love them."

Katie took another bite of sandwich and made a noncommittal "Hmm . . ."

"If you like, I could introduce you to them," Seth offered.

Katie swallowed, her eyes widening. "Sure. I wouldn't mind. I could invite them to join the Merchants Association. It *would* be in their best interests."

"Of course," Seth agreed.

Katie polished off the first half of her sandwich. "When?"

"I beg your pardon?"

"When could you introduce me to your friends? Tonight? Tomorrow?"

"Whoa—whoa! What's the rush?"

"Oh, come on, Seth, you know I've been dying to get my hands on that place for years. If somebody else is going to have it, I want to be in on the plans. I need to. I love that old house. It was meant for *me,* but if I can't have it, I want to make sure the new owners are going to love it and take care of it just like I would have."

"That sounds very noble, but are you sure you won't become a pain in their—" Like Davenport, he paused in his description.

"Does everybody go around McKinlay Mill thinking of me as some kind of a nuisance?"

"Not at all," Seth assured her. "It's just . . . you *do* have a dynamic personality. It's a big part of your charm."

"Flattery will get you everywhere with me. You and Andy both know what buttons to push."

"All part of being a good lawyer." He sipped his iced tea. "I'll give Nick a call and try to set something up. Are you free every night this week?"

"Usually I would be, but Tuesday I'm cooking dinner for Andy."

"You—cooking? Isn't that an oxymoron?" he asked, aghast.

"I'll have you know I dug out my aunt Lizzie's favorite cookbooks and bought several new ones, too. I've been working my way through them. The way to a man's heart *is* through his stomach, right?"

"I've heard it said, but it doesn't work with me," Seth muttered.

"I might just invite you to dinner so you can see how much I've improved. But the truth is you'd melt."

"How would you like to come to my place to cook? I've got central air-conditioning."

"I might just move in with you," she countered.

"Let's not go that far," he teased. "You could seriously cramp my lifestyle."

"And you, mine."

They both laughed.

"Are you coming to the potluck at the Alley on Saturday night? Everybody's going to be there."

"Everybody?" Seth asked.

"Everybody who's anybody on Victoria Square."

"That doesn't include me," he said sadly.

"You're the Alley's lawyer. And I'm looking for a tenant for one of my empty storefronts inside the Alley," she reminded him.

"You know how fond I am of Artisans Alley, but that's not the ambiance I want my clients to experience when they come for legal services."

Katie sighed. "You can't fault a girl for trying. But the invitation is still open. I would love for you to be there. You can bring the mansion's new owners."

"I'll think about it."

"Think hard," Katie said, and ate another potato chip. She watched as Seth stabbed another piece of lettuce and realized just how much she enjoyed his company. Now if she could just get him to spill the beans on the new owner of Wood U. But now wasn't the time to badger him. He'd tell her in good time.

If she didn't uncover that fact for herself first.

• • •

Seth dropped Katie off at the front of Artisans Alley, and she was grateful that the front of the building was air-conditioned. If she stood there and soaked in the cool dry air for a few moments, she might actually cool down from the quick but hot ride in Seth's car before she had to face the hot box that was her office. Seth gave a wave and turned the car around. He was headed to the new marina and his sailboat, which he'd named *Temporary Relief.* He'd have fun on the lake, with the wind blowing through his hair, while she toiled away in her own little sweatshop.

Swell.

As she walked through the lobby toward Artisans Alley's entrance, she could once again hear Ida ranting. Enough was enough.

"And there she is!" Ida accused, pointing a finger as Katie entered the store.

She took Ida by the arm and escorted her back into the tag room.

"I told you, I will not work under these conditions," Ida said.

"I'm not asking you to," Katie shot back, and instead she picked up Ida's purse, which had been sitting on the floor beside her chair, and handed it to her. "It's time for you to go home, Ida."

"I can't go home. It's the middle of the day."

"You're not staying here if all you're going to

do is complain and say disparaging things about me in front of the customers."

"Was I doing that?"

"Yes."

"Oh. Well. Oh."

"You may come back tomorrow, but only if you're dressed appropriately and don't talk to customers. Do I make myself clear?"

Ida slung the strap of her purse over her shoulder and stalked out the door in a huff. Katie didn't have the time or the energy to deal with her anymore that day and soon followed, turning right and heading toward the back of the building and her office.

As she ducked into the vendors' lounge, she ran straight into the opened refrigerator door. "Hey, watch it," said a surly voice she recognized. Vance Ingram straightened. "Oh, Katie. It's you. Sorry," he said and slammed the fridge door.

"Is something wrong?" she asked.

"Yeah. My lunch. It's gone. I've been thinking about those leftover barbecue ribs for hours and I just searched every shelf and my container is definitely missing. So now I'm out lunch *and* my Tupperware. Janey"—his wife—"is going to kill me when I don't come home with it."

With his snow-white beard and wire-framed glasses, Vance always reminded Katie of Santa Claus, but in his present mood he was definitely not emulating Jolly Old Saint Nick, and that was unusual for Vance, who seldom got angry about anything.

"We've had a rash of food and pop thefts for the past few days. I've been meaning to put a sign up on the fridge to warn people not to take what doesn't belong to them." She sighed and shook her head. "I feel like a grade school teacher—I shouldn't even have to do that."

"You print it—I'll hang it," Vance offered, and followed Katie to her office. "Have you thought about putting up a video camera?" he asked, as Katie stowed her purse in her desk drawer and tapped the spacebar on her keyboard to awaken her computer.

"No, but it's a good idea. The truth is, I don't have the money to put one up. And if I did, I'd probably train it on one of the exits to catch shoplifters."

"I've got a fake one in my booth. It's battery operated and has a little red light that blinks every couple of seconds. Since I put it in, I haven't had as many items disappear."

"Yeah, but everybody here knows it's fake. It wouldn't be much of a deterrent in the vendors' lounge."

"I guess you're right," Vance admitted.

Katie typed the message, changing the font size so that it filled the page, and then hit print. The page came rolling out seconds later. She glanced over it to look for typos before handing it to Vance.

"You and Janey and Vance Junior will be at the potluck on Saturday night, right?" Katie asked.

"We wouldn't miss it. Janey's bringing her memaw's ambrosia pudding. Rose has me manning the barbecue. Thanks for supplying the burgers and hots."

"It's my pleasure." Katie hadn't yet decided what else to bring to the dinner. It had to be some kind of dessert. She'd have to figure it out soon before Rose got on *her* case. "Anything happen since I went to lunch?" she asked.

"Just Ida and her nonsense. Detective Davenport was poking around Wood U for a while and then came in to talk to some of the vendors."

Katie shook her head. When Ezra Hilton died, she couldn't get Davenport to even think about the murder . . . but then, he'd had enough on his plate. It was just days after his own wife had died. He really should have taken his retirement then. But maybe he figured he could work through his grief better if he kept involved. That was how Katie had survived her husband's early demise.

"Have you spoken with him?"

Vance nodded. "But I didn't know Wheeler well—despite the fact we both worked in wood. I admit, I went in his shop a few times to check out his merchandise, but it was usually a woman working behind the till. We just never crossed paths." He brandished the piece of paper and swiped a piece of tape from her desk dispenser.

"I'll hang this up—then I guess I'll hightail it over to McDonald's and get me a Big Mac and some fries. I'm starved."

"I'm not confident the sign is going to stop the pilfering," she called at his retreating back. No more than it would deter Nona Fiske from hauling out her parking signs again. Katie turned back to her computer. Maybe she should enlist Detective Davenport's help in capturing the fridge food felon—that was one case he might surely solve before he was to retire at the end of the week.

She sat down at her desk and glanced at her list of things to do and decided to ignore it for just a while longer. Instead, she logged on to the Internet and clicked the bookmark for her favorite local TV station. She clicked on the update for the Wood U murder but found nothing new reported. A murder out in the sticks didn't draw as much attention as one in a more affluent suburb.

She sat back in her chair and stared at the computer screen. It was still there on the corner of her screen—the Excel document that was simply labeled INVENTORY. It called to her on a regular basis. It and the file of pictures that was located elsewhere on her hard drive. She straightened, grabbed her mouse, and clicked on the icon. Seconds later, the inventory popped open. There, in loving detail, was every item she'd purchased for The English Ivy Inn. The bed frames. Claw-foot soaker tubs that needed to be painted on the outside with a new finish on the inside. Sconces. Dishes. Glassware. Cutlery. Two China cabinets. Dressers. Hand-painted Limoges dresser sets. A trunk full of doilies and other vintage linens. She'd even gotten a deal on a gross of padded hangers, figuring she could hang them in the closets and the armoires she'd purchased at auctions.

Her gaze fixed on the bottom of the spread-sheet, where all the figures were totaled. She'd spent nearly twelve thousand dollars on her treasures. She'd spent thousands more on the rent for the storage unit.

A rivulet of sweat trickled down her temple.

If she could sell the items in the storage unit, she could not only fix Artisans Alley's HVAC problems, but eliminate the monthly storage fees.

They're only things, she told herself.

Things that were doing her no good.

Things that would deteriorate in long-term storage.

Things that she loved but had no personal use for.

I'm not ready to part with them, she thought and closed the file.

She could afford to carry the rent on the unit for a few more months. Maybe in the fall she'd be ready to make a decision on selling them. Or maybe she'd cave in and move in with Andy if he would let her store her treasures in the apartment over the pizza parlor for the same discounted amount she was paying him for rent.

But she didn't want to do that either.

She surely was channeling Scarlett O'Hara, because she turned away from the computer and refused to contemplate the situation anymore. She'd think about it tomorrow. Or next Wednesday. Or in October.

More sweat trickled down her face.

She bent down and turned the fan on higher.

Five

Katie counted out the day's receipts for the third time. She liked to do it at least three times in case she made an error, but each time she'd totaled the day's cash, checks, and credit card receipts, they'd matched. She added Saturday's receipts to the blue bank bag and totaled up the numbers for the morning's bank deposit.

No doubt about it, she could cover the checks to the vendors and there'd still be a couple grand left over to pay some of the bills. One more week to the month and then she'd see how far ahead she was when it came to paying on the last of the loans still outstanding. That had to come first before she even thought about taking out another loan for the HVAC. And anyway, there were only another eight or ten weeks of hot weather until she'd have to start thinking about heating bills. Why waste the money on air-conditioning now?

Because she was *hot!* And she was sick and tired of being *hot!*

After locking the receipts in the back of the file cabinet, Katie shut down the computer for the night. But before she left to go to Angelo's Pizzeria to visit Andy, she decided to wash her hands. There was nothing as filthy as cash money, and she'd handled quite a bit of it. She rose from her chair and headed for the washroom behind her office.

Soon after she'd become a vendor at Artisans Alley, Edie Silver had decorated the small washroom. She'd put up pretty wallpaper, hung a few floral pictures in gold frames, and installed a rectangular basket for the folded paper towels. After a day's use by customers and vendors, the little basket was now empty—and the wastebasket was full. Katie shook her wet hands until most of the droplets had fallen, and opened the vanity's cabinet door to reach for a new package, but instead of the towels she found a small, shabby, imitation alligator-skin suitcase.

She withdrew it and set it on the vanity. Flipping the old-fashioned latches, she opened the case and found it filled with personal items. Soap, clean washcloths, a purple toothbrush, a whitening toothpaste, and a pink disposable razor.

"Now who would have left this under the sink?" she asked herself. Had one of the vendors had somewhere to go after closing one night, dolled up, and then left the case to collect some other time? She'd put a note in with the checks on Tuesday and hope the owner would collect it. In the meantime, she closed the case and put it back under the sink. She filled the basket with towels and emptied the wastebasket. She'd give the room a more thorough once-over in the morning before opening.

She turned out the last of the lights and locked up, pocketing her keys. It was still light—and hot—out. The tarmac held the heat of the day even when it had been in shadows for hours. The lights were on at Angelo's and she could see several customers lined up to pay for their pizzas. After leaving the deadly after-hours quiet of Artisans Alley, she looked forward to the boisterous noise Andy and his workers made.

Angelo's Pizzeria wasn't quite as hot as Katie's office at Artisans Alley, but it came close, despite the air-conditioning unit chugging along outside. Andy kept his pizza ovens at a temperature of seven hundred degrees. They were well insulated, but sometimes the place still felt like a sweat-shop.

"Good evening," she called, and received a

chorus of greetings from Andy, his number one helper, Keith, and two of the boys waiting for pizzas to deliver.

"What'll you have tonight?" Andy asked.

"Nothing for me. I'm too hot to eat."

"We're just too hot," said Tony, one of the delivery boys. "I can't wait to get back in the car and crank up the AC."

"Me, too," agreed Blake, the other driver.

Andy finished putting a pizza into an insulated bag and handed a stack to Tony. "Here's yours." He grabbed the other stack and handed it to Blake. "And here's yours. Go forth and deliver."

The boys yelled a good-bye to Katie, and she gave them a wave as the door closed on their backs.

"So what'll you have tonight, Katie?" Andy asked. He usually seemed pleased to see her, but this evening he looked preoccupied.

"I told you, nothing. But if you're going to force me, I'll have a pepperoni calzone." That was an easy order. Andy had them made up in advance, and neither he nor Keith would have to fuss with making something special for her. Besides, she had a date with a big bowl of cold, wiggly raspberry gelatin and whipped topping later on and she wanted to leave room for it.

"One calzone for the lady, Keith."

"It'll be ready in five minutes," he called.

The phone rang. Andy took the order, hung up,

donned a new pair of gloves, and started making another pizza.

Katie sidled up closer to him. "I've known you long enough to tell when something's bothering you. Do you want to talk about it?"

Andy nodded, quickly looking to see if Keith was eavesdropping. He was singing along with the radio as he checked the progress on the pizzas in the ovens.

Andy leaned closer and dropped his voice. "I think one of my boys could be in trouble."

Andy hired at-risk boys from the local high school, not only giving them work to keep them out of mischief, but mentoring them, too. He had been just such a kid and working in a pizza parlor had kept him out of reform school. Well, mostly. He felt the need to offer that same kind of help to other young men.

"Which one?"

"Blake."

The boy who'd just left. For someone in possible trouble, he'd seemed rather cheerful. "What happened?"

"Blake was one of Dennis Wheeler's students. They didn't get along and everyone knew it." Andy frowned. "Blake was out delivering a pizza when the fire started. The thing is . . ." He paused, his expression darkening. "The customer called to complain that the pizza was an hour late and cold. Blake showed up at the shop and said the air in his tire was low and that he'd had to stop at a gas station to get it filled."

"The closest gas station is at the corner of Manitou Road," Katie said.

Andy nodded. "I know it. And that's the opposite end of Route 8 from where the customer lived."

"What are you saying? That he's been accused of setting the fire—or murder?"

Andy shook his head. "I don't believe it for a minute." But he didn't look as convinced. "Detective Davenport has already paid the kid a visit."

"Surely the gas station has surveillance cameras. Their video could prove he was there," Katie said.

"And what if he wasn't?" Andy shook his head. "I'm sure as hell not going to suggest Detective Davenport take a look."

"He doesn't need your encouragement. You know he's going to check Blake's alibi."

"He hasn't always shown that kind of initiative," Andy offered.

"This is his last case. He's going to want to go out on top by solving it quickly and delivering a suspect the district attorney can convict."

Andy looked even more uncomfortable. "I've had thirty kids work for me since I opened the shop and not one of them has gotten into trouble."

Katie had to bite her tongue to keep from saying

there's always a first. Instead she said, "So what does Blake say?"

"His father warned him not to say anything— even to me," Andy complained.

"That doesn't sound fair. You've given him a chance to prove himself."

"As with any of my boys, it's always a case of guilty until proven innocent," he said bitterly.

"Someone died," Katie reminded him.

"And there's no proof Blake is responsible. Now, can we talk about something else?"

"Like a new breaker box in my apartment?" Katie asked hopefully, and took a can of Coke from the fridge.

"That wouldn't be my first choice of topic," Andy admitted, looking sour. "You know, if you'd like to move, I'd be happy to let you out of your lease."

"And where would I go?"

"To my house. I have plenty of room for you. I'll even let you bring your cats. And you'd save a fortune on rent."

"I appreciate the offer, but for now I think I'll stick with our current arrangement." *Even if I have to live in my shower just to keep from melting.* He wasn't going to get rid of her that easily.

"Katie, your calzone is up," Keith called as he maneuvered a wooden paddle and slid the steaming pastry into a small box. He handed the box to Andy, who passed it along to Katie, along with a handful of paper napkins.

"Thanks."

"Are you going to eat it here or upstairs?"

"Definitely here. It's at least ten degrees cooler down here." Was that rubbing it in too much?

Katie sat down in one of the chairs Andy provided for customers who came too early to pick up their food. She opened the box, broke the calzone in two, and blew on it to cool it. Movement outside the big glass window caught her attention. "Will you look who just parked outside?" Katie said.

Andy squinted, gazing past the big red vinyl lettering on the plate glass window at the front of his shop.

Detective Davenport got out of his car. He'd lost the suit coat, and was wearing a brown, short-sleeved polo shirt. He was definitely out of uniform. "Do you think he wants to order a pizza?" Katie asked.

"I doubt it," Andy said, sounding worried, and peeled the plastic gloves off his hands.

The strip of sleigh bells jangled as Davenport opened the shop's door. "Good evening, all," he called, his voice jaunty.

"Detective, did somebody slip happy juice into your afternoon coffee?" Katie asked, and took a bite of her calzone.

Davenport managed a crooked smile. "Not at

all. Short-timer's syndrome has made a new man of me."

New or old, it was obvious Andy wasn't at all pleased to see the detective.

"What are you doing here on the Square so late?" Katie asked, and wiped the corners of her mouth with a paper napkin.

"My job." Davenport slouched against the counter, directing his attention to Andy. "I thought the Taylor kid was supposed to be working here tonight—at least that's what his parents told me not ten minutes ago."

"He's out on a delivery," Andy said. Katie could tell by the grim set of his mouth that he wasn't likely to help Davenport—not if it meant ratting on one of his charges.

"Why the interest in Blake?" Katie asked the detective.

"Seems he and Dennis Wheeler almost came to blows a couple of times during the past school year."

And who had told him that?

"That's not surprising. The jerk—and I'm talking about Wheeler—loves to bait his students."

"And how would you know that, Mr. Rust?" Davenport asked.

"Because I was once one of his students. The guy's a ball breaker—and he can get nasty."

Katie blinked. She had no idea Andy had

known Dennis before he joined the Merchants Association. She'd always found Dennis to be an amiable kind of guy. To hear he wasn't . . .

Davenport's gaze was penetrating. "Did you ever have a beef with the man since high school, Mr. Rust?"

"No."

Katie studied the set of Andy's mouth. Was he telling the truth?

Davenport's gaze remained riveted on Andy's face. "Here's what I know. You said the Taylor kid was out delivering a pizza last night." Andy nodded. "So how come when I talked to a Mr. Olsen, the guy whose pizza was delivered an hour late and colder than an iceberg in January, he says he didn't see the kid until almost ten o'clock? So where was the kid from the time he left here with a hot pie 'til he ended up at Olsen's house, where he didn't get a tip?"

"I can honestly say I don't know," Andy said with annoyance.

"Did he ever pull that kind of crap before?" Davenport demanded.

Andy shook his head. "Until today, I thought he was my greatest success story."

"Hey, what about me?" Keith asked, who'd obviously been eavesdropping on the conversation.

"Did I say greatest? I meant second greatest," Andy said and shot Keith a weak grin.

Davenport's tongue seemed to be massaging the gums along his front teeth. He poked around at his molars, too, before he spoke again. "Do you mind if I hang out here and wait until the kid returns?"

"Be my guest," Andy said, and waved a hand toward the plastic lawn chairs sitting against the wall under the front window. "Would you like to order a little dinner while you wait? My pizza is the best in the area."

"You know I can't take free food. It might be looked at as a bribe," Davenport said, his voice level.

"I wasn't offering it for free," Andy grated and jerked his right thumb over his shoulder in the direction of the sign that hung on the back wall listing his prices.

Katie sipped her Coke, every nerve in her body on alert. She couldn't remember when she'd seen Andy so tense.

"I'll have a small cheese and pepperoni pizza. And a can of orange pop, too," Davenport said.

"Coming right up," Andy said, and turned his back on the detective.

Davenport craned his neck to watch Keith, who was pulling a pizza out of the oven. He looked like he'd just gotten caught with his hand in the cookie jar. But then, Davenport seemed to have that effect on most people—making them feel guilty for things they hadn't done.

Davenport turned around to gaze over Victoria Square in the direction of Wood U.

"Have they positively identified the body found in the fire?" Katie asked.

"Not yet," Davenport answered succinctly.

There was something about his expression—or perhaps it was his eyes—that hinted of a willingness to talk . . . if she asked the right question.

"Is there any possibility that Wheeler *isn't* the victim?" Andy asked.

Davenport frowned. "Until we get a positive ID, anything's possible," Davenport admitted. But then why was he so interested in Blake? Did he have any other suspects?

"That'll be seven fifty-five, Detective," Andy said, and shoved a can of pop across the counter toward Davenport. "Your pizza will be up in a few minutes."

Davenport dug out his wallet and handed Andy a ten. He made change and gave it back. Davenport grabbed his pop and turned to Katie. "Is there a bench or somewhere where we can sit and talk?" he asked, sounding downright friendly.

Katie nearly choked on her calzone.

"Not really. Although the Merchants Association is looking at plans to do just that. And maybe add a gazebo."

"That would be lovely."

Lovely? Katie hadn't known the detective even knew—let alone used—the word.

"Is there anyplace else we can go?"

"There's a ratty old swing on the old Webster mansion's front porch, but I'm not sure if it could hold both our weights. The rope looks pretty worn."

"And it would be trespassing for us to use it. Oh well . . . another time then."

Another time? Katie met Andy's puzzled gaze. At least he was a witness to Davenport's apparent change in demeanor. She *wasn't* simply going crazy after all.

"You're welcome to eat your dinner here in my shop and wait for Blake," Andy offered the detective, waving a hand in the direction of the chairs where Katie was already sitting.

Davenport shook his head. "That's okay."

"And it's ready," Keith said, sliding Davenport's pizza into a box. He handed it to Andy, who gave it to the detective.

"Thanks. I think I'll wander on back to Wood U and take another look around while I wait for the Taylor kid to show up."

"Suit yourself," Andy said, and he and Katie watched the detective leave.

"I'm glad he's gone," Keith said from his position in front of the ovens.

"You and me both," Andy said, "but he'll be back."

"Keith, what happened between Blake and Dennis Wheeler at the school?" Katie asked.

"Old Man Wheeler ragged on Blake on a regular basis," Keith admitted. "Criticized everything he did—made him look stupid in front of the whole class. Blake's folks kicked up a fuss, had a meeting with the principal and got old Woody Wheeler—that's what everyone called him behind his back—in trouble. Wheeler held a grudge and made life even worse for Blake. He baited him until Blake hauled off and punched him. Everybody was talking lawsuits for a while there."

"What happened?" Katie asked.

"Blake said he can't talk about it. I hope that means they were suing the bastard."

"School was over. If Blake withstood a whole year of harassment, why would he kill Wheeler a month after school ended? Chances are he'd never have to put up with him after that," Katie suggested.

"Didn't Wheeler retire at the end of the school year?" Andy asked.

Keith nodded. "I don't think anybody—even the teachers—was sorry to see him go."

Katie frowned. Her late husband had been a teacher at the high school. Had any of the students felt the same way about him? She couldn't imagine him picking on a child in his class. Except for his killer, everybody had loved Chad.

"What are you thinking, Katie?" Andy asked. "That the kids are wrong and Wheeler was a saint? Believe me, he wasn't. Wheeler's been picking on students for years—me included—so I tend to believe what Keith says."

Katie nodded. Did Andy realize he might now look like a suspect—especially as he'd just lied to Detective Davenport? Then again, if the body wasn't Dennis Wheeler . . .

She looked down at her calzone and realized it had grown cold.

"Any chance you can toss this in the oven to warm it up?"

"Sure thing," Andy said, taking the box from her. He slid the pie onto a paddle and popped it back in the oven.

If Andy had looked preoccupied before, now he looked downright worried.

He shouldn't have admitted he'd had trouble with Dennis. Davenport was sure to think he held a grudge and maybe *he'd* lie for Blake. Or worse, if he held a grudge against his former teacher, he might be willing to protect his protégé—by any means.

Was Davenport feeling so chipper because he was about to make an arrest?

Katie swallowed, realizing she'd lost her appetite.

Six

Blake never came back to the pizzeria that night. Katie had sat in her hot apartment, watching the parking lot and waiting. Davenport came into the pizzeria a few times, but eventually he left Victoria Square.

Katie didn't sleep much that night—and it wasn't just the heat that kept her awake.

As always, the first thing Katie did when she woke up in the morning was to gaze out her apartment's front window to take in the Webster mansion. She never got tired of the view. That wreck of a house would one day be a painted lady once again, but sadly, it wasn't she who'd pick out the paint palette.

With a sigh of resignation, she went downstairs, retrieved her newspaper, and then breakfasted on a banana and coffee as she perused the local section. A two-paragraph story on the lower side column confirmed what Detective Davenport had said the night before: The body found in the fire had not been identified.

It turned out to be a good thing that she'd held off sending flowers to Abby Wheeler.

She refused to believe that either Blake or Andy had anything to do with the death at

Wood U. There had to be another explanation.

Suppose . . . just suppose the body in the county morgue wasn't Dennis Wheeler. Just because facial recognition wasn't available to them didn't mean a body had no other recognizable features. Surgery scars, tattoos, bones with old breaks, jewelry, or even clothing could be identifiable. And yet Davenport seemed to be pursuing the idea that Blake Taylor had killed his former teacher.

So what if the victim at Wood U wasn't Dennis Wheeler? What if he'd had a motive to disappear? He'd certainly been secretive about selling his business.

The idea intrigued her. Katie picked up a pen and began jotting down ideas on the newspaper's margins.

If Dennis was missing, he had to be the one responsible for firing the bullet that had killed the man found in the shop, and he'd set fire to the place to cover the crime? But why would Dennis need to hide? He hadn't taken his car. What if he'd taken the dead man's car in an effort to keep the authorities from identifying the body before he could get away? And where would he go? He did have the money from the sale of his shop. If the murder had been premeditated, could he have escaped to Canada? He'd need a passport to cross the border. Could he have gotten on a plane later that night and escaped to some country that didn't have a treaty of extradition?

That was a lot of supposing.

Feeling mildly depressed, Katie wondered if she should attempt to alleviate it via her favorite pastime—baking—but already the kitchen felt like an oven on low. Still, she hadn't brought a snack into the Alley in several days and her sweet tooth was hankering for something with chocolate.

Funny how bringing in a sweet treat could soothe frayed nerves and promote general happiness among the vendors. It worked and she was sticking with that successful formula. And if she had to deal with Ida once again, she was going to need something to settle her own nerves. But instead of making liquor-infused chocolates, she settled on peanut butter buckeyes, which required no baking. She could melt the chocolate and shortening in the microwave. She wasn't in the mood to deal with cleaning the top half of the double boiler—at least not that morning.

Half an hour later, the buckeyes were in the fridge firming up nicely.

As Katie got ready for work, she couldn't stop thinking about what she now knew about Dennis Wheeler. Was a man who picked on his students—children who wouldn't ordinarily fight back as Blake had done—as easily capable of murder?

• • •

Katie opened Artisans Alley's vendor entrance at precisely eight o'clock. Sometimes she found vendors waiting to get in to straighten their booths or add new merchandise, but that morning she was alone. She took her plate of buckeyes to the vendors' lounge and popped them in the fridge. She'd wait until there was a pot of coffee brewing before she brought them out for everyone to sample.

In the meantime, she donned her rubber gloves and, armed with disinfectant and paper towels, cleaned the washroom behind her office. Sure enough, the little suitcase was still there.

Afterward, Katie heard people coming and going in the vendors' lounge while she got lost in the weekly ritual of printing out the inventories and checks for each of the vendors, adding a note to remind everyone to attend the Christmas potluck on Saturday—and that she'd found the suitcase under the sink. She married the copies of the note with the checks and inventories, and put them in the proper envelopes—all of which took up far too much of her time. She'd have to start delegating some of the menial work. Putting labels on each of the envelopes was time-consuming. It might be just the kind of job for Ida—that is, if she could tear herself away from her precious sales tags for an hour or so a week. If not, maybe it was something the girls on the register could do between waiting on customers. She should also look into offering reduced rent in exchange for a little clerical work. She'd put that on the list of things to do, too.

The phone rang at just past ten. Katie picked it up. "Artisans Alley. Katie Bonner speaking. How may I help you?"

"Katie, it's Fred."

"Hi, Fred. What's up?" she asked, pleased to hear his voice.

"The closing on the Webster mansion was this morning. I know I said I'd bring the new owners over to meet you, but something's come up. They're already on their way to the house if you want to meet them. They should be there any minute."

"Thanks. I'll go over and introduce myself."

"They're eager to join the Merchants Association, so why don't you take over one of your welcome packets."

"Great idea. I'll do just that. Thanks."

"I'll be dropping off the check for the one-night rental on that empty storefront later today or maybe tomorrow."

"Whenever," Katie said. "See you then." She hung up the phone and stood, turning to her file cabinet and the drawer she kept that contained her files and other information on the Victoria Square Merchants Association. She grabbed a packet for the newcomers. New blood. Just what the Square needed.

Since she hadn't offered the buckeyes to the vendors yet, maybe she should take them over and give them to the mansion's new owners. Chocolate and peanut butter—nothing said "welcome to the neighborhood" any better.

But when Katie went to the refrigerator, the cookies (or were they technically candy?) were gone—and so was the charming rose-patterned plate she'd put them on.

"That does it!" she said to no one in particular. "Something's got to be done to stop whoever's filching food from the fridge!"

But what that something was, she wasn't sure.

She stormed off to lock the vendors' entrance before opening for the day and heading over to the Webster mansion, or rather Sassy Sally's. Ugh. The name made her shudder.

As she began her trek across the Square's lengthy parking lot, a Big Brown truck pulled in. Katie waved at the man behind the wheel, expecting it to be the regular deliveryman, but that day it was someone else. The lucky bum was probably on vacation—something that wasn't likely to happen to her anytime soon. She watched as he hopped from the truck, package in hand, and hoofed it into Gilda's Gourmet Baskets.

As Katie passed The Quiet Quilter, she noted that the note she'd attached to the front door the day before had already been removed. Sure enough, Nona's car was parked at the side of the building. So far there was no sign of the contraband signage either.

Good.

An unfamiliar car was parked outside of the Webster mansion, and two men stood with their backs to the Square, admiring the building.

"Anybody home?" Katie called cheerfully as she approached. The walk across the lot had cooled her anger over the missing buckeyes.

The men turned. "Sure are," the fairer of the two said.

Katie extended her hand. "Hello, I'm Katie Bonner. I manage Artisans Alley on the other end of the Square. I'm also the president of the Merchants Association. I've come to welcome you to the neighborhood."

"Oh, you're the one who hates us," the sandy-haired man said and grinned as he shook her hand.

Katie's mouth dropped open in shock, the fingers of her left hand clenching the welcome packet, wrinkling the envelope. "I beg your pardon."

"For buying the property you've had your heart set on for so long," said the dark-haired man. He had a touch of gray at his temples, making him look distinguished. He offered her his hand, and she took it.

"I—I . . ." Katie couldn't seem to say another word.

The sandy-haired man's smile was warm. "Hi, I'm Nicholas Farrell—you can call me Nick—and this is my partner, Don Parsons."

"I—I . . . I don't know where you got the idea that I—I . . ." She couldn't even bring herself to repeat the four-letter word.

"Okay, maybe hate *is* a little strong. We were told, by our mutual friend Seth Landers, you were upset to see the building get sold out from under you once again. We apologize. But you have to admit, it is a diamond in the rough. Can you blame us for wanting to bring this old girl back to life?" Don said, gazing fondly at the old home.

Katie shook her head.

"Would you like to come through with us now and hear what we've got planned?" Nick asked.

Katie nodded. She was beginning to feel like a mime. She certainly wasn't at her articulate best.

Nick held out his hand and she took it. "Careful walking through the yard. The first thing on the list is to get rid of all this debris and start the demo." He led her through the tangle of weeds and other detritus littering the small courtyard.

"I understand you're an old friend of Seth's," Katie said as they mounted the creaky wooden steps.

Nick's grin was broad. "He was my first boy-friend—back when we didn't know what being boyfriends was all about—and were afraid to act on it anyway. He stuck up for me, like a big brother. We've remained friends all these years. He was my best man at Don's and my wedding."

Seth had said he'd attended the wedding. He hadn't said he'd participated in it. And she could identify with Seth acting like a protective older brother. She looked at him in the same light.

"Seth tells me that you're his best friend here in McKinlay Mill," Nick told Katie.

She smiled. "I'm flattered."

Nick produced a set of shiny new keys from his jacket pocket and inserted one into the deadbolt. He turned it, then selected another key from the ring and inserted it into the lockset. "That's got to go," he said, indicating the handle.

"Maybe the door, too," Don agreed, "unless our contractor knows how to make a Dutchman to repair the hole for an antique glass doorknob and mortised lock."

"You sound like you know a lot about construction," Katie said.

"Don?" Nick laughed. "He just watches a lot of episodes of *This Old House*."

"Hey, you do, too!" Don protested.

Katie stifled a smile. Fred Cunningham had been right. Already she felt comfortable with Nick and Don and bet Fred's prediction they'd become friends would indeed come true. "So what have you got planned for the entryway?" she asked, once they'd all trundled inside.

"Restoration. That means tearing out all the drywall that broke this beautiful home into apartments."

The former owners had started that work—until Katie had helped them with their sweat-equity demo, knocked a hole in a piece of Sheetrock, and found the remains of a human body. That ended their demolition, and they'd put the house back on the market in a matter of days.

"First things first. Up the fire insurance on this place," Don said seriously. "I admit it, I was extremely upset to hear about the fire on the Square the other day."

"Make that *we* were upset," Nick echoed. "Especially if it *is* arson. Do you know anything about it, Katie? I mean, other than what's already been on the news?"

"I'd like to reassure you, but at this point, I have no idea."

Nick nodded. "Seth said you had lots of ideas on remodeling and redecorating this old place. I'd love to hear them."

Tell them about the stuff in your storage unit, a little voice within her urged. *Maybe they'd want to buy it.*

"You might not be able to shut me up," she said instead.

"Seth said you know where to buy antique furniture and accessories."

Tell them about the stuff in your storage unit! the voice said louder. *Offer them a great price to take it off your hands.*

"I sure do. There's a great shop in Greece on the Ridge. And there are some wonderful architectural salvage places in Rochester, too. You'll want to check out the weekly sales at Donahue's Auction Barn in Parma, as well."

Are you going to tell them about your stuff or not? the voice taunted.

"No."

"No?" Nick asked, confused.

Katie gave a nervous laugh. "Sorry. Just thinking aloud. I had to stop going to auctions and sales. I downsized to a tiny apartment earlier this year and I just don't have any more room."

"And we have plenty of rooms to fill," Don said, waving a hand to take in the empty, cavernous house. "We might have to go on buying trips to New York."

"You'll pay a lot more. You'll find wonderful furnishings locally for a fraction of the big-city prices. I'll make up a list of places for you to check out."

And one of them had better be your storage locker, the voice taunted.

"And before I forget . . ." She handed Nick the slightly crumpled envelope she'd been holding in her sweaty hand. "I understand you're eager to join the Merchants Association?"

"We sure are," Don said. "We want to become a contributing force on Victoria Square and figure the best way to do that is to become friends with all the other merchants."

"They're a great bunch of people. We're having a meeting on Wednesday night at Del's Diner. We'd love to have you join us. We have dinner before the official meeting starts. Conrad Stratton from The Perfect Grape always brings a nice selection of wines, too."

"Sounds great," Nick said. "We'll have to patronize his shop."

"He gives discounts on bulk sales," Katie said.

"We'll be buying sherry by the case for our guests," Don said.

Katie laughed and thought of the lovely crystal glasses and decanters swathed in bubble wrap in a box in her storage unit. "I was going to do the same thing."

"Great minds think alike," Nick said.

"Or read all the same books about innkeeping," Don agreed and grinned.

Nick nodded toward the kitchen. "The room that seems to need the most work is right through here."

"Don't I know it," Katie said. It was going to have to be a total gut job before they could open for business.

"Seth said you had a lot of good ideas. Come on in and tell us about them. We can compare notes," Nick said, and led her through the dining room toward the back of the house. She'd walked through these rooms so often she could have done it blindfolded.

"Uh-oh," Nick said as they entered the dusty kitchen. A window in the back door had been broken, and glass littered the old yellowed linoleum. That would have to go, too.

They all looked at the gaping hole where the window had been, then around the room, which showed signs of someone having been there in the not-too-distant past. Candy wrappers and fast-food bags littered the counters, as well as a nearly empty take-out coffee cup sitting in the dirty sink.

"When did you say you did your walk-through?" Katie asked.

"Friday," Don said, sobering. "This stuff wasn't here then."

Nick gave him a knowing glance. "Methinks a trip to the hardware store is in order to replace this glass."

"Calls to the locksmith and the security company are in order, too," Don agreed.

"I can't imagine who'd want to break in now, when the house has been sold," Katie said. "It's been empty for years and thankfully was never vandalized."

"Let's hope whoever was here didn't do any

other damage. We'd better do a thorough walk-through," Nick said. Don nodded.

"You might want to call the Sheriff's Office, too," Katie recommended. "It's probably not related to the arson at Wood U, but you never know."

"We'll do that," Nick agreed.

Katie studied their somber faces. "I'm so sorry this has ruined what should have been a happy day for you."

"Not ruined, but . . . it does put a damper on it. Still, we're determined to open Sassy Sally's on time, and neither this—nor renovation night-mares—will deter us."

"*Nothing* will discourage us," Don said with determination.

On the one hand, Katie was happy to hear that . . . but it also meant the death knell to all her dreams for The English Ivy Inn.

And why would someone have broken into the place? To hide? Someone who had reason to disappear but didn't want to go far?

Was it possible her harebrained theory about Dennis Wheeler could actually be true?

Seven

Katie returned to her office and immediately noticed that not only had her vintage rose plate not been returned, but that her small heater had once again gone missing. This time she didn't bother searching Artisans Alley and marched directly to the tag room.

Sure enough, Ida sat before her folding table, diligently working on attaching the sales tags to small squares of paper, with the heater chugging along merrily behind her. She had not taken Katie's suggestion to dress warmly, this time wearing a matching shorts and sleeveless shirt combination.

Katie stomped over to the heater, and turned it off. She was angry enough to rip the cord from the wall, but didn't want to damage the little machine.

As before, Ida seemed oblivious to her presence until the heater's fan stopped running. Her head jerked up and her breath caught in her throat at being startled. Her left hand snapped up to clutch her chest. "That's the second time you've nearly scared me to death," she complained.

"And that's the second time you've stolen my heater."

"I told you, I'm cold!"

"And I asked you to dress warmly."

"And I told you, I can't do that."

Katie crossed her arms over her T-shirt, but took special care to keep her voice level. "Then if we can't come to a compromise, I'm afraid you'll have to leave Artisans Alley."

Ida's eyes became so wide, Katie thought they might pop out of her skull. "You can't do that!" she hollered.

"Yes, I can," Katie said, making sure to keep her voice level.

"Then I'll bring in my own heater."

"Ida, I don't think you understand what I'm , telling you. If you wish to remain a vendor here at Artisans Alley and work in the tag room, you'll have to dress appropriately for the air-conditioning. If you don't wish to do so, then you will no longer be welcome here."

"But I've been a vendor here for years, and you've only been here a few months. I have more rights than you."

Katie sighed. "Ida, I *own* Artisans Alley."

Ida's mouth dropped in shock. "How can this be?"

"I explained to you last fall that when Mr. Hilton died, I inherited the business. That means I'm the boss."

"But you're a woman!" she cried, aghast.

Good grief! Hadn't Ida ever heard of equal opportunity?

"I'd be happy to open the glass display case now so you can gather your lace," Katie offered.

"To take it home?" Ida asked.

"As of right now, you are no longer a vendor here at Artisans Alley."

"But who will be the tag room manager?"

"We don't need one. I'll have one of the walkers take over for the rest of today, and we'll all take turns during the day from now on."

"But it's *my* job," Ida said, tears filling her eyes. Her lower lip trembled and the gigantic wart on her cheek began to wobble. It gave Katie the creeps.

"Not anymore. Pick up your purse and come along with me," Katie said.

Ida's mouth opened and closed and then she burst into loud, wailing sobs, making Katie feel like ten different kinds of a brute.

Steeling herself, she unplugged the heater, picked it up, and left the tag room. She tried to ignore the stares of the other vendors as she walked away, with the sounds of Ida's howling following her.

Back in her office, she deposited the heater back under her desk, grabbed the master key ring from the hook on the wall, picked up an empty paper box she'd stashed alongside the file cabinet, and walked back through the vendors' lounge and out into the main showroom, making her way to the back display cases.

Unlocking the case, she removed Ida's dusty stock. Not one piece had sold since she'd helped Ida put it on the shelf some ten months before.

Once everything was in the box, she closed and locked the case, and headed for the tag room once more. Rose had left the register and was attempting to calm a still-weeping Ida.

Katie placed the box on the table. "Here are your things, Ida. I wish we could have parted under better circumstances. But I can't have you taking my things without permission, as well as being unwilling to work with me on the air-conditioning problem. It's better that we part company now. I'll walk you to your car."

"Go away," Ida shouted, her tearstained face flushed with anger.

"I'll walk her to her car," Rose said, looking at Katie with disapproval.

"Thank you, Rose."

Then Katie turned and left the tag room.

She quickly came to an abrupt halt. Bad news travels fast, and every vendor present in the Alley stood outside the tag room, looking shocked. Katie held her head high and walked back to her office, where she shut the door and fell into her chair. Her hands were shaking badly, and she wished she kept a bottle of sherry or maybe even something a little stronger in her desk drawer. Instead, all she had were peppermints in her jar.

She unwrapped two of them, popped them in her mouth, and crunched.

A knock on her door startled her, and her heart began to pound even harder in her chest. Was she having a heart attack?

The door cracked open. "Katie, are you all right?"

It was Liz Meier, whose booth was filled with stained glass art. Was she, too, going to berate Katie for being heartless? She wasn't sure she could take that.

"Is Ida gone?" Katie asked.

"Rose took her over to the tea shop. She'll be okay."

Katie nodded, tried to look Liz in the eyes, but found she couldn't.

"I think I speak for many of the vendors when I say . . ." Liz sighed. "It's about time you chucked Ida out on her derriere."

Katie's head snapped up. "What?"

"That woman," Liz said through clenched teeth. "I know she has issues, and we're supposed to have compassion for her—and I do—but she has made life here at the Alley unbearable at times. For years her disruptive personality has caused problems with the vendors, and she's upset quite a few of our customers, too."

"I do feel bad for her. I wish I could've helped her more," Katie began, "but—"

Liz held up a hand to stop her. "Mr. Hilton

turned a blind eye to the problems Ida caused. He turned a blind eye to a lot of the things that were wrong with this place. I'm happy to say that most of the problems that used to exist are gone since you took over."

Most? Katie wasn't sure she wanted to hear a litany of what else needed fixing at Artisans Alley—at least not then.

She forced a smile. "Thank you, Liz." But somehow, she really didn't feel better about the situation. She felt she should have been able to come up with a better solution. It would be hard to overcome the guilt. But honestly, she had to look out for what was best for Artisans Alley— not just for herself, but for *all* the vendors, too.

Doing what was best for the greater good didn't always feel that great.

"I'd better let you get back to work," Liz said. "And I'd better get back out on the sales floor. We have customers to take care of and need to stop the drama once and for all."

"I appreciate you stopping by."

Liz gave her a quick smile and left the tiny office.

Despite Liz's reassurance, Katie felt she'd handled the situation badly. She found her hands were still shaking as she picked up a stack of papers and sorted them into tidy piles. She'd neglected her filing for a few days and decided now was as good a time as any to do it.

The desk was clear and she was about to start compiling the list of antiques and other furnishing stores for Nick Farrell when she turned to find Andy standing in her doorway with a grease-stained brown paper bag in hand. "Need a little pick-me-up?" he asked.

"And a friendly face," she admitted, then stood and gave him a quick kiss on the lips.

"What's wrong?"

"I had another run-in with Ida. I've asked her to leave the Alley for good."

Andy sobered. "Then it looks like I came at just the right time." He proffered the bag. "Did you have breakfast? Sorry it's a little smooshed. It wasn't perfect enough to send out with the rest of this morning's batch, but it'll still taste as good."

"Thank you," Katie said, and accepted the bag and peeked inside. Sure enough, it was one of his heavenly cinnamon buns.

Andy took the only other seat in the office. "Boy it's hot in here."

"No worse than standing out in the parking lot in full sunlight," she said, and rooted through her desk until she came up with a few crumpled paper napkins. "Besides playing brunch deliveryman, what brings you over to the Alley so early?"

"Blake," he said, his eyes filled with worry. "He must've gotten wind that Detective Davenport was looking for him. He never came back from his run last night."

"I know. I was watching for him. He collected money for those pizzas. Does that make him—"

"A petty thief?" Andy answered. He shook his head. "The kid's good for it. He's scared. And who can blame him? Talking with Davenport doesn't inspire confidence. More like dread of a life sentence—even if you haven't done anything wrong."

"He's been very nice to me these last few days. It's almost creepy," Katie admitted, and took a big bite of her cinnamon bun. Oh! Heaven.

"We've got to figure out what happened over at Wood U before the detective does," Andy said.

"To protect Blake?"

"Of course."

"But what if he was somehow involved?"

"I'll never believe that."

"But you yourself said Dennis bullied some of his students. What if he pushed Blake too far?"

"I might believe that if school was still in session. The kid doesn't strike me as someone who'd hold a grudge."

"How well do you really know Blake?"

"He's worked for me almost every week for the last eleven months. I think I know him—and the rest of my boys—pretty well. I'm not a terrible judge of character."

"Of course not. You love me," Katie said, scraping a bit of frosting from her bun and dabbing it on Andy's nose.

He was not amused. Grabbing one of her napkins, he brushed away the offensive topping.

"How can a teacher get away with bullying a student—especially in this day and age when the topic seems to be in the news so often?" Katie asked.

"Back in the day—a whole thirteen or so years ago—pretty easily. Now, I'm not so sure. I questioned Keith a bit more after you left last night—asking him to clarify what he meant when he said Wheeler was always ragging on Blake. He said Wheeler said all the right things, as though to encourage Blake to try harder with his projects—but it came out sounding very condescending and critical. I can believe that, having gone through the same thing myself."

"Do you think kids today are more fragile than when you were in school?" Katie asked, and nibbled on her second breakfast.

"Maybe. I don't like the fact that Wheeler got away with it for so long."

"If they forced him to retire, he finally paid for his behavior."

"It was the threat of lawsuits that finally made the school act. And of course, the teacher's union backed him up over the years whenever there was a complaint—but I think the possibility of lawsuits made it hard for them to keep making excuses for his bad behavior."

Katie decided it was time to change the subject.

"I met the Webster mansion's new owners this morning. They're nice guys. And get this—the house had been broken into over the weekend. The kitchen had a bunch of fast-food wrappers and it looked like someone had slept on an old mattress upstairs."

"Interesting."

"Demo on the place will start tomorrow, so whoever is squatting can't come back. And let's face it, with no electricity or plumbing, the house isn't all that pleasant a place to stay right now."

"Are you suggesting Wheeler has been hiding there?" Andy asked.

"Well, they haven't identified the body at the morgue as being his."

Andy shook his head. "I think you're on the wrong track. I honestly think it's Wheeler who died on Saturday. After all, any son of a bitch that can pick on kids can pick on an adult, too. We just have to figure out who he was picking on."

"If he was picking on anyone. We don't know that he had any enemies. I mean, apart from his wife, none of the other merchants seems to have really known him. I sure didn't."

"Can you come up with something else? I mean, you've done this kind of thing twice before," Andy said.

"It seemed like there was a lot more to go on when Ezra Hilton was killed, and Rose was close to her deceased niece. I'm not sure I want to bother Abby Wheeler right now. And what would I ask her? If she knew her husband was a bully? What was he capable of?"

"You can bet she knew firsthand what the man was capable of. She wouldn't be the first wife who stayed in an abusive marriage."

"We don't even know if they had a dysfunctional marriage," Katie pointed out. "I don't even know if they ever had children."

"Who could you ask?"

Katie shrugged. "Maybe Rose or Gilda."

"Would you ask them?"

Katie polished off the last of her cinnamon bun and nodded. "I'll try, but Rose didn't approve of me ousting Ida, so I might have to wait a day or so to hit her up. Gilda might be more receptive."

"See what else you can find out about the guy, too, willya?" Andy pushed.

Katie scrutinized his face. If she was a naughty girl, she could tie her acceptance to a new breaker box for her apartment. But she decided it was better—nobler—to be nice. "Okay. But don't get your hopes up."

"I know it sounds dopey, but . . . I don't have children of my own, and yet I feel as protective as any parent when it comes to the boys who work for me. They're just kids. They don't realize that what they do now could follow them for the rest of their lives. I just don't want them messing up and regretting it for as long as they live."

Katie nodded, and didn't for a second doubt Andy's sincerity. But if Blake was involved with the murder and arson at Wood U, it was already too late for him.

Eight

Katie finished getting the checks ready for distribution the next day, and locked them inside the file cabinet before she ventured out of her office. By then it was nearing the noon hour and she figured things might be slower for Gilda, giving her an opportunity to talk.

Rose wasn't at the cash desk when Katie passed the front register. She'd probably already gone to lunch—or could she still be consoling Ida? When she got to the parking lot, Katie noted that Ida's car was gone, and that Rose's red Mini Cooper was parked in its usual spot. At least she hadn't hightailed it out of the Alley. As it was, she worked most days, although she wasn't assigned, and thank goodness for that. Getting the vendors to show up on their allotted workdays was difficult enough—but even more so during the heat wave.

They'd show up if you sold your treasures to Nick and Don to pay for the AC upgrade, taunted the logical voice within her.

She ignored it. Or tried to. Ignoring good advice went against her better judgment, especially if the person giving her the good advice was . . . herself.

When Katie opened the door to Gilda's Gourmet Baskets, she was immediately assaulted with a blast of frigid air. It felt jarring after walking across the blast furnace that was the Victoria Square parking lot. Gilda was with a customer, ringing up a sale, but the rest of the shop was empty. Katie poked around the finished baskets, admiring the time and care Gilda employed when assembling them.

"I'm sure your nephew will love this basket. It's got everything a new homeowner could ask for," Gilda said to her customer.

Katie looked up. A new homeowner. One day she'd own her own home and not have to live in a tiny apartment—especially over a very hot pizza parlor. But then, that was her own decision. Most days she didn't regret it. Most days.

If the woman were dressed with a bit more panache, she could have won a Carol Channing look-alike contest. She wore what Katie's aunt Lizzie had called a muumuu—a tentlike purple floral dress. The sheen of her platinum hair was just a tad off, giving away that it was a wig. The woman's lipstick was a bright magenta that clashed with her outfit, and her eyes were hidden behind large sunglasses. "I'm sure I'll be back soon," she said and gave a wave as she exited the store.

"Have a great day," Gilda called as the woman exited the shop.

Katie hightailed it to the counter. "Did you get a load of that outfit?"

"I wasn't paying attention," Gilda admitted. "All I cared about was the color of her credit card. Gold. Now, what are you doing here during business hours?" Gilda asked, but her voice held no reproach.

"I had to escape my oven of an office for a while. And I was hoping you might have a few minutes to talk about Dennis Wheeler."

Gilda glanced around the empty shop. "A few minutes. Would you like a cup of coffee or something?" She waved a hand in the direction of a shelf against the wall that held airpots of coffee and hot water for cocoa. If Gilda had asked the question when Katie first entered the shop, she would have said no—but she found herself chilled in the frigid air.

"Thanks." She helped herself to a cup of coffee and doctored it with hazelnut creamer. "I haven't been cool enough to drink coffee for over a week," she admitted.

"Why do you think I have the AC set so low in here?" Gilda asked. "Between the cold air and the free samples, I'm selling the artisan-ground coffees like hotcakes. It more than pays for my utility bills." Gilda always was a sharp business-woman. "Now, what did you want to know about Dennis? Have they figured out if it was him who died in the fire?"

Katie shook her head. "Not as far as I know. I heard some rather disturbing news about Dennis last night and I wondered if you'd heard the same."

"What kind of news?" Gilda asked.

"Word is that he was bullying his students over at the high school, which is why he was forced to retire early."

"Oh my," Gilda said, shocked.

"One of the first things Detective Davenport asked me was if Dennis and Abby had a good marriage. I didn't give the question any relevance until I'd heard about Dennis bullying his students. Do you think they could have had a bad marriage?"

"Even if they did, what's that got to do with the murder and arson at Wood U? Especially if they haven't even identified the body *as* Dennis? Besides, Abby Wheeler was genuinely distraught when she arrived on the scene on Saturday night. No one could fake that kind of worry and tears."

Katie nodded and sipped her coffee. No doubt about it—the night of the fire Abby had been beside herself with worry and grief. "Abused wives are often reluctant to leave their husbands. It's all about emotional manipulation. Sometimes these women are brainwashed into thinking they deserve the abuse."

"Abby Wheeler doesn't come across as that gullible," Gilda pointed out.

Katie had to agree with that assessment. She took another sip of coffee before she tried a different tack. "Do you know how long Dennis owned the business?"

Gilda frowned. "I've been on the Square for almost five years now, and Wood U was here before I was. But I'm not sure if Dennis was the first owner."

"Did you know the business had been sold?"

"No," Gilda said, sounding genuinely surprised.

Again Katie nodded.

"Who bought it?"

"I haven't found out—yet. Seth Landers represented the new owner, but he won't say who it is."

"And you're such good friends, too," Gilda teased.

"Something about ethics and all that stuff."

"Oh, yes," Gilda said and chuckled. "A lawyer with ethics. That's kind of an oxymoron, isn't it?"

"It's bound to come out any day now. I mean . . . what if that person had the motive and the opportunity to kill Dennis? Or what if Dennis killed the new owner?" Katie asked, postulating what had only occurred to her at that moment.

"But why?"

Katie shrugged. "Who knows what drives people to kill? An argument over money? Maybe Dennis got caught pilfering merchandise after the business was sold."

"Oh, he'd never do that," Gilda protested.

"Until last night, I would have never thought him capable of bullying his students either," Katie pointed out.

Gilda shook her head. "All this speculation is useless until the police identify the dead man found at the store."

"I suppose you're right," Katie admitted. She polished off the last of her coffee and tossed the paper cup in the trash next to the makeshift coffee station.

"Why do you obsess about these things, Katie?" Gilda asked.

Katie shrugged. "I don't know. Maybe it's because I don't have anybody left to care about."

"What about Andy?"

Katie smiled. "Yes, there is Andy. But with no one else, I feel like I have to look out for my vendors—or at least those who are helpful and kind." *And not maddening like Ida,* that irritating voice inside her reminded her. "And those in the Merchants Association, too. You're all I've got."

"Oh, that's so sweet," Gilda said. "Although you haven't been a part of Victoria Square for very long, Katie, we feel the same way about you."

Katie felt a blush rising up her neck to color

her cheeks. She hadn't meant to get maudlin. "Thanks, Gilda." She glanced at her watch. "And thanks for the coffee, too. I'd best be getting back to the Alley. No doubt I'm needed to solve yet another crisis."

"Have you already had one today?"

Katie nodded. "A doozie. I had to tell Ida Mitchell to leave."

"Well, that was long overdue," Gilda said, her expression darkening. "Ezra let her walk all over him. Now don't you go feeling guilty about it either. I give you a lot of credit for juggling so many balls. There's a reason why I work alone in my shop for most of the year. I've found dealing with employees to be the most exasperating part of the business, so I'm glad I only have to deal with them during the holidays."

"The situation became intolerable," Katie said, but was determined not to go into the details. She was sure everyone on the Square would know about the altercation before the end of the day anyway. "I'd better get going."

"I'll see you Wednesday at the Merchants Association meeting, if not before," Gilda called as Katie opened the door. A blast of heat hit her in the face with the force of a sucker punch. She waved a quick good-bye and hurriedly shut the door.

She wondered if she'd have better luck talking to Rose.

One thing was for sure—if she couldn't get Rose to come up with more information than Gilda had, Andy would be less than pleased to hear the poor results of her sleuthing efforts.

Rose was back at her post at Cash Desk 1, ringing up a sale, when Katie arrived back at Artisans Alley. Since there was no one standing behind her to wrap the fragile blown-glass ornaments, Katie stepped up to the counter, grabbed a piece of paper, and wrapped the first of several colorful orbs. With the sale complete, Katie handed the customer the package and said, "Have a nice day."

"You, too," the woman answered and headed for the exit.

Rose hadn't turned around, and unlike other times when Katie had stepped in to help, she hadn't thanked her either.

"Are you angry with me?" Katie asked.

Rose sighed—rather theatrically, too. Finally she turned to face Katie. "No. Just a little disappointed. Then again, I know how maddening Ida can be. She's caused me to lose my temper more than once in the past. And it wasn't right of her to say disparaging things about you to the customers."

"Thank you for that. If it makes you feel any better, I'm not happy about the situation either. But I couldn't back down. Not this time."

Another customer arrived at the cash desk,

holding one of Chad's small floral paintings. Rose rang up the sale and Katie took one long last look at it. Pink poppies. They'd seen them in a churchyard on a day trip to Fair Haven, New York. Chad had snapped several photographs and used them as the inspiration for the painting. There were only four or five paintings left now, and when each one sold, Katie felt a pang of regret. But she had no room for more and, in fact, had put ten or twelve of the larger paintings in her storage unit, with the intention of hanging them at The English Ivy Inn.

That wasn't going to happen now.

"Take good care of it," Katie told the man, who said it was to be a birthday gift for his wife.

"It hurts to see them go, doesn't it?" Rose asked.

Katie nodded. "But hopefully that man's wife will enjoy it for years to come." She found she had to swallow down a lump in her throat.

"Is there something else you want to talk about?" Rose asked.

"Actually, there is. Dennis Wheeler."

"Has there been a break in the case?" Rose asked eagerly.

"Not that I know of. But I heard some rather disturbing news about Dennis, and I wondered if you'd heard something similar." Without naming names, she conveyed what Andy and Keith had told her the night before.

Rose listened, nodding now and then. Finally, she shrugged. "If Dennis had been a vendor here, I'm sure I would've known all the dirt. Not much escapes me—and we're a gossipy group. But being as he was one of the merchants . . . Sorry, I can't help you, Katie."

"That's okay."

"Your husband was a teacher at the high school. Do you know any of the other teachers there?"

"Not really. But I met Kevin Hartsfield back in April while we were trying to find out what happened to Heather. He used to teach math at McKinlay Mill High School."

"Oh, yes, I remember him. Another sterling example of the quality of teachers they've hired around here. Do you really think he'd be a good character witness for Dennis Wheeler?"

Katie shook her head. "I guess not."

"I suppose you could go up to the school and speak to a secretary or maybe even the principal, but they aren't likely to talk about a man who was asked to retire, now, are they?"

"No," Katie agreed.

"And you're not thinking of talking to Abby Wheeler, are you?" Rose asked with disapproval. "That poor woman has enough on her mind."

"I agree," Katie said.

"Good. Now, as long as you're here, we should talk about the potluck on Saturday."

Katie sighed. "I can't thank you and Edie enough for taking charge of this."

Rose waved a hand in dismissal. "You have far more important things on your mind than organizing a party. And it's fun. Of course, I've had a heck of a time getting people to commit to a specific dish to pass. Too many people want to bring dessert. I've had to put my foot down and insist that we get some good side dishes."

"Oh, dear. I was going to bring a dessert."

"What were you thinking of?"

"Since it's been so unrelentingly hot, I thought I'd make a no-bake treat. Maybe homemade peppermint patties."

"Oh, they're my favorite. And they're candy, not dessert, so I think I can make an exception. But if you have some extra time, we could sure use a side dish, too," she stressed.

"I'll see what I can do," Katie promised.

She returned to her stuffy office and turned on the fan once more, thinking about her conversation with Gilda. What if Dennis had killed the new owner and then taken off? There was only one person she knew of to call to check. She picked up the receiver and punched in Seth Landers's office number.

"I'm sorry, Katie, but he's tied up with clients all morning. Is this something important? An emergency?" Seth's secretary, Carrie, asked.

"No." Whoever had been killed had been dead

for almost thirty-six hours. She could wait to ask her questions.

"I'll ask him to call you," Carrie said.

"Thanks." Katie hung up the receiver. It rang almost immediately. She sighed and picked it up. "Artisans Alley—"

"She's at it again," came the angry woman's voice. Vonne Barnett. *She* had to be Nona, and *it* had to be that she'd once again set out the signs in the parking lot.

"I'll be right over," Katie said, then hung up the phone and rued the day she'd ever accepted the job of president of the Victoria Square Merchants Association.

Nona Fiske might consider herself The Quiet Quilter, but she was also a major pain in the butt. And right now, Katie's butt was in agony. She hated playing the bad guy, and if she'd known she'd have to do it so often between dealing with the vendors at Artisans Alley and the merchants on the Square, she might have refused her inheritance of another forty-five percent of the Alley. Well, probably not, because she'd quit a job she'd despised, and most of the time she enjoyed the interaction with the people on the Square. This week? Not so much.

She donned an Artisans Alley promotional baseball cap and dark sunglasses before she left the building—like taking on the persona of a bad cop. She knew she'd find it easier to confront Nona if the woman couldn't see her eyes. She needed to be the intimidator—not the intimidated. As she walked across the Square, Katie wondered if she should have borrowed a piece of gum from one of the vendors. Didn't people look tougher when they chewed gum?

Her first stop was at Afternoon Tea, where, sure enough, she saw the professional-looking signs Nona had paid someone to make. They even had the Victoria Square logo added to the bottom to make them look official.

The door to Afternoon Tea burst open and Vonne Barnett came out to join Katie. She was a little taller than Katie, with glasses and short dark hair. She wore a soiled apron with the name of the tea shop on it, and there was the hint of flour dusting the left side of her cheek. "See, see," she said, waggling her hand as she pointed to the offending signs.

"I see them, all right."

"I know I've only been to one Merchants Association meeting so far, and I don't like to look like a complainer right out the gate, but I did read the charter and—"

"It's okay, Vonne," Katie said, holding up a hand to interrupt. "You've done nothing wrong. In fact, you've done everything right."

Vonne sighed. "Thank you. But honestly, what can you do if she won't take them down? If you toss her out of the Merchants Association, she can essentially do as she pleases."

"I'll remind her about the snowplowing and other perks she gets as a member."

"And if she decides they aren't worth it?"

Katie didn't answer. "You'd better go inside. Nona isn't the most reasonable person I know. I don't want her screaming at you and making a scene potential customers can witness."

Vonne nodded, turned, and reentered her shop.

Katie approached The Quiet Quilter's covered porch and climbed the two steps up. She was about to enter the shop when the door swung open and Nona Fiske barreled through, nearly knocking her over. Though small in stature, and nearing the end of her sixth decade, Nona seemed to have boundless energy. She reminded Katie of a tornado—all force and fury but with no constructive mission.

"Good morning, Nona," Katie said, keeping her voice bland. "It seems we have a problem with parking."

"Yes, someone removed my signs, hiding them in back of my store. I'll bet it was those cretins who bought the tea shop next door."

"No, it was me," Katie said, still keeping her tone even.

"You!" Nona accused, then lowered her voice. "I should have known."

"Now, Nona, you know why they had to be removed."

"No, I don't think I do," Nona said, raising her chin, perhaps as a way to look taller.

"According to the Merchants Association's charter, every parking space on Victoria Square is open for any potential customer who wants to park there. This encourages them to visit more than one shop during their stay."

"My customers don't shop at other stores on the Square."

"Are you absolutely sure of that?"

"My shop is very busy," Nona began. "I don't have time to follow each and every customer out to their cars to see what they do."

Katie raked a glance around the immediate area. Not one car was parked anywhere near The Quiet Quilter.

"Nona, you've been told more than once not to put out signs designating parking for The Quiet Quilter only. Do you want to tell me why you've decided to violate the charter?"

Nona folder her arms across her sweater, her stance defiant. "I think it's stupid."

"The charter, or the parking rules?"

"Both." Did she realize just how childish she sounded? It certainly wasn't flattering.

"Nona, what is your problem with following the rules?"

"It's not the rules I despise, it's you!"

"Me?"

"You walked in, took over Artisans Alley, took over the Merchants Association—"

"As I recall, Gilda begged someone—anyone—to step forward and take over the Merchants Association, and when no one did, she suckered me into it."

"And haven't you enjoyed every day of it, you power-hungry bitch?"

Katie forced herself not to react. Her first inclination had been to bleat, "Yeah, it takes one to know one!" Instead, she silently counted to ten and wondered how many more times that week she'd be referred to with the *B* word. "I'm going to try to forget you just said that, Nona, and chalk it up to the stress we've all endured during this lengthy and oppressive heat wave."

"Don't make excuses on my account," Nona said.

"Very well. If you need a copy of the charter, which you helped draft I might add, I would be glad to see that one is delivered to you. I'd like you to review the section on the parking policy. If you have a grievance, you need to bring it to the Association. Do I make myself clear?"

"Perfectly," Nona said.

"Thank you. Will we see you at the monthly meeting tomorrow night?"

"You better believe it," she said, and turned. Without another word, she reentered her shop, slamming the door.

Katie turned and started down the steps for the parking lot. So much for looking tough with a cap and dark glasses. Now, who could she get to walk a copy of the charter over to Nona? Too bad she'd already sent Ida home; this might have been the perfect job for her. She didn't want to saddle such an unpleasant task on just anyone at the Alley, and she was damned if she was going to walk across the lot and deliver it herself.

If Godfrey was hanging around, she'd get him to do it. It seemed as though he and Nona were made of similar—annoying—cloth.

Nine

The first thing Katie did when she returned to Artisans Alley was put out a call on the building's public address system, asking Godfrey to meet her in her office. He didn't. That meant she'd have to find someone else to do her dirty work. She made a copy of the charter, placed it in a flat envelope, and headed for the cash desk. On her way, she met up with Liz Meier.

"Just the person I was hoping to find," Katie said. "Can you run an errand for me across the Square?"

"Sure. I'd love to go outside and cool off for a few minutes," Liz joked.

"Take this over to the owner of The Quiet Quilter, and then stand back in case she explodes."

"Sounds like you're not having a good personnel relations day."

"You've got that right," Katie said, and handed her the envelope.

Liz smiled. "Don't worry, I'm wearing invisible armor. Completely impervious to jerks and other unintelligent life-forms."

Katie smiled. "I really appreciate this."

"I'm glad to help," Liz said, and headed for the exit.

Katie returned to her office, checked her voice mail, and found no return call from Seth.

Swell.

She sat down at her computer, opened a new document, and began to work on the agenda for the next Merchants Association meeting, making sure that Nona's parking problem would be addressed, as well as welcoming the newest members to the group. She checked her notes from the last meeting and included the unfinished business. With that wrapped up, she figured she'd better get to the bank before it closed. She hadn't yet banked the weekend's receipts and needed to make sure the checks to the vendors wouldn't bounce the next morning.

That errand ate another forty-five minutes, and when Katie returned, there was still no message from Seth. Okay, so she didn't expect him to be at her beck and call, but surely he had to allow himself a couple of down moments during any given workday. Or was she just spoiled since it seemed like most of her day could be considered downtime when it was eaten up by petty errands and often just as petty people?

Katie dawdled, deciding not to start anything new. First she neatened her desk, then tidied the vendors' lounge, and even emptied the waste-basket in the restroom behind her office.

It was twenty minutes before closing by the time Seth finally returned her call with a casual, "You rang?"

"Yes. I didn't realize you had such a busy practice. I would've thought you'd be out on the golf course or something. Isn't that what lawyers do in the summer?"

"Only if they want to swelter. I've got top-notch air-conditioning, and people flock to my office just to sit in my waiting room."

"I believe it," Katie said.

"Now, tell me what's up," Seth urged.

"I had a conversation with Gilda Ringwald-Stratton this morning, talking about Dennis Wheeler. Now, try to have an open mind about this—but what do you think about the possibility that Dennis might have killed the new owner of Wood U?"

"Not a chance."

"Have you seen or talked with the new owner since Saturday night?"

"No, but I know someone who has."

"Damn. That completely negates my theory."

"Sorry. Is there anything else you want to tell me?"

"I met your friends Nick and Don this morning after they closed on the Webster mansion when they came to check out their new home. They're nice guys."

"Didn't I tell you that?"

"Yes, but since you've been tied up all day, I'll bet you haven't heard that someone broke into the house since they'd done their walk-through on Friday."

"Was there any damage?" Seth asked, concerned.

"Just a broken window. They were going to have it fixed and see if they could speed up the installation of their security system."

"Good."

The silence dragged.

"Are you doing anything tonight?" Katie asked, the thought of the long, hot evening ahead and nothing to do but watch the walls of her apartment sweat holding no magic for her.

"Unfortunately, I've already got plans. Let me see how the week shakes out and maybe we'll get a chance to cook together in my nice air-conditioned kitchen in a day or two."

"That sounds heavenly. Thanks."

"Sorry to cut this short, but I've got to run. Talk to you later," Seth said and hung up.

Katie hung up her phone, too.

Swell.

There must be something mildly interesting she could do to pass the evening. And then it came to her. The village library was air-conditioned. She could spend a couple of hours there reading cookbooks. Surely she'd find some kind of recipe for a side dish to bring to the potluck on Saturday and win her points with Rose.

With that decided, Katie made her store-closing announcement, and shut down her computer for the night. After that, she went up front to help take care of the last of the day's customers, collected the cash from the registers, locked it in her file cabinet, and closed her office door.

Since Liz had acted as the Alley's security officer for the day, she did a final walk-through with Katie before Katie locked up for the night. They walked out together and bade each other good night. Before Katie could make it to her car, she saw Francine Barnett charging across the parking lot toward her.

Swell.

Francine always seemed frazzled. As the tea shop's kitchen manager, she didn't interact with her customers as much as her daughter did, which was good because Katie was sure the tea shop, which was supposed to be a haven of serenity,

133

would be so charged with tension it would drive the customers away in droves.

Was that part of the shop's current lack of patrons, or was Vonne's assessment correct that the heat and Nona's parking signs kept the customers from their door?

"Katie—Katie!" Francine frantically called. Maybe the reason Nona and her new neighbor didn't get along was because they were too much alike—high-strung and prone to hysteria.

Francine was out of breath by the time she caught up to Katie. "We've"—*gasp, gasp!*—"got to talk." *Gasp, gasp!*

"Take your time, Francine. I'm in no hurry."

Francine leaned against the car and then yelped.

"Watch it, it's hot," Katie warned. After all, the white Ford Focus had been sitting in the sun all day.

Francine rubbed her fanny and turned a sour gaze on Katie. "I was warned not to open a shop here on Victoria Square. But no, Vonne didn't want to locate near the new marina. She said Victoria Square was the place to be. And then I found out about all the deaths."

Katie felt sure she was in for a thorough tongue-lashing.

"I mean, really—who opens a death store?" she said, her hand taking in the small bungalow that housed The Angel Shop, which was filled with angel figurines, garden memorial stones, stained glass panels, and such. Reaching out to other grief-stricken people had helped the owner through the loss of her mother after a long battle with cancer. It was a business that served an ever-growing niche population.

"I go to visit my mother for three days and what do I find when I return? Someone else on the Square has died. Violently!" She glared at Katie, as though it might be her fault. What was she supposed to say? "Poor Mr. Wheeler."

"They don't know for sure if it was Dennis who died. At least, not that I've heard," Katie said.

"Well, *somebody* died. I'll be afraid to be on the Square by myself. And I sure as heck won't let Vonne work at the shop alone at night anymore. She's my only child," she cried.

What intruder would be dissuaded from breaking in by the sight of this wisp of a woman?

"And now—now we've got that horrible woman from the quilt shop harassing us. Are you going to do something about her?"

"I've already spoken with her."

"Did she promise she wouldn't put those signs out in front of our shop?" Francine demanded.

"Not exactly, but I did warn her that she was in violation of the parking policy and that it would be brought up at the Merchants Association meeting on Wednesday."

"Fat lot of good that's going to do if she refuses."

"Let's give it a try, shall we?" Katie said diplomatically.

Francine glowered.

"Now, is there anything else you'd like us to talk about at the meeting? I've started the agenda, but there's plenty of time to amend it."

"I'll think about it," Francine said, marginally mollified.

"Excellent. I'll be looking forward to your input."

Francine turned a jaundiced glare at Katie. "Are you making fun of me?"

Katie sobered, feeling sweat trickle down the back of her neck. "Never. I take everything brought to me by the merchants seriously, especially this parking problem. There's no reason any merchant should feel intimidated or bullied." Like Dennis had bullied his students and perhaps his wife? "And I intend to take steps to put an end to it."

Francine nodded. "Thank you."

"Now, will you and Vonne be coming to the Artisans Alley Christmas in July gathering on Saturday?"

"We haven't decided."

"You're welcome to come—and bring an appetite. There's going to be tons of food, music, and I hope, fun."

Francine let out what sounded like a bored breath. "Maybe. We'll think about it. See you later, Katie." And she turned and started back for Afternoon Tea.

Crisis averted!

Katie sorted through her key ring. She'd only been standing in the parking lot talking with Francine for a few minutes, but she felt as though she'd been on the hot seat long enough. Only now she'd have to literally sit on the hot seat of her car for the five-minute drive to the library on the edge of town.

Her reward for the day would be a few hours of uninterrupted peace and quiet.

No complaining merchants.

No complaining vendors.

No worries at all.

Fingers crossed.

McKinlay Mill's library was located on the west end of Main Street, where it reverted to Route 8. Housed in the old elementary school building, it was big, brick, and ugly. The main floor housed the library and the second floor doubled as the senior/community center. Whose bright idea had it been to force the village's elderly to traverse up a flight of stairs? There was an elevator, but it was creaky and slow and Katie wondered how safe it really was.

But for such an old building, it did have reliable air-conditioning. Katie felt positively frozen her first five minutes inside the building, but she soon grew acclimated. Taking a stack of ten or twelve books from the shelves, she commandeered one of the upholstered chairs and settled in for a good read. Before she'd left the Alley, she'd tossed some Post-it Flags in her purse to mark the pages of any interesting recipes.

From her vantage point, Katie had a good view of the library's entrance, the circulation desk, and the computer carrels, where every seat was occupied, and stationed nearby was a large bottle of hand sanitizer. The thought of all those strangers manhandling the keyboards day in and day out was sobering, and Katie was glad she didn't have to share her computer at the Alley with anyone else. Well, occasionally Vance or Rose would use it for Alley business, but it was usually to take on a task that Katie had delegated. She knew she needed to do that more often, too.

She'd flipped through half of a Martha Stewart cookbook when she looked up to see Abby Wheeler standing at the returns portion of the circulation desk, handing in a pile of books through the return slot.

Katie piled her cookbooks on her chair, hoping to save it from another patron's encroachment, and hurried over to the circulation desk. "Abby," she called.

Abby looked up, her expression one of startled fear, and then she recognized Katie and visibly relaxed. "Katie, you don't know how good it feels to see a friendly face."

Had she seen a host of unfriendly faces of late?

"How are you doing?" Katie asked, concerned.

"Not so good," Abby admitted. "A reporter and camera crew were camped out on my front lawn most of yesterday and again today. What must my neighbors think?"

"Haven't any of them checked in to see if you need anything?"

Abby shook her head and fed another one of her books into the return slot. "I always heard that when trouble struck, people banded together to help someone in grief. So far, no one's offered me so much as a bagel in a grocery bag."

Katie swallowed down a pang of guilt. "Maybe they're hoping that it's all a mistake and Dennis will show up with amnesia or something." Katie winced. That was the most idiotic thing she could have said, yet Abby didn't seem to be listening all that hard. She fed yet another book into the drop slot.

Abby's gaze strayed. Katie turned to her left to see a couple of library patrons staring in their direction. "I have to get out of here," Abby said, sounding panicked. "Would you return the rest of my books?" She shoved them at Katie and fled for the exit.

Katie watched her bolt and then looked down at the pile of books before her. They appeared to all be mysteries. She fed them one by one into the slot before returning to her seat, feeling oddly disconcerted by her encounter with Abby.

She picked up a Rachael Ray cookbook and studied the table of contents. When she looked up few minutes later, she saw Detective Davenport standing at the circulation desk, leaning close to speak to the woman checking out books. She kept shaking her head, her expression stern, and yet neither spoke loud enough for their voices to carry.

Finally, Davenport moved away from the desk and looked around the library at large, spying Katie. She waved. His grim expression didn't waver, but he did march toward her.

"What are you doing here, Mrs. Bonner?" he asked.

"Escaping the heat. How about you?"

"Uh . . . well, to be honest, I'd followed Mrs. Wheeler here."

"You aren't thinking Abby killed her husband?" Katie asked, aghast.

"It's a possibility," he admitted. "I was hoping the library staff would volunteer to tell me what books she'd just returned, but they're not about to say without a warrant—if I could even get one. Libraries have fought hard for First Amendment rights for their patrons—damn them."

"I don't know. I don't think I'd want just anybody to know what I'm reading," Katie said.

Davenport looked down at the stack of books that sat beside Katie's chair. "So, you like to cook. So does one of my kids. Big deal."

"I spoke to Abby before she left," Katie said.

Davenport's eyes widened. "Oh?"

"A couple of people were staring at her and pointing. It seemed to frighten her. She fled and I had to feed her books into the return slot."

"Oh?" Davenport said again, and this time she feared his eyes might actually pop out of his skull.

"She reads mysteries. And doesn't everybody?"

"I don't," he said, scowling.

"Well, I've been known to. I like the ones where the heroines bake. They include recipes."

Davenport actually grimaced.

"Do you really suspect Abby of killing her husband?" Katie asked.

"Under these circumstances, the spouse is always a suspect, although more often it's a man, not a woman, who commits homicide."

"I saw Abby on Saturday night—and so did Gilda Ringwald-Stratton. She was terribly upset. There's no faking that kind of hysteria." Odd. Katie had labeled both Nona and Francine with that descriptor. But Abby had been truly upset and frightened. Perhaps she needed to amend her description of the two Victoria Square merchants. Perhaps they were just plain nuts.

"You're probably right," Davenport admitted.

"But until we make a positive ID on the body, it's open season on suspects."

"And do you have more than one suspect?" Katie asked.

"Yes," Davenport answered without hesitation, yet he didn't elaborate. "I need to get home. My girls are keeping the dinner warm, and I hate dried-out meat and vegetables. It'll be good to sit down and eat a decent meal once I retire."

"I envy you having someone to share dinner with," Katie said.

"Don't you have a boyfriend, Mrs. Bonner?"

"He works nights, and I work days. But we try to eat together a night or two every week." One meal here or there. Well, it could be worse. She could eat all her meals alone, like she had during the months she and Chad had been estranged, and then just as many after he'd died. She and Seth had become close during the past ten months, going to lunch on a regular basis, and as she'd told Davenport, she and Andy tried to eat together as often as his job allowed.

"Have a nice dinner, Detective."

"You, too, Mrs. Bonner." Davenport nodded and exited the library.

As he left, Nona Fiske entered with a big canvas bag draped over her shoulder, heading straight for the book return.

Katie turned away, aiming for the seat she'd so recently abandoned, and yet as she sat down, she could see the covers of the books Nona favored. Romances with bare-chested heroes and swooning heroines. She smiled. Nona and Rose favored the same kind of fiction, and yet Rose was a sweetheart and Nona was not.

Katie dived back into her cookbook, content to immerse herself in nonfiction and the relative safety of decadent, butter-drenched recipes. Well, maybe they weren't safe for her heart, but they were safe for her psyche.

In comparison, Dennis Wheeler's death—or disappearance—was far too horrific to contemplate.

Ten

Katie didn't leave the cool comfort of the library until she, and all the other patrons, were chased out at closing time. She staggered to her car with a load of new-to-her cookbooks and spent the rest of the evening in front of her fan, with one or more cats on or sitting next to her, reading recipes, looking for a fun side dish to placate Rose for Saturday's potluck dinner. Yet in the end, she decided to bring an old standby that her aunt Lizzie used to make, apricot carrots.

The next morning, Katie got up at first light, put the kettle on for tea, and perused the morning paper, hoping to find an update on the Wood U fire and murder. There was none. On TV dramas, the crime teams always processed DNA evidence in what seemed like minutes. Too bad real life didn't imitate art—if those shows could be called art.

She'd just polished off a third slice of toast and a second cup of tea when a loud roar outside caused Katie to look up from the Jumble she'd been about to start. The cats, who'd been looking out the window overlooking the Square, jumped down just as a gigantic thud rumbled through the ground.

"What in the world?" Katie looked out the window to see a huge Dumpster now sitting in front of the Webster mansion. Hadn't Fred Cunningham said the new owners intended to start work the day after they closed on the property? Would they actually start demolition this morning?

To answer that question, a shiny white pickup truck with BURFORD CONTRACTING emblazoned on the side pulled up in front of the mansion. Nick and Don hadn't been kidding when they said they wanted to open by Thanksgiving.

Katie fought the urge to cry. She'd known this was going to happen, and everybody around her had been tiptoeing around her delicate feelings, but it was time to toughen up. Fred was right. There would be another opportunity for her to open an inn someday . . . *but never on Victoria Square.*

"You can sit around and mope about it or you can get on with your life."

How many times had her aunt Lizzie uttered those words when she'd had some minor disappointment? But that was the difference. Losing The English Ivy Inn—well, she'd never really had it to begin with—was the biggest disappointment of her life.

She set the newspaper aside without even attempting the Jumble. It was time to go to work anyway. She showered and dressed, locked her apartment, and headed down the stairs. At ground level, the Dumpster looked even bigger. She turned away and headed for Artisans Alley.

No one was waiting to get in to straighten his or her booth, so Katie headed directly for her office . . . and found the door open. She stood staring at it for a long moment, sure she'd closed it the night before. Was she having a senior moment? She shrugged, went inside, and booted up her computer. Next, she gathered up the checks she'd processed the day before and headed for the tag room, which also housed pigeonhole mail slots for each of the vendors. She doled out the envelopes, and was about to head back to her office to get the cash for the tills when she saw Rose Nash standing at the door to the vendor entrance and the corridor that led outside.

"Good morning, Rose." Katie scrutinized her friend's face. "Is something wrong?"

Rose craned her neck to look outside once again. "I wasn't sure how to tell you this but . . . Ida has returned."

Katie felt her blood pressure start to rise, as well as her anger. She, too, looked out the door but saw nothing outside. "Surely she has something else to do rather than tape down sales tags all day."

"Oh, yes, she's found something else to do all right. I think you'd better take a look."

Katie turned to head back to the tag room.

"You won't find her there," Rose called, and Katie stopped, turning to face the older woman.

"Where is she?"

"Out in the parking lot in front of the entrance."

Katie blinked in disbelief, but instead of commenting, she turned and hurried out the vendor entrance, her annoyance building with every step.

She burst through the doors to the parking lot to find Ida, dressed in long pants and a long-sleeved shirt, holding a sign and marching up and down in front of the building. The sign said: BOYCOTT ARTISANS ALLEY—UNFAIR LABOR PRACTICES.

Unfair labor practices! For asking the woman to dress appropriately? And there she was—clad in warmer clothes, risking heat stroke. Didn't she know anything about dressing for the weather conditions?

"Ida, what do you think you're doing?" Katie demanded.

Ida kept up her pace. Five steps toward the north, pivot, five steps toward the south. "Protesting."

"What for?"

"I want my job back!"

"We've been over why you were asked to leave. You took my heater and refused to dress appropriately for the temperature in the tag room."

"I'm dressed appropriately now."

"But could I trust you to do so tomorrow?"

Ida didn't answer. Instead, she kept on marching.

Katie resisted the urge to throw her hands up in disgust, but turned and went back inside the building. Rose was standing just behind the door. "Aren't you going to try and stop her?"

"I've learned from bitter experience that talking to Ida is like talking to a rock. She can't be persuaded to do anything she doesn't want to do."

"But it's already awfully hot out there, especially standing on the tarmac. She doesn't have a hat on. When the sun gets higher, she could get heat stroke."

Somehow Katie managed to hold on to her temper, but she couldn't think of anything to say to improve her standing with Rose, with Ida, or with anyone else. "Then maybe you should lend her one. There's cold water in the fridge, too. If you'd care to give her some, I'm fine with it."

"But—"

Katie held up a hand to stave off any more discussion. "I'm going back to my office. If you want to offer Ida any other assistance, I'm fine with that, too. But as far as I'm concerned, the discussion about her is over."

Rose nodded, her pale blue eyes looking watery. After their discussion the previous day, Katie hadn't thought Rose had much more tolerance for Ida than she had herself.

No sooner had Katie returned to her office than Detective Davenport showed up at her door.

"What happened with your former, now disgruntled, vendor? Collective bargaining fall through?" he said and laughed, although his expression held no mirth.

"We had a disagreement about taking and using other people's property without permission, among other things. I'd much rather talk about why you're here."

Davenport shrugged. "Just doing my job."

"You've been hanging around McKinlay Mill quite a bit since the fire. Taking a more in-depth interest than usual, Detective?"

"I told you—this is my last case, Mrs. Bonner."

"Why now?" Katie asked. While she'd

suspected in the past that Davenport's seeming lack of interest in his cases was due to being burned out or a short-timer's attitude, she also knew that he had three daughters. Daughters in college—or about to go to college. That took money. "You still haven't told me what you plan to do next."

Davenport actually managed a wry smile. "A little of this, and a little of that. But I've only got four days to wrap this up, and the Taylor kid has gone to ground. His parents say they haven't seen him since Sunday afternoon."

Katie's gut tightened. Could Blake have been the one to break into the Webster mansion and leave the food wrappers? He would have had to move on now that work had commenced on the house.

"I suppose you want to pick my brains because Andy Rust—Blake's boss—is my boyfriend."

"It couldn't hurt," he admitted.

She sighed. "Andy believes the boy is one hundred percent innocent."

"And how about you?"

Katie hesitated. "I hope Andy's right. He's got a lot of faith in the kids he hires. I'd hate for his trust to be misplaced."

"So he said."

"Have you looked into the allegations that Dennis Wheeler bullied his students?"

"I've spoken with the school principal. It's a

possibility one of the kids took his revenge, but it's not the only angle I'm looking at."

And Katie would bet he wasn't going to share that angle with her either.

He eyed her, his mouth twisting into a frown. "Are you sure there's nothing else you want to tell me about the fire or what's happening on the Square?" he prodded.

"Only . . ." She sighed, resigned, and then told him about her walk through the Webster mansion with Nick and Don.

"Why didn't someone report this?" he demanded angrily.

"I suggested they do just that, but I haven't spoken with them since yesterday so I have no idea if they did. And who would make the connection anyway?"

"Crap. Whatever evidence was there is probably sitting in that Dumpster. I'll head on over there right now."

"If I hear of anything else, I'll give you a call," she promised.

"I'd appreciate it." Davenport gave her a parting nod and hightailed it out of her office.

Feeling as though she'd just betrayed Andy, Katie sat down at her desk and wondered what to do next. She didn't have time to ponder the question long because a knock at the door drew her attention.

"Got a minute?" Vance asked.

"For you? Always."

Vance entered Katie's tiny office and parked himself against her file cabinet. He crossed his arms over his golf shirt. That defensive posture didn't bode for a happy conversation. "About Ida . . ."

Katie closed her eyes and hung her head, wondering how much it would hurt if she pounded it against the top of her desk. Probably no more than the throbbing headache Ida had already given her with her disruptive nonsense.

A warm hand touched her shoulder. "If it's any consolation, I know exactly how you feel."

She looked up at him and could see he was trying not to laugh. It didn't make her feel better. "Tell me how Ezra used to deal with her."

"He let her do anything she damn well pleased, and maybe you should, too."

"I'm not Ezra, and I can't run Artisans Alley the way he did."

"I realize that, but she's a demented old lady. She's got no life, she's got no friends, and she's got nowhere else to spend her time. Like it or not, we're all she's got."

"I *don't* like it." She sighed. "I'm not a complete monster. I do feel sorry for the woman, but she obviously has a lot of problems—something we're not in a position to deal with or correct."

"That's true," Vance agreed with a nod.

Again Katie sighed. "What is it you want me to do? Take her back?"

"Eventually."

Katie raised an eyebrow. "And in the meantime?"

"I've got an EZ-UP tent in the back of my truck. She can sit under that so she doesn't get heat stroke, and if we park it near the vendor entry, it'll keep her from blocking the front entrance."

Katie thought it over. It was a reasonable compromise—for now. "How long do we put up with this?"

Vance shrugged. "She's stubborn. She may never give up."

"Then maybe we'll just have to find her another job. Somewhere she can *go* on a daily basis. Something she can *do* that will give her a sense of purpose—something more than just taping tags on sheets of paper."

"Great idea. Are you willing to do it?"

"I have more important things to do with my time, but if I want her off my hands, it looks like I'll have to do something." She frowned. "I do feel sorry for her, but she's really not my problem," Katie reiterated.

"As long as she's picketing outside of Artisans Alley, she's *definitely* your problem," Vance said.

Why did he have to be right *all* of the time? Perhaps that was why she counted on him—for advice and for his friendship.

Katie nodded. "Okay. Put your little tent up.

When you're ready, I'll help you take a table and chair out to her."

He waved a hand aside. "I figured you'd say yes. I already set it up and took out the chair and table. She's sitting there like the Queen of Hearts from *Alice in Wonderland*."

"Lovely. I suppose next she'll be advising people to come after me—off with my head!"

Vance stroked his beard thoughtfully. "She's already doing that."

Katie rolled her eyes. "Swell."

Katie found it hard to concentrate that afternoon. Her mind kept flitting to various subjects: Dennis, Blake, the upcoming potluck dinner, the demolition going on at the Webster mansion, and the menu for her dinner with Andy later that night. She made the latter her top priority, and wrote out a grocery list for later.

Too restless to work, she got up and made a circuit around Artisans Alley. Her vendors were right. You could go from blazing hot to searing cold walking the length of the long aisles of booths. The ducting for the air-conditioning had been concealed in some areas and was exposed in others. It had been a sloppy, inadequate job. She wondered who had done the initial work but hadn't been able to find any of the paperwork in her files. Then again, she had tossed out a lot of the decades-old papers when she'd first taken over, before she knew what to save and what to keep. It didn't matter in this case, she'd contacted a trusted firm with more than seventy years of experience. If she had the work done, she would go with them.

If she had the money to do the work, she would get it done in a heartbeat.

You could have the money, the voice inside her harped. She ignored it. Or tried to. Living in denial. Yes, that's what she was doing—and quite well, too, she decided.

As she made her final round of the second floor, she neared the large storage closet where her late husband had lived illegally during their months of estrangement prior to his death. Ezra had called it Chad's Pad. He'd called her on a number of occasions and asked her to come and claim Chad's belongings, but she never had. And when she'd taken over Artisans Alley, she'd left everything as it was. If they pulled down the walls, they could make room for more vendor space, she decided. Since she currently had four empty booths, that could wait awhile—and for cooler weather in the fall. But since she expected to fill that vendor space before the holidays, she thought it might be a good idea to list that on her calendar for a day in September. She tried the door handle and, as expected, found the room locked. Good.

Katie trundled down the steep back stairs and

made for her office, finding the mail had been delivered and someone had stacked it neatly on her desk. On top of the pile was a handwritten note with one word written on it: "Ida."

Katie glanced at the clock. It was nearly four. She'd been a good sport about letting the woman demonstrate, but it was time for Ida to end her protest for the day. The problem was, Ida wasn't going to listen to Katie. She needed an ally to convince the woman to go home. Was Vance still around?

Without even looking at the mail, Katie headed for the front of the store, where Rose was taking a break, reading one of her romance novels. "Rose?"

Rose held up a finger as her gaze dodged back and forth across the page. Then she grabbed her bookmark and slammed the book shut. "That rotten scoundrel," she said and shook her head. "Of course all will be forgiven in a couple of chapters."

"Sorry to interrupt," Katie said. She had no problem with her cashier reading when there was nobody to wait on. Rose did, after all, put in more time at Artisans Alley than any other vendor. Well, except for Ida, but that was another—unhappy—story. "Is Vance around?"

Rose shook her head. "He had to leave for the day. He said he'd see you either tomorrow or Thursday. He's not scheduled to work again until then. Is there a problem?"

155

"Yes, it's Ida. I'd like her out of here and Vance's little tent down before we close tonight."

"That could be a problem. I'm not sure I know how to take down an EZ-UP."

"Me either. I'd hate for it to blow over and get ruined or for one of us to break it."

"Are you sure Vance didn't think about it before he left?"

"I don't know. I found a note on my desk that just said 'Ida.' I assumed she was still out there."

"You'd better go out and look."

Katie frowned, and headed out the door. Sure enough, the EZ-UP was gone, and so was Ida. But where she'd sat was covered in trash. Empty coffee cups, candy, and fast-food wrappers. It looked like Ida had also taken her petty ire out on a few of the begonias that were planted in front of the shrubbery.

Frustrated, and with growing anger, Katie picked up the mess and threw it away. She watered the flowers, but had little hope they'd revive. And what was she going to do if Ida showed up in the morning? Threaten to have her evicted by the Sheriff's Office? She might be able to level charges of trespassing and malicious mischief, but that might only incite Ida to attempt more petty revenge. Perhaps Vance was right. She needed to find Ida something else to do with her time.

But what?

Eleven

Although the local grocery store was fine for most of what you'd want to fill your larder on any given day, their seafood department was hardly impressive. Katie didn't want to buy frozen scallops for the dinner she planned for Andy, so after closing Artisans Alley for the day, she drove to the neighboring town of Greece and hit their biggest and best store. Since she was already there, she decided to do her shopping for the week, and spent far more than she usually would. Maybe it was better to stick to her home grocery store after all.

When she'd been married to Chad, Katie had been too busy working and going to grad school to care about cooking, but she found she enjoyed making dinner for Andy, who seemed to appreciate the effort she put into the meals they shared. On the other hand, maybe he was as sick of eating pizza and calzones as she was and just didn't want to offend her.

Upon her return home, the cats greeted her with tales of starvation and she fed them before she began preparing her own meal. Mason was particularly fond of seafood, and would bother her to no end if she didn't make sure he was already satisfied before she took out the scallops to get them ready for the oven.

Food prep always relaxed her—and after what she'd put up with that day from Ida, she felt she deserved a nice quiet evening. Of course, the strawberry wine cooler she downed helped not only to keep her cool, but also to reach her quiet zone even faster as she puttered around the kitchen for more than an hour. She had everything ready at the appointed time, and though Andy was ten minutes late in arriving, that was okay. After all, she had nowhere to go, and it wasn't like she didn't know where he was.

She took another wine cooler out of the fridge and cracked the screw cap. She took a sip and then pressed the sweating glass container against her flushed cheek. It felt wonderful. If only she had a life-sized bottle to sidle up against, she would be cool—and keep cool—in no time flat.

She heard footsteps on her stairs and went to the door to open it. "Greetings, and welcome to my most humble abode," she said, and leaned forward to give Andy a kiss. His face was just as flushed as her own, with sweat beading his forehead.

"Sorry I'm late. We had a rush—"

Katie pressed a finger against his lips to silence him. "No shop talk tonight, okay?"

He laughed. "You got it." He stepped into the

kitchen and sniffed the air. "Something smells good. Is that garlic in the air?"

"Yes. Sit down and I'll get you a nice cold beer."

"I could use one after the day I've had."

She shook her finger at him. "No shop talk. Remember?"

He nodded, took a seat at the small table, and accepted the bottle from her. He opened it, taking a long drag. "That hit the spot. Too bad I can't have more than one."

"Mustn't be a bad influence on the boys," she said, referring to his band of high school misfits in the shop below.

He shook his head, his lips pursing, and for a moment Katie thought he might cry. She took the seat opposite him. "What's wrong?"

"It's Blake. One of the boys told me he keeps a small gas can in the trunk of his car."

"Isn't that dangerous?"

"Yeah . . . and convenient—if you want to start a fire."

In that hot kitchen, Katie suddenly felt cold. She wasn't sure how to respond.

"It turns out Blake has had a fascination with fire since he was a kid."

"He's still a kid," Katie insisted, but Andy shook his head.

"He's eighteen, and I'm scared shitless he might go to jail as an arsonist."

"He's been caught before?" Katie asked. Andy

159

nodded. "How many fires are we talking about?" she asked, dreading the answer.

"Five that are documented."

Katie's heart sank. "Oh, Andy. I'm so sorry. I know how hard you've tried to reach these boys, and you've had a wonderful success rate—"

Again he shook his head, and then took another long swallow of beer. "I knew he was a troubled kid, but nobody told me about the fires."

"Has he been arrested?" Katie asked.

"I don't know. He didn't show up for work tonight. Nobody's seen him since Sunday night, and his parents are worried sick. Things don't look good. If this had been his first offense, he might be sent for therapy, but he was caught starting those other fires. And he lied to Detective Davenport about his whereabouts on the night of the Wood U fire."

"Where was he?"

"I'm not sure. I heard that secondhand from one of the other boys."

"Oh, Andy, I'm so sorry." Katie reached over to rest a hand on his arm. His skin felt hot to the touch.

He didn't look at her. His eyes seemed watery. He looked away. He probably didn't want her to see him cry.

It was time to lighten the conversation. Katie got up from her seat. "How about some hors d'oeuvres?"

Andy cleared his throat. "You made hors d'oeuvres?"

"Isn't that what a good hostess does?" She opened the fridge and took out the glass plate that held an assortment of finger foods, removed the plastic wrap, and placed it on the table before him. "It's really nothing fancy," she said as he reached for one of the deviled eggs.

"You piped in the filling?"

She shrugged. "I may not rival the chef at the Ritz, but I can wield a pastry bag just as well as Martha Stewart. I bet I could decorate a cake as good as or better than that domestic diva, too."

Andy laughed and then took a bite and chewed. Katie studied his face, waiting for a reaction, but he seemed determined to make her wait.

He swallowed and then nodded with what seemed like pleasure. "Curried?" he asked.

She nodded. "My aunt Lizzie loved curried deviled eggs. We had them all the time."

"Not bad." He reached for a baguette slice topped with cream cheese and roasted red tomatoes, popped that into his mouth, and chewed. Already he was smiling. He swallowed. "Didn't you once tell me you didn't *like* to cook?"

"Deviled eggs and a visit to the grocery store's olive bar is hardly cooking. And it's not that I don't like cooking so much, as that I never had the time. Now I seem to have way too much time on my hands in the evenings."

He frowned. "Is that another hint that I don't spend enough time with you?"

"No! When we first started dating, I knew you had a business to run. You knew I had one, too. I admit, I'd love to spend more time with you, but when you're free, I'm not. And when I'm free, you're not. That makes the time we *can* spend together all that more special. I hope you feel the same way."

He looked pensive. "Why did I fall for a girl on the wrong side of the clock?"

"Woman," Katie corrected, "and I could ask the same thing. But I'm not in a hurry to change things either. Are you?"

"No." He reached for her hand and drew her down to sit on his lap. It felt like sitting on a heating pad in that sticky kitchen, but Katie didn't move. He kissed her. He tasted like salty sweat and curried eggs, and he smelled like pizza—comforting. "I love you, Katie."

"And I love you, too."

He smiled, but his eyes wandered to the clock. "I told the boys I'd be back to the shop within an hour."

"That's okay, the scallops only take twenty minutes in the oven."

"Oven? No wonder it's so hot in here," he said.

Katie shook her head. "The oven you bought for this place is very well insulated—it doesn't leak much heat at all. Besides, it's always this warm in this kitchen."

He frowned. If he expected her to do a pitch for a new circuit box, he was going to be disappointed. She was determined not to mention it. "I'd better pop those scallops into the oven right now. Then I'll sauté the peapods and mushrooms."

"More garlic?" he asked.

She smiled. "If you had time to stay, I might hold the garlic, but as you have to get back to work . . ." She let the sentence trail off.

"You just don't want me to kiss any of my customers."

"On the contrary, go ahead and kiss Vance or Godfrey—or even Seth Landers."

Andy frowned. "As you know, *none* of them are my type."

She laughed as she grabbed a sauté pan from the cupboard, set it on the stove, and turned the heat up. She'd already washed the peapods and mushrooms. All she had to do was cook them. She grabbed the butter dish from the fridge, hacked off a couple of tablespoons' worth, and put them into the pan to melt.

"We ought to do this more often," Andy said. "I like to watch you cook."

"I would love to cook for you on a regular basis. That way we'd get to spend more time together. How about Monday night after Danny comes back from vacation? Then you won't have to hurry back to work. And maybe you could stay longer than for just dinner."

Andy's smile widened. "You've got a date."

Once Katie had kissed Andy good-bye, washed the dishes, and tidied her kitchen, she had nothing left to do and figured she might as well go back to Artisans Alley and catch up on the mountain of work that she'd been too restless to tackle earlier in the day.

Entering the Alley after hours once felt creepy and a little frightening, but since Katie had moved into the apartment over Andy's pizzeria, she'd found she got a lot more work done when there were no interruptions from vendors or a telephone that seemed to constantly ring. Besides, working kept her from thinking about certain things. Like missing out on buying the Webster mansion . . . again. And the fact that she really ought to sell off everything in her storage unit and pocket the money. Or rather, pay off Ezra's final loan or fix the HVAC.

She slipped the key into the door at the main entrance and let herself in. She preferred entering the building through the lobby after hours. The lamps from the parking lot shed good light on the entrance and she could see everything around her. Of course, the fact that Andy would watch her lock herself in also gave her a feeling of added security. He insisted that she call him so that he or one of his employees would walk her back to the outside stairs to her apartment—all ten or twelve feet of a journey. Still, it felt nice that someone worried for her safety.

She walked past the closed storefronts, through the Alley's lobby area, and unlocked the French doors that led inside. The security lights seemed dim and cast wan shadows as she made her way through the booths to the back and her office. She didn't bother with the lights in the vendors' lounge. It, too, had a security lamp, and she went into her office, which she hadn't bothered to lock.

She sat down at the computer and hit the on switch. As she waited for it to boot up, a crack issued from the floor above her. The old building creaked and cracked at all times of the day, especially during weather extremes. But when the sound came again, she cocked her head and listened more carefully, her mouth falling open as though to give her an increased ability to hear. She could swear she heard footsteps up on the second floor. She'd locked up the Alley more than four hours before. Vance had a key, but if he was going to be in the building after hours, he always informed Katie, and she hadn't seen his truck out in the lot.

She tiptoed out of her office and into the vendors' lounge, but heard nothing. Next, she ventured onto the sales floor. Another crack made her pause, listening hard. When nothing happened for another minute, she moved toward the back of the building until she came to, and stood in, Vance's booth, straining to listen. She definitely *did* hear footsteps on the floor above.

With exaggerated care, she quickly walked back toward her office, wincing every time the old wooden floor creaked beneath her. If she could hear creaking and cracking, so could whoever was up on the second floor.

Back her in office, she quickly shut the door and picked up the phone, dialing 911.

"I want to report a trespasser," she whispered when the dispatcher came on the line. "I'm alone in my workplace on Victoria Square in McKinlay Mill."

"Can you get out without being seen?"

"I don't know." Damn. Why hadn't she thought of just running out the front door and calling from the pizzeria?

"Then it might be best to stay where you are. Can you barricade yourself in?"

Katie glanced at her file cabinet. Maybe. Her crummy office chairs certainly weren't going to do the trick. "It would probably cause too much noise, and I don't want to draw attention to myself."

"Can you turn off your lights and hide under your desk?"

"Yes."

"Do it. An officer can be there in a few minutes. I'll stay on the line with you."

Katie turned off the lights. The lamps from the back parking lot cast weird shadows, and she was glad the darkness in her office was not absolute. Still, she fumbled her way along the desk and crawled under it.

Something seemed to crash in the vendors' lounge and her breath caught in her throat. "He's coming closer," she whispered into the phone.

"Stay calm, don't make a sound."

Katie could hear the footsteps coming closer and closer to her office, and then . . . they veered and whoever was there went into the bathroom. She listened and distinctly heard the toilet seat bang into the tank and then . . .

"Good grief! Someone's peeing in my john!" she cried.

For a second, Katie was sure she heard laughter in her ear.

The lid banged down and Katie heard the toilet flush. Next she heard the water come on as the person behind the wall washed his or her hands. Well, at least this person was neat. And he or she had known where to find the restroom. Could it be a vendor?

The water switched off, but Katie could still hear the toilet refilling. The person exited the restroom and the footsteps started off again.

Katie felt foolish sitting in the dark when the

person in the next room had to be someone she knew. "I'm going to go see who it is."

"No, don't!" the dispatcher cautioned. "Please wait until the deputy arrives."

"How will I know when that happens if I'm hiding in the dark in my office?"

"They'll break in the door."

"Oh no they won't! I'm not paying for that kind of repair—and I know the Sheriff's Office certainly won't!"

"Ms. Bonner, please!" the dispatcher pleaded, but Katie had had enough. She hung up the phone, opened the door a crack. There was no one in the vendors' lounge. She listened for a minute and heard no sound. She fumbled to open the desk's bottom right drawer, where she kept some tools, and grabbed a claw hammer. Her plan was to hightail it out the back door and run around to the front of the building to wait for the deputy to arrive. The hammer was her insurance.

She opened the door a crack and again peeked into the vendors' lounge, but there was no sign of the intruder. Feeling like a sneak, she tiptoed into the lounge, unlocked the back door, and scooted out into the parking lot, then ran as fast as she could around the side of the building.

It was far too soon to expect the sheriff's deputy, but as she looked around the lot, she recognized Detective Davenport's car parked in front of Wood U. She made a run for it. By the time she got there, she was breathless and had a stitch in her side.

Davenport was snooping around the side of the dark building. "Detective," she called, panting. "Someone's in the Alley. Someone's sneaking around inside the Alley and it's supposed to be empty at this time of night."

"Do you always jog with a hammer?" Davenport asked with a frown.

"Only when I feel my life might be threatened."

"What did this person do that was threatening?"

Katie bit her lip. "He—he peed in the Alley's downstairs restroom."

Davenport's eyes widened and then he burst into laughter. "You were threatened by a peeing man?"

"Detective, will you please be serious? Someone either broke into the Alley or hid inside after closing."

"Did you call nine-one-one?"

"Yes, there's a sheriff's deputy on the way—but who knows how long it'll be before he gets here? And—"

Davenport grabbed her by the arm, his fingers moist from the humidity. "Come on." He dragged her over to his car and they got in, neither bothering with their seat belts for the short drive across the parking lot.

"I left the back door open," Katie said, and Davenport steered for the back parking lot. He pulled up to the back door with the screech of brakes, nearly tossing Katie through the windshield.

About the same time, the sound of a siren could be heard.

Davenport jumped from the car with more speed than Katie thought him capable of. She followed suit. "Flag down the deputy. I'm going in," he said.

Katie nodded and made a run for the side of the building once more, jumping up and down, waving her arms and shouting. The deputy got the message and pulled his car up to meet her.

"What's going on?" Deputy Schuler demanded, eyeing the hammer still clutched in her hand.

"Someone is trespassing in Artisans Alley. Detective Davenport has gone in to investigate."

"He should have waited for backup," Schuler said and scowled.

"Tell *him* that," Katie said as the deputy slipped out of his car, grabbing his billy club in the process.

"You stay here," he ordered, and ran for the back stairs.

Katie felt foolish standing there with her hammer, especially when she noticed Andy running along the tarmac and heading for her.

"What's going on?" he demanded.

"There's someone in the Alley."

"At this time of night?"

"Exactly. I heard footsteps up on the second floor and called nine-one-one," she briefly explained.

"Good girl," Andy said, making Katie wince at his word choice. He craned his neck to see around her. "Is that Davenport's crate?"

She nodded. "I saw him poking around over at Wood U and we jumped in his car and drove right over. Then the deputy showed up." She gave the back door a worried look. "I wish they'd hurry up and find that creep." She shivered, even though the temperature had to still be in the high eighties. "The thought of somebody being there when I was all alone . . ." Again she shivered.

Andy rested a floury arm around her shoulder. "You could've called me."

She smiled at him and kissed his cheek. "My hero."

The back door opened and a sweaty-faced Davenport exited the building. "He must've heard the siren. I heard running footfalls on the second floor, and tore up the stairs," he said, still panting. That wasn't a good idea for a man his age and especially in this heat. "Looks like he got away through an emergency exit at the back of the loft. Your alarm's blaring—you'd better call your security company."

"I'll do that right now," Katie said, and went back inside the building, while Davenport opened his car door and switched on his radio transmitter to talk to dispatch.

The heat inside the building was at least ten degrees higher than outside, and practically slammed Katie in the face. Back in her airless office, she looked up the number for the security company in her old and worn Rolodex, called them, and explained the situation, telling them that sheriff's deputies were already on the scene.

As she hung up the phone, she noticed a key she kept on a hook next to her bulletin board was missing. That explained a lot.

Katie left her office and headed out the back door once again, looking for Detective Davenport, who was conversing with Deputy Schuler. They stopped talking as she approached.

"I just noticed the key to Chad's Pad is missing," she told Davenport.

"Chad . . . your husband? Hasn't he been dead for over a year?"

She nodded. "We were living apart at the time of his death," she reminded him. "He was staying here in the Alley."

"Illegally," Davenport put in.

Katie nodded. "I didn't like the idea either, but . . . that's beside the point right now. I keep the key to the door of the room he stayed in on a hook in my office—it's missing. But I checked the door to that room earlier today and it was definitely locked."

"Let's go have a look at *Chad's Pad,*" Davenport said.

"Now that I know you're okay and that the detective is here, I'd better get back to work," Andy said. "Stop over before you go upstairs tonight," he told Katie, who nodded.

Katie led Davenport through the Alley and up the stairs to the stifling hot loft. Tucked in the far corner was the room that Chad had occupied. The door was closed, but when Katie reached for the handle, it turned.

"Damn," Davenport muttered, "I shouldn't have let you do that. You've just ruined any fingerprints that might've been on there."

"If someone's been living inside, there'll be plenty more—and in the bathroom downstairs," Katie said and swung the door wide. The room was dark, and she used her elbow to flip the switch. Sudden light blazed in the sixty-watt bulb that hung from the ceiling. The room stank of stale sweat and Katie forced herself to breathe shallowly. Davenport pushed past her to enter the tiny room.

The covers on the bed were a jumbled mess. The remnants of past meals—lunches and other food swiped from the vendors' lounge's refrigerator—filled the overflowing wastebasket. Gwen's missing pop cans and Vance's Tupperware bowl were tossed in a pile as well. A heap of dirty clothes filled one corner of the tiny room.

Davenport pulled out a pen and poked at them. "Do you recognize any of these shirts?"

Katie bit her lip. "I think so. That striped one. I think Dennis Wheeler has one like it."

The detective looked up sharply. "Do you think he's the one who's been hiding here in your loft?"

"I don't know. All I know is he has a shirt like that. I don't know if it's actually *his* shirt."

Davenport straightened and frowned. How could he stand to be in that close, hot space and not keel over? "Would *you* have told him about this hiding place?"

"Of course not. But it was no secret that Chad stayed here for two months when we were apart. He went to a couple of the Merchants Association meetings. He might have told Dennis about it then. I don't know—I wasn't part of the group then. But Gilda Ringwald-Stratton would know. She's a walking encyclopedia when it comes to the Victoria Square Merchants Association."

"I'll have a talk with her, and then I'll speak to Mrs. Wheeler again," Davenport said, scowling.

She made a mental note to call the woman herself the next morning. If Abby was going to be grilled by Detective Davenport, she might feel the need for a little moral support.

Davenport glanced at his watch. "I hope you weren't planning on doing anything important tonight, Mrs. Bonner, because I want to get the crime team out here to fingerprint this place. I know you won't want the area around this storage space to be cut off from your customers in the morning."

"You've got that right," Katie said. She'd found sleep hard to come by in her sweltering apartment, and she had plenty of work to keep her occupied while the crime team did their thing up here. And she blinked in astonishment. Detective Davenport had actually shown sympathy for complications that could arise for her business.

He must be feeling really ill, she decided. Or had his pending retirement finally made him see that even after a violent death, the living needed to make money to *keep* on living?

She moved aside as Davenport exited Chad's Pad and pulled out his cell phone, punching in a number.

"I'll wait for you downstairs," she said.

He nodded, turned his back to her, and began speaking into his phone.

Katie had no desire to eavesdrop and headed for the back stairs and her office. She had a feeling it was going to be a very long night.

Twelve

It was well past twelve when the lab team finished their work in Chad's Pad and started on the washroom behind Katie's office. An hour later, she inspected the space and shook her head. She was far too tired to deal with the mess they'd made. She locked up Artisans Alley and walked across the darkened parking lot toward home.

The lights were still on at Angelo's Pizzeria, but there was no one out front. Andy was probably in the back preparing the dough for the next day's batch of cinnamon buns. Katie withdrew her cell phone from her pocket and punched in Andy's cell number. Instead of answering, his head popped around the corner of the door. He saw her and hurried toward the front of the shop. She pocketed her phone as he unlocked the door.

"Hey, you were supposed to call me *before* you left the Alley," he chided her.

"Sorry. I forgot."

"Don't do that again," he admonished. "I worry about you."

She smiled. "Thank you."

"That took a long time," he said, and gave her a quick kiss.

"It sure did."

"Come on inside, you're letting the mosquitoes and moths in," he said. Once inside, he locked the door and gestured for her to follow him to the back room. Sure enough, he was working on a new batch of dough. "I might have to hire a backup backup," he said as he washed his hands at the slop sink. "I'd forgotten how much work it was to run the shop *and* keep the cinnamon buns going."

"You got spoiled fast."

"Thank God Danny will be back on Monday."

"Then you'll be able to make the potluck?" Katie asked, sudden hope coursing through her.

"Wouldn't miss it. I'm bringing my world-famous pepperoni pasta salad."

"It's supposed to be a Christmas party," Katie reminded him.

"I celebrate Christmas in December. You and your vendors can celebrate it whenever you want."

"Party pooper."

She watched him work. He looked tired. He always looked tired. He worked too hard, for too long, and this whole situation with Blake was also wearing on him.

"That was a great dinner tonight," Andy said. "Thanks for going to so much trouble."

"I'm glad you liked it. Only now it seems like it must have happened three or four weeks ago," she said and eased herself into the room's only chair. It was a duplicate of the plastic lawn chairs Andy had out front for customers.

"So what did Davenport have to say about your intruder?" Andy asked as he went back to work.

"Not much. But there was something on his mind. He was . . . different. His attitude. Of course, he's been acting weird—nice—since Sunday. Tonight was just another facet of his weirdness."

"Cut the guy some slack. He's retiring in a couple of days. It'll be a big change."

"It's not just that. The other deputies were very standoffish. Like he had cooties or something. They didn't seem to want to talk to him."

Andy added another hunk of dough to one of the rising trays. "That's odd."

"I kind of felt sorry for him," she added. "And you're right. Leaving the Sheriff's Office has got to be a big change for him. And worse, he lost his wife last fall. I'm sure they must've made plans for when he retired. And he's still got kids in school. Why retire now with all that expense hanging over him?"

"You ever heard of student loans?"

"How do you think I went to college? But most parents want to help their kids through school. I get the feeling he would, too."

"Maybe he got forced out," Andy suggested, and pulled out another empty rack, filling it, too, with dough to rise.

"I suppose that could have happened. He does

have a rather brusque personality," she said and yawned.

"You need to hit the sack."

"Hey, you've been up as long as I have, if not longer. I don't know how you manage."

Andy smiled. "I love to work. At least for myself. I never would have worked this hard at the accounting firm. But I get a lot of satisfaction being here. I have this old building, I'm happy with the kids that work for me—for the most part—and I even love that you've living here now. When I leave at night, I know that you're here and you're safe and that I'll see you every day, no matter what."

Katie smiled and swallowed down a lump in her throat. A year ago she had no clue that she would ever love again. Chad and Andy were so different. Chad had kept secrets. Andy was an open book. No disrespect to her late husband, but she much preferred Andy's style.

"I wish I wasn't so tired, and that Monday wasn't so far away."

"Monday?" Andy asked, puzzled.

"Yeah. I did invite you for dinner and to stay over," she reminded him.

"Oh, yeah. Isn't it terrible that we have to schedule our time together?"

"Yes, but it also means that our time together is that much more precious—and intense." They shared a knowing smile.

"I love that kind of intensity," Andy said.

"So do I."

Oh, how she yearned for those moments of longing and desire to stretch on, but then she yawned again and the need for sleep pulled at her overtired body. "If I don't go upstairs in the next couple of minutes, I'm going to keel over and fall asleep right here," she said.

"Go. I'll see you tomorrow," Andy said and peeled the plastic gloves from his hands. He tossed them aside and stepped close, pulling her to him and planting an oh-so-gentle kiss on her lips.

She pulled away enough to nestle her head against his neck and plaster the rest of herself against him. "I love you."

"I love you, too, Katie Bonner."

They hung together for a long moment before Andy pulled away. "Go home. Go to bed. And don't think about any of the crap you went through tonight."

She'd already done that—until he'd mentioned it, that is.

"Yes, sir," she said anyway.

Andy led her back through his shop and out the front door to the stairs that led to the apartment above. "Good night." He leaned forward for one last kiss before Katie mounted the steps. At the top, she blew him a kiss before she unlocked the door to go inside.

The cats were waiting for her, feeling needy after having been abandoned for so many hours. She retrieved the pouch of cat treats from the kitchen counter and filled their empty bowls before heading to her tiny bedroom.

She had a feeling the next day was going to be just as long and with just as many surprises. And with everything that had been happening of late, those surprises weren't likely to be happy.

Not happy at all.

Morning came far too early, and yet already the sun was sleeping in later each day. Summer in western New York was far too brief, and the extended heat wave made it difficult to enjoy the season. The thermometer outside her kitchen window already said seventy-four degrees. The paper predicted a high of ninety-seven, and the extended forecast called for showers on the weekend, putting the Christmas in July potluck party in the Victoria Square parking lot in jeopardy.

Swell.

Katie's morning schedule was the same as always. Breakfast, shower, dress, and out of the apartment by seven fifty-eight. She'd heard noises in the pizzeria and had inhaled the aroma of baking cinnamon buns. Andy must be exhausted. If he wasn't counting the hours until his assistant manager returned from vacation, Katie was.

A rumpled-looking Godfrey was the only vendor waiting for Katie to open Artisans Alley. "About time you got here," he grumbled.

Katie glanced at her watch. "I'm a whole minute early."

Godfrey shrugged.

Katie unlocked the door and Godfrey rushed in ahead of her. She went directly to the main breaker in the front of the store and turned on the lights and fired up the air-conditioning, for all the good it did. Godfrey was exiting the vendors' lounge as Katie approached her office. She heard the sound of water running. Godfrey must have used the restroom. She cringed. All the surfaces were still covered in black fingerprint powder. Well, there went her morning. That stuff was not only filthy, but defied dust cloths and the suction on her mini-Shop-Vac.

Before she faced the washroom cleanup, Katie put on the coffeepot—not that she would partake. She checked the status of the water bottle in the fridge and found it still nearly full, and then hauled out her Shop-Vac and began the washroom project.

By the time she emerged from the now tidy restroom, almost all the coffee was gone. She made a fresh pot and finally sat down at her desk and booted up her computer. What should she tackle first? Finalizing the agenda for the Merchants Association meeting that evening or analyzing the cost of ads for the upcoming Dickens Festival, which began in November? She chose the agenda. Since she'd heard from no one else who wanted to add items, she finished the list and e-mailed it to the Association's secretary, Sue Sweeney, owner of Sweet Sue's Confectionery. Next she called the rental company to check on the chairs and tables that were to be delivered on Saturday morning for that evening's potluck. Everything was in order. Another hurdle leapt.

There were many other items that needed her attention, but Katie suddenly remembered she hadn't stocked the cash registers with money to start the retail day—which was to begin in less than five minutes.

She'd shut the register drawer and looked up. Ten o'clock. She strode to the French doors that separated the store from the building's lobby and unlocked them. No sooner had she done that than the Big Brown delivery guy approached the door with a carton under one arm. He came inside and dropped it off at Cash Desk 1.

"Hi, I'm Katie Bonner, manager of Artisans Alley." She offered her hand to the young, muscular guy. He looked cute in his regulation brown shorts and shirt. A brown corporate hat covered his short-cropped blond hair.

"Greg Mason. Guess I'll be seeing you on a regular basis."

"What happened to Jerry?" Katie asked.

"Retired."

Katie frowned. "Funny. He didn't mention it to me last Friday."

"Yeah, it was sudden. But now I've got a regular route, so I wish him well and thank him, too."

Katie shrugged. "Well, welcome to the neighborhood."

"Thanks. See ya," he called and headed out the door.

No sooner had he left than Crissie Hunter, the tanned, thirty-something mailwoman, arrived with a stack of mail and circulars. "Hey, Katie," she said, handing them off. "I hear you guys are going to have another one of your famous wingdings on Saturday night."

"We sure are. Would you like to come?"

"Oh, no. I wasn't fishing for an invitation," Crissie said. She walked her route and already her uniform blouse was damp and sticking to her. "Just wanted to tell you to have a happy one."

"We'll do that."

Crissie turned. "See you tomorrow."

"Bye."

Rose Nash wandered up to stand beside Katie. She spent almost as much time at Artisans Alley as Katie did. "She's such a nice young woman."

"Yes," Katie agreed.

"I wanted to let you know that I've twisted a

number of arms and we will have a bunch of side dishes for the potluck on Saturday."

"I thought I might bring a dish of apricot carrots. They're pretty good."

"Oh, goody. I'll add that to the list. I want to make little tent cards so that all the food is labeled. I've managed to borrow a bunch of warming trays and some extra slow cookers. If you've got one, can you bring it, or put your carrots in one?" Rose asked.

"Sure. That's a great idea."

"Good. Do you want a list of all the dishes?"

Katie was about to say no, but then saw how much it meant to Rose to share all that she'd done to ensure everyone at the party could eat, drink, and be merry. "Sure. Thank you."

Rose beamed.

Katie slapped the pile of mail in her right hand against her left palm. "I'm off to my office to try to get some work done. Holler if you need help come lunchtime."

"Will do," Rose said, and turned to Cash Desk 1. She stowed her purse under the counter, took out her romance novel, and withdrew her bookmark. *Another day at Artisans Alley,* Katie thought wistfully, wishing she could goof off for even part of one day. But then, she found she thrived on the work. Well, most of the time.

Back in her office, she sat down at her desk and rifled through the mail, putting the circulars into the recycle pile and sorting through the rest of the envelopes. Most of them were bills or credit card offers, but one of them was a square, buff-colored envelope that had been addressed by what looked like a teenager's hand. Intrigued, Katie reached over to the chipped coffee mug that held pens, pencils, nail files, and a letter opener. She slit the top of the envelope and removed an invitation to . . .

"Detective Davenport's retirement party!" she read aloud.

Why on earth would the detective want to invite her to his party? Was it because she had been a thorn in his side for the past nine months and he wanted to celebrate the fact that he'd never see her again? Had one of his teenaged daughters written out the invitation?

Did she really *have* to go to the party?

She glanced at the address. Oddly enough, it was being held right here in McKinlay Mill. She'd thought the detective lived on the east side of the city. Maybe he had moved, or was thinking of moving.

She inspected the invitation. It had been specifically addressed to her. No mention of bringing a date, not that she thought she could extricate Andy from his pizza business on a Friday evening. But maybe she could take someone like Rose. There was a number to RSVP and she decided to call it and ask.

She dialed the number. "Hi, we're the Davenports," said a cheerful young female voice. "We can't come to the phone right now, but leave a message and we'll get back to you."

Katie hung up the phone. The bouncy voice probably belonged to one of the detective's daughters. He had two . . . or was it three?

She thumbtacked the invitation to the small overloaded corkboard that hung next to her desk. She'd try calling later.

Katie opened all the bills, putting them into a folder to be dealt with next week, on bill-paying day, but her gaze kept going back to the party invitation and the address for the gathering. "Holy smoke—that's our address," she said aloud, and pulled the invitation off the bulletin board once again. The party was going to be held at Artisans Alley?

Was Detective Davenport the person who'd rented her empty rental space?

She dialed Fred Cunningham's number, but it was voice mail that picked up on the fourth ring. "Fred, it's Katie Bonner. Why didn't you tell me it was Detective Davenport who wanted to rent my storefront for his party?" No sooner had she said it than she wondered why she was so upset. "Give me a call," she said, and hung up the phone.

Why *was* she so upset? The detective knew she'd had financial problems in the past. Was he throwing her a bone? And maybe she ought to consider letting the space for more short-term rentals. After all, the whole idea was to maximize her income stream—and it really didn't matter how that was accomplished as long as it was legal.

Katie pinned the invitation back up and had just settled down at her desk when a rap on her doorjamb caused her to turn. Rose Nash stood in the doorway, and a tall, large—not fat, but big—man stood behind her.

"Katie, this is Detective Hamilton. He'd like to speak to you about the fire at Wood U." Rose ducked around the man and made a quick escape.

Dressed in a blue sport coat that could have doubled for a circus tent, Katie wondered if Hamilton's shoulders were too big to fit through her office doorway. She rose from her chair and offered her hand in a rather tentative manner. Was he likely to crush it? "How can I help you, Detective?" And what was he doing here instead of Detective Davenport?

The big guy clasped her hand gently, and despite the humidity, his hand was dry to the touch.

"Ma'am, I'm taking over the investigation of the murder at Wood U on Saturday night. Do you have a few minutes?"

"But I've already spoken to Detective Davenport."

"I've read his report. I wanted to go over your statement with you. I'll be talking to everyone who knows anything about the fire and the murder."

"Where's Detective Davenport?" Katie asked, growing concerned.

"He's retired, ma'am," Hamilton said in a bored monotone.

"But I understood he'd be working until the end of the week."

"I believe he's on paid leave until his official retirement date. I'm in charge of the investigation as of today. Now, I have a few questions." He withdrew a notebook and a capped pen from the oversized pocket of his coat. "May I sit down?"

"Sure." Katie stood back, and sure enough, Hamilton had to sidle through the door to enter the small office. He took the seat she offered, which was a tight squeeze. Did the Sheriff's Office have to buy oversized furniture for this guy? How had he ever made it through the ranks to the post of detective? As a rookie, had he driven the paddy wagon instead of a cruiser? The logistics were mind-boggling.

"I understand you're not a stranger to reporting crimes," he said in the same monotone. Was he bored or just reciting the dialogue from an old *Dragnet* episode?

"You got that right," Katie said, and had a feeling the following conversation was going to

189

be difficult. She settled back in her chair for what promised to be a long and boring interview.

He went over what he knew about the investigation so far, including the trespasser who'd been residing in Chad's Pad. "You may be interested to know that Mrs. Abby Wheeler identified the shirt that was found in your upstairs storage room as belonging to her husband."

"Oh. Well . . . good. I guess." And then it occurred to Katie. "I just remembered. I found a suitcase full of stuff in my bathroom Sunday night. Soap, deodorant." Had the lab team found it the night before? She hadn't looked under the sink when she'd cleaned the room only an hour earlier. She jumped up and scooted around the corner, but found the door to the washroom was locked. She knocked.

"It's occupied," came a woman's voice.

Katie turned to find Hamilton looming over her. "There's no telling if it'll still be in there. I mentioned it yesterday in my note to the vendors. It could have already been claimed."

"I think you should let me handle this," Hamilton said, and motioned for her to stand aside. He knocked on the door. "Ma'am, this is Detective Hamilton of the Sheriff's Office. Could you hurry it up, please. This is official business."

They heard the toilet flush, and then water run in the sink. Seconds later a chubby woman who looked to be in her late sixties opened the door, giving them both a glare. "Can't a person pee in privacy?"

"Sorry, ma'am, but as I said, this is official business."

The woman stood rock still. "Oh, yeah? Like the cops who speed and run their sirens until they hit the McDonald's parking lot for a burger and fries?"

Hamilton's face remained impassive.

"Now, if you'll step aside, maybe I can get out of here," the woman said with indignation.

Katie stifled a smirk as she and Hamilton backed out of the way, allowing the woman to leave. As soon as she was gone, Hamilton entered the washroom.

"It was in the cabinet under the sink," Katie said.

Hamilton crouched down, opened the cabinet door, and then didn't move. "What did you say this suitcase looked like?"

"A small, faux alligator-skin job in brown."

He stood and Katie looked around him. There was no suitcase under the sink.

Hamilton glared at her.

"I swear, there was a suitcase there on Sunday night."

"Why didn't you report this to Detective Davenport last night?" Hamilton growled.

"I forgot all about it until just a minute ago."

His expression said, *A likely story.*

"I have no reason to lie," Katie said defensively.

"I'd like to see the storeroom where the suspect was hiding, if you'd be kind enough to show me the way," Hamilton said.

"I'd be happy to," Katie said, and exited the doorway with Hamilton striding right behind her. Did he think she was going to try to get there before him and hide some other evidence?

Katie took the steep back stairs two at a time while Hamilton maneuvered up the narrow enclosure. She had to wait for him to catch up at the top before she threaded her way through the aisles to the back loft to Chad's Pad.

The room was as it had been left the night before by the lab team—messy, and still contaminated with fingerprint dust. She waited for him to catch up.

"Here you go," she said, and opened the door to the small storage space. She flipped the switch just inside the door, and the single lightbulb hanging from the ceiling did a poor job of illuminating the gloom.

Hamilton entered the stifling hot space and poked around for what seemed like forever. Katie stood watching him while the sweat beaded on her scalp and then ran down the back of her neck. It wasn't even noon yet and already the temperature had to be in the nineties in the loft. She'd have to get a thermometer and chart the temperature by the hour. Maybe that would convince her to sell her treasures to Nick Farrell.

I don't want to sell my stuff! It had taken her years to collect the furniture and other items. She had paid a king's ransom storing the things. She'd never get her money's worth out of them if she sold now.

I am not selling my stuff!

She wiped the back of her hand across her sweaty forehead and realized she had to get out of the loft before she became dehydrated. "I'll be in my office if you need me, Detective," she called, and saw Hamilton wave a hand in dismissal.

Katie hurried down the back stairs and reentered the vendors' lounge, glad to escape the heat—but not the guilt of dragging her feet to upgrade the HVAC. But that cost money, money she didn't have.

But could have—*if* she sold her treasures.

She entered her office, determined not to think about it. She had far more important matters to ponder. The potluck dinner, the trespasser who'd been hiding in the Alley, and if it *was* Dennis Wheeler, then who'd been killed at Wood U just four days before?

Thirteen

It was almost lunchtime when Katie decided to take a break and head back to her apartment. Now that she'd restocked her cupboards—and refrigerator—there was more than just kitty treats to snack on. She was hankering for a ham and cheese sandwich on rye. The cats would be happy to have company for a half hour or so, and maybe she'd stop and see Andy, too.

She was just leaving her office when she saw a familiar figure threading his way through the sales room, heading for the vendors' lounge. Detective Ray Davenport, retired.

"Good morning, Mrs. Bonner," Davenport called brightly. "Or should I say afternoon?"

"Hello, Detective." Katie studied his face, which seemed impassive. "Are you allowed to talk to me anymore . . . in an official capacity, I mean?"

"You've heard," he said and frowned. "Who says we're talking officially? I'm now a man with lots of time on my hands."

"And a hankering to solve your last case . . . even if they did take you off it. And why was that?"

"I can't go into that right now. But everything

will become clear as soon as this murder is solved."

"And you don't think your colleague Detective Hamilton can do the job?"

"He's very capable. He's known around the office as Fine-tooth-comb Hamilton. He's extremely meticulous. Likes all his i's dotted and t's crossed. It'll just take him several years to come up with the killer."

"And you don't want to wait that long?" Katie guessed.

"Got it in one."

Godfrey walked into the vendors' lounge, making a beeline for the fridge. He grabbed a mug from the rack and poured himself cold water from Katie's bottle.

"Why don't we go into your office to talk," Davenport said, and pointed the way.

The two of them entered and Davenport shut the door, parking himself against her file cabinet.

Katie took her chair and leaned back, marveling at how their relationship had changed since the first time she'd met him some ten months before. He'd been obstinate, disagreeable, and apparently uninterested in solving Ezra Hilton's murder. And now . . . she wasn't so sure she'd judged him fairly. "What's your plan?"

"I'm not sure I have one . . . yet. But don't you think it's disturbing that a dead man is found in Wood U and the owner goes missing? Yet his car is still behind the shop. There's no credit card trail to follow, so where did he go and how is he surviving?"

Katie's eyes narrowed. "Right here only steps from his store—in Artisans Alley?" As if she hadn't come to that conclusion the night before.

"It's more than plausible. So who among your vendors would have helped him? Was he particularly friendly with anyone here?"

Katie shook her head. "Not that I know of."

"What about that guy who sells the wood in Booth 37?"

"Vance Ingram? I already asked him about it. He told me he didn't know Dennis."

"What if he lied?" Davenport asked with a raised eyebrow. "He wasn't exactly truthful during the Hilton murder investigation."

"Things were different then. I trust Vance—and he trusts me. He wouldn't lie to me."

"I've had a lot more experiences with liars," Davenport grumbled. "We're going to have to go at this differently."

"We?" Katie repeated.

"I need you to speak to people that I can't officially talk to."

"So that I can get in hot water with Detective Hamilton instead of you?" she asked.

Davenport shrugged, adopting what was probably supposed to be an innocent expression. "Who says he has to know?"

Katie sighed. "If I pulled this crap while you were working an investigation, you'd have a fit."

"You're probably right," he admitted. "But I'm not asking you to do anything that will hamper the investigation. I would encourage you to tell Hamilton everything you learn."

"And is he going to be just as receptive as you were after Ezra Hilton's murder?"

"Probably. But that isn't likely to stop you either. Will it?"

Again Katie sighed. "As head of the Merchants Association, I do have a stake in getting the killer caught and hopefully *clearing* our former member's name. That's just good business."

"I agree," Davenport said with a nod.

Something about his affability smelled as rotten as a week-old dead trout. "Still, if you can't be honest with me, I see no reason to help you poke around."

He sighed. "What do you want to know?"

"The name of Wood U's new owner," Katie demanded. She hated being the only one who didn't seem to know.

Davenport shook his head. "I'm well aware of who now owns the business. There's no connection to the death at the shop. The new owner had taken over the business in name only and has an iron-tight alibi."

"Who told you the identity of the new owner? Fred Cunningham? Seth Landers?" she demanded.

"That's none of your business, *Mrs. Bonner.* Now, are you going to help or not?"

So much for the detective being her newfound friend. "Not unless you tell me," she said petulantly. Goodness, she sounded like a spoiled ten-year-old.

"I can't," Davenport nearly shouted.

Katie sat back in her chair and folded her arms across her Artisans Alley T-shirt and waited. Davenport was going to have come clean if he wanted her help.

She started silently counting backward from ten. Nine. Eight. Seven. Six. Five. Four. Three. Two . . .

"Okay, it's me," Davenport admitted.

Katie's jaw dropped. "You? Why on earth would *you* buy the business?"

"Because I'm retiring. I'm not ready to be put out to pasture. I figure I can make this a second career. And I'll tell you one thing, I'm a hell of a lot better woodworker than your friend Dennis Wheeler ever was."

"He wasn't my friend. He was an associate."

"Whatever," Davenport said hotly. Katie had never seen him so riled before.

"Good grief, Detective, no wonder you've been relieved of duty. It had to be a huge conflict of interest for you to be the chief investigator of a murder committed on property you own. How come your superiors allowed this transgression in law enforcement protocol for the first three days of the investigation?"

Davenport said nothing.

It couldn't have been Seth who turned him in. Although he was an officer of the court, if questioned, he could also play the attorney-client confidentiality card.

How long had Davenport dabbled in wood-working as a hobby? He'd never mentioned it. Then again, they weren't exactly buddies. The only reason she knew about his deceased wife and his college-age children was because one of the deputies had mentioned them to her days after Ezra Hilton's death. Davenport had never revealed anything to her that could be construed as personal, and now he was going to be her neighbor here on Victoria Square. The thought of him arguing with her at upcoming Merchants Association meetings filled her with dread.

"Why all the secrets?" she asked finally.

"Because somebody broke into my shop and killed another human being. Someone set fire to my shop. It's my obligation to find out who did these things and bring that person to justice."

"But you can't do it as a member of the Sheriff's Office because it's a blatant conflict of interest for you to be investigating, right?"

"Yes. But just because I've been officially taken off the case doesn't mean I can't poke around on my own."

"Oh, come on, Detective. Aren't you doing what you've chided me not to do in the past?"

"The stakes are much different."

"I don't see how. You've been exonerated—at least I'm assuming so. But when Ezra Hilton was killed, you were thinking *I* might have done it."

"I ruled you out right away," he grumbled.

She let out an exasperated breath and crossed her arms over her T-shirt once again. "Well, you might have let *me* know it."

Davenport glared at her.

"So what happens now?" Katie asked.

"I'm supposed to go back to the office and pack up my things. They're going to let me loose a few days early," he said bitterly. "A reward for a job well done or some kind of crap like that."

His expression was a mix of anger and deep disappointment, and Katie actually found herself feeling sorry for the man.

"Well, if it's any consolation, you can now join the Merchants Association and become a full-fledged member of the Victoria Square family." Odd how just minutes before, the thought had repelled her.

"I was planning on doing that . . . eventually. I thought it best to let Wheeler make the decisions until I had a better handle on how the store operated. He was supposed to mentor me—for a fee."

"Which you already paid?"

Davenport nodded.

"You don't need to pay a fee for mentoring from anyone in the Association. And I'd be glad to give you any advice and information you might need. I haven't had as much experience as some of the members, but I seem to have had a bit more success than some of them, too."

" 'No brag just fact'?" he quoted from an old TV Western.

"Yup," Katie replied. "Maybe we *would* make a pretty good team."

Davenport rubbed his chin. "Yes. We might. And maybe we should start working together right now."

Katie's eyes widened in surprise. "Now, Detective—"

"*About-to-be-retired* detective," he corrected bitterly.

"Wouldn't going after a murderer put us both in danger?"

"I think I know how to handle myself. And I can take care of you, too."

Katie frowned. *What an ego!* "Okay, what do you want me to do?" she asked, resigned. After all, she wanted to know how all this turned out, too.

"First, we need to ascertain that it was indeed Dennis Wheeler who's been hiding in Chad's Pad."

"According to Detective Hamilton, Abby

Wheeler confirmed that the shirt we found last night did belong to Dennis. And didn't you say it could take weeks before the state lab results come through with fingerprint and DNA evidence?" Katie reminded him.

"Exactly. And that's why we need to trap him."

"And how do we do that? We frightened him away last night. You don't seriously think he'll return, do you?"

"He might. If we bait him."

"With what?" she cried, her exasperation level rising.

"He may have left something behind that he needs. I want to have another look at that room."

"There wasn't anything in there—besides what Chad left—except for some dirty clothes and dirty dishes. But there is something I forgot to tell you." She told him about finding the suitcase on Sunday night—and how when she'd mentioned it to Hamilton and they'd gone to look, the suitcase was gone.

"Damn. No sign of it in Chad's Pad, I suppose . . ."

"You suppose right. I didn't see what the lab team took as evidence, but there couldn't have been much in there. And the place was as hot as a sauna. If Dennis was staying in there day and night, he probably lost half his body weight in sweat." But it did explain the thefts in the vendors' lounge refrigerator.

"It is a pretty miserable place to stay," Davenport agreed. He sighed in exasperation. "Would you be willing to talk to Abby Wheeler?"

"What about?" Katie asked suspiciously.

"Things!"

"What do I say? 'Hello, Abby. Looks like your husband is wanted for murder. Tell me about that and every other crime he may or may not have committed.'" She frowned. "Can't you see her slamming her front door in my face?"

"Mrs. Bonner," he said, his voice dropping to a tone of admonishment.

"Katie. If we're going to be partners in this, you'll have to call me Katie."

"Katie, I'm sure you'll think of just the right thing to say. You always have in the past," he added snidely.

She ignored the dig. "What's my excuse for showing up on her doorstep?"

"You feel bad for her, because no matter what happens, it's likely she's lost her husband. Or how about pulling the comfort visit from the head of the Merchants Association? Use your imagination," he encouraged.

Katie's frown deepened. "How soon do you want me to talk to her?"

"How about now?"

"Detective—"

"Ray," he corrected. "If I have to call you by your first name, you have to call me by mine."

"Ray," she said, and oh, it felt so wrong on so many levels, "I have a business to run. And besides, this just doesn't feel right."

He grabbed her by the arm with one hand and opened the office door with the other. "Sure it does. You're one of the most curious women I've ever met in my life—next to my late wife—and you have a knack for getting people to spill their guts. Get Mrs. Wheeler to spill hers." He pulled her into the vendors' lounge. Luckily there was no one there to listen in on their conversation.

"But what if she's too heartsick to talk?" Katie asked.

"Compare notes. Your husband really disappointed you before his death—"

"As far as we know, Dennis Wheeler is still alive," Katie pointed out, ignoring the dig.

"He won't be if she gets her hands on him," Davenport said. "She's got to be pretty pissed off by now—especially if he's been hiding from her, too."

"What if he fled to their house and she's now harboring him?"

"It's a possibility. Damn, I wish I could send you in there with a wire."

"Surely you met the woman. You did buy her business."

"*His* business," Davenport corrected. "It was in his name alone."

Katie frowned. "That seems strange. I mean,

during the winter months she was at the store every weekday while he worked at the high school."

"Maybe he paid her to work there."

"And maybe he didn't," Katie grated. The injustice of the situation annoyed her.

"Let's go," Davenport urged her, giving her a slight shove in the back.

"You can't come with me."

"I'll stay in the car," he said.

"Oh no you won't. If she sees you, she's likely to clam up for sure."

"Then I'll park down the block. I can drop you off."

"I'll drive myself."

"All right. Then we can meet back here."

"I really don't want to talk about it here."

"Your place?" he suggested.

"I really don't want to talk about it *there* either."

"Well, there's nowhere else to talk around here."

"Okay, my place. But if Andy wants to know why I've invited you up there, you're going to have to come up with a reasonable explanation. He won't be thrilled to hear I'm helping you and I want to put off the moment of telling him for as long as possible."

"Whatever," Davenport said, and urged her to move.

"We have to stop at Tanner's bakery first."

"What for?"

"When I spoke to Abby at the library the other night, she said that because nobody knew if Dennis was dead or alive, none of her neighbors or friends had consoled her or even brought over as much as a bagel."

"So you're going to bring her a bagel?"

"I was thinking about taking some cupcakes. Cupcakes are always comforting, especially if the frosting looks like a rose, don't you think?"

"No. I'd prefer macaroni and cheese, but there's no time for you to make it. I'll check out Chad's Pad while you go to the bakery. But hurry it up. We haven't got all day."

"Excuse me, but I'll be doing *you* a favor by talking to Abby."

"And I appreciate it," he said, giving her a nudge. "But we aren't finding out what she knows if you aren't there actually talking to her."

Katie sighed. Being friends with Davenport was going to be a major pain in the butt. But then it seemed like just about everybody she knew was being a major pain in the butt of late.

"Cupcakes. The more frosting the better," Katie said, and marched out of her office. And maybe she'd score one for herself as well. If she was going to have to put up with Davenport, she was going to need some kind of reward.

Fourteen

Sweat trickled down the back of Katie's neck as she tapped the dull brass knocker on the Wheelers' front door. She held the bakery box tight and took a look around her, taking in the weeds that grew along the side of the house. No one had cut the lawn or whacked the weeds in a few weeks. That was probably Dennis's job. But the rest of the place looked unkempt, too. Paint was peeling around the soffit and around the trim. It looked like more than a few household tasks had been left undone of late.

Abby's car was still in the drive, so surely she had to be home. Katie knocked again and looked around once more. She saw the curtain at the window move. She couldn't blame Abby for being careful, or for simply ignoring people intruding on her heartache—especially if they were from the local press. She started counting, figuring if she got to twenty, Abby wasn't going to open the door. She got to eighteen when the handle turned. The door opened on a chain. "Katie, is that you?" Abby whispered.

"It's me, and I'm alone. Can we talk?"

The door closed and the chain rattled. Abby

threw open the door and quickly ushered Katie inside before slamming it shut again.

Unlike the outside, the inside of Abby Wheeler's home was immaculate. Perhaps Abby had whiled away the hours relentlessly cleaning while waiting for word on her husband's fate. Despite working a sixty-hour week at Kimper Insurance, Katie had occupied the rest of her spare time during her separation from Chad cleaning and baking. The apartment had been spotless and the larder full—and she'd had no one with which to share either of them.

"I hope I haven't come at a bad time," Katie said, following Abby into the dim living room. After being exposed to ninety-degree temperatures for hours on end, the air-conditioned room felt downright cold. Abby, dressed in a sweater, slacks, socks, and penny loafers, turned on one of the lamps and seated herself on the couch. Katie took one of the matching wing chairs that faced the curtain-shrouded picture window. "I brought you some cupcakes from Tanner's." She offered the box.

"Thank you, Katie. That was very thoughtful of you," Abby said and accepted the box, setting it on the coffee table. "To tell you the truth, I could use a friend right now. This whole ordeal has really shaken me. I don't know what to think— who to talk to that can understand what I'm going through."

Katie nodded. Although she could guess, she really *didn't* know what Abby had endured these last few days. "Losing trust in someone you love can shatter your world," she began. "That's how I felt when my late husband invested all our savings in Artisans Alley."

Abby sighed. "This isn't the first time I've been shattered by Dennis's actions."

"I was surprised to hear Dennis had sold Wood U." Katie could feel a blast of cold air coming from the register on the floor nearby and gave an involuntary shiver. Had Abby worked up a sweat dusting and polishing and set the temperature to sixty-five? With little humidity, it felt arctic cold.

"No more than me. But then I always wondered why a man who disliked children would become a teacher." She shook her head. "Dennis's father constantly belittled him while he was growing up. He did the same to his students. I'm surprised he wasn't fired long ago," she said bitterly. "I'd always wanted children, you see. I didn't know Dennis's feelings until we'd been married for over a year. I'm Catholic. I don't believe in divorce. That's why I concentrated on my career. These last few years I looked forward to our retirement. Now it looks like everything we'd planned for the future will never happen." She sighed. "At least I don't have the shop hanging over my head anymore."

"You didn't like running the business?" Katie asked, surprised.

"I hated it. I had no choice when my career was taken away from me, thanks to layoffs. Dennis had the shop *and* his teaching career—and he was intent on keeping them both until he retired."

"Which was last month," Katie said. Abby nodded. "What *were* his plans for retirement?"

"To buy a condo in Key West and get away from winters in western New York."

Not surprising. A lot of people did just that.

"Do you think he might've taken off for Florida?"

Abby ran a hand through her bleached blonde hair, suddenly looking very tired. "I don't know. If he killed someone at Wood U, he'd be smart to disappear. He'd have to know I'd mention his plans to that detective. He knows that I'm a real law-and-order freak and I can't stand it when criminals get away with stuff. Look at how they treat shoplifters with just a slap on the hand and maybe make them go to a few group therapy sessions. They don't even make these people pay restitution. How does that stop crime?"

It sounded like Wood U had had more than a few light-fingered customers for Abby to be so angry about it. She never came to Merchants Association meetings, and Dennis had never mentioned it when the subject came up during the holiday rush back in December. Funny how it bothered his wife more than him. And yet when people thought of Wood U, they usually thought of Abby, not Dennis, as the owner simply because she ran the shop on a day-to-day basis.

Abby sighed. "I just can't come to terms with the idea of Dennis killing anyone. But everything the officers told me last night points to that fact."

"Such as?" Katie prompted.

"The shirt they showed me. I bought it as a birthday gift for Dennis in May. And the fact that every cent Dennis made from the sale of Wood U was withdrawn from our bank account the day this whole mess began," Abby continued. "I wonder if he took off for a country with no extradition."

Katie had wondered the same thing. "Do you have enough money to get along in the meantime?"

Abby shook her head, her face crumpling. "Not if Dennis doesn't come up with some kind of support—which isn't likely if he's skipped the country, or if he ends up going to jail. I'm going to have to find a job pretty quick if I'm going to make the next mortgage payment. And what can I do? I gave up any hope of continuing my career to help Dennis in the shop."

"What did you do?" Katie asked.

"I was an office manager for a construction company in Rochester. Right now my skills are rusty. Nobody is going to hire me to do more than a minimum-wage keyboarding job. I sacrificed so much for that man and look how he repaid me."

"I'm so sorry, Abby," Katie said and shivered. It was downright *cold* in the room. Abby could save some money by turning off the air-conditioning.

"Still, it doesn't make sense—especially if he's guilty of murder." Abby shook her head. "I believe Dennis has taken off. With everything that's happened, I wouldn't be surprised if he had a girlfriend on the side and had been planning on leaving me all along. I mean, what if the woman couldn't leave right away? Maybe that's why he'd be hiding at the Alley."

Katie clasped her arms. "Maybe."

"Are you cold?" Abby asked.

"A little," Katie admitted.

"Sorry. I hate this whole menopause thing. I've been having wicked hot flashes. They make me absolutely miserable. I'm either boiling hot all the time or freezing." She indicated her sweater. "You caught me in one of my freezing moments. But any minute now I'll be peeling it off." At Katie's startled expression she laughed. "I have a sleeveless shell on underneath." She pulled back the neck of her sweater to show off the light blue shirt. She sank back into the couch. "Menopause. The time of life when your husband looks at you with a jaundiced eye and wonders what happened. Where the wrinkles came from. The weight you just can't seem to take off. And he thinks, 'I'm going to be stuck with this old woman for the rest of my life.'" She gave an ironic laugh. "It's a pity that kind of man doesn't look in the mirror and see that he's deteriorated, too."

This wasn't a conversation Katie was interested in continuing. She stood. "I'm sorry, Abby. I've taken up way too much of your time."

"I'm glad you stopped by," Abby said, then stood and walked Katie to the door. "I feel so cut off from everyone and everybody. I even miss working at the store, which is something I never thought I'd say. And I miss being on the Square. The smell of chocolate and jellies and fresh-baked bread. I miss waving to my shop neighbors. I miss hearing the gossip. Speaking of which, besides the fire, has anything new happened on the Square?"

"The Webster mansion has been sold. It's going to be a bed-and-breakfast called Sassy Sally's. It's supposed to open in November."

Abby's eyes lit up. "Just in time for the holidays. And what a great name. Oh, darn. I'm going to miss seeing it transformed from a wreck to the beauty it deserves to be."

"Artisans Alley's Christmas in July party for the vendors and the Square's merchants is on for Saturday evening. We'd love to have you join us."

"I'll think about it," Abby said with a wan smile.

"Oh, and we have a new Big Brown delivery guy."

Abby blinked. "What happened to Jerry?"

"I heard he retired."

Abby looked thoughtful. "That seems odd. He never mentioned it to me the last time I saw him."

"That's what Gilda Ringwald-Stratton said, too."

Abby shrugged, and then she bit her lip for a moment. "I know I've never worked with you at the Alley or at the Merchants Association, but would you mind if I put you down as a character reference on a job application? I've decided that first thing Monday morning I'm going to seriously start looking for work."

Katie hesitated but saw the look of fear in Abby's eyes. Her future livelihood might depend on it. "Sure." She dug into the pockets of her shorts and came up with a wrinkled business card. "You can use this number."

"I don't know how to thank you, Katie. Dennis always said you were one hell of a woman. Now I know he was speaking of more than just your physical appearance."

"Oh . . . well, thank you. I think." She smiled. "If you need anything, the Merchants Association is . . ." She was about to say willing to do anything it could to help. But technically Dennis was no longer a member and no longer eligible for assistance. Katie forced a smile and changed tacks. "Call me."

"I'll do that," Abby said and opened the door.

Katie caught sight of Davenport's car halfway down the block. She turned back to face Abby. "We'll talk soon."

"I'd like that," Abby said. Letting out a big puff of air, she began unbuttoning her sweater.

Katie could see a light sheen of perspiration on her forehead. "Another flash?"

"Hardly a flash. They seem to last for at least five minutes."

"You have my sympathy."

"And you have mine. You've still got this to look forward to."

Hadn't Rose said the same thing? Katie didn't want to think about it.

The door closed and Katie walked down the stone path to her car at the curb. She got in and buckled her seat belt. She looked back at the Wheelers' house, but there was no one peeking through the curtains.

She started the car and pulled back into the street, eyeing her rearview mirror. When she got to the stop sign, she could see Davenport's car slowly rolling behind her. She turned and steered the car toward Artisans Alley, wondering what she was going to tell Davenport. She'd learned nothing of any real value—except that Abby believed her husband to be a louse. Well, Katie had been leaning that way for the past day or so anyway.

But she didn't like the idea of facing her new pal Davenport. Would he be angry? Would he think her incompetent? Or maybe her lack of anything interesting to report would convince him that he should work on this little project by himself.

She could but hope. And Andy was sure to be just as disappointed when she told him of the conversation with Abby.

It was turning out to be one very disappointing day.

As predicted, Davenport was distinctly unhappy. He paced the confines of Katie's kitchen, scowling, the wrinkles in his forehead multiplying in an alarming number. Was this the look his gave his children when he was upset with them? Had they needed extensive psychiatric care during their young lives because of it?

"I had hoped for better," he said, using a distinctly fatherly tone. A disappointed father.

Katie wasn't buying into that and shrugged. "Sorry. What's the next step?" she said, and cut her ham sandwich into triangles. "Do you want one?"

Davenport shook his head and continued to pace her small kitchen/dining area, his footsteps heavy on the creaky old wooden floor. The term "flatfoot" seemed appropriate. What would Andy think as he sliced and diced his veggies and meats for that night's pizza sales down below?

"I'm going to have to think about what we do next."

Katie sat down at the table. "Well, while you're thinking, think about joining us at the Merchants Association meeting tonight. As a member, you can *nicely*"—she stressed the word—"interrogate everyone under the guise of educating yourself on the organization." She bit into her sandwich, chewed, and swallowed.

"That's true," he said.

"And you'll have a nice meal and a couple of glasses of wine. But not too much wine, you have a long drive home."

Davenport merely grunted.

"We're meeting at six thirty at Del's Diner."

"I know the place."

"And you'll be there?"

Davenport sighed. "I'll be there."

"And try to be nice. But don't smile too much. You'll freak everyone out."

Fifteen

As usual, the dinner conversation around the big table in Del's Diner's function room, for the Merchants Association's monthly meeting, was boisterous. The group had given Nick and Don a warm welcome. However, Katie wasn't exactly sure the welcome mat was out for Detective Davenport. Was it reticence on his part, or were the other members actually avoiding talking to him? Since he'd been seated on one end of the table, with Katie on the other, there wasn't much she could do to include him in the various discussions—at least not without shouting.

Nona Fiske sat as far away from Katie as she possibly could, while Vonne and Francine sat to Katie's left, as far away from Nona as they could be. Vonne kept shooting daggers at Nona, who seemed oblivious. That was just as well. Katie wasn't eager for open warfare to break out before the meeting even began.

Andy had not joined them, but then, he rarely did. His business hours were on the opposite end of the clock from that of most of the Association members.

Conrad walked around the table, topping everyone's glass with a lovely pinot grigio. No one seemed in a hurry to start the meeting, probably because Del's air-conditioning was in tip-top shape and not everyone's home would be as cool or humidity free. Katie consulted her watch. They usually started the meeting well before seven thirty.

She picked up her own glass and struggled to come up with yet another topic of conversation. She turned to her right. "Gilda, did you know Jerry Murphy, the Big Brown delivery guy?"

Gilda scraped the last of the peanut butter mud pie from the dessert plate in front of her. "Oh, sure. Everybody on the Square knew him." She set down her fork. "I saw him every day. Not only do I ship with Big Brown, but I get deliveries from them just about every day."

"Did you know he retired?"

"Yes," she said and sighed. "The new guy told me. I was surprised he never mentioned it to me. We talked a lot. I understood he intended to stay on the job until he could no longer heft those fifty-pound cartons, and believe me, he did that for me just last Friday. He must have changed his mind."

Katie took another sip of wine. "Maybe there was a family emergency or something."

"I could be wrong, but I don't think he had much family. I know he was single, and he liked to flirt, so I'm sure he had plenty of female admirers." She giggled. Was it the wine or had

Gilda—who herself was newly married—fallen for Jerry's glib tongue?

Jordan Tanner—who owned the Square's bakery—took a knife and clinked his half-full water glass until the conversations had quieted to a murmur. "Hadn't we better start the meeting, Katie?" he asked. "We have a lot to cover tonight."

"So we do," she agreed, and stood, knowing there was also a baseball game on ESPN that he probably had TiVo'd. Taking her gavel in hand, she struck the table twice. "We'll now bring the monthly meeting of the Victoria Square Merchants Association to order. Sue, will you hand out copies of the agenda to everyone?"

Sue bounced to her feet and collected a sheaf of papers from a bag she'd set against the wall before taking her seat for dinner. She handed one to everyone before sitting once again.

"First of all, I'd like to officially welcome our newest members, Nick Farrell and Don Parsons, owners of Sassy Sally's Inn, what we've known for many years as the old Webster mansion." A smattering of applause greeted her announcement, and both men nodded at the enthusiasm shown by all.

"I'd also like to welcome Ray Davenport. Many of you know Ray as a detective with the Sheriff's Office." There was no applause as everyone turned to look at the detective. "Mr. Davenport—

Ray—bought Wood U from Dennis Wheeler and the transaction was recorded more than a month ago, but I'm not sure if he's actually a member or needs to join the Association. Nothing in our charter says that when a business is sold, the membership must go along with it—"

"Probably because we've never had a situation like this before," Gilda put in. As one of the founding members of the Association, she had helped draft the charter. "Most of the businesses that fail on the Square just die without a change of hands. The people who next buy or lease the building usually join under a new business name."

"Then it's something we ought to address. Business has picked up on the Square in the past nine months—"

"Thanks to you, Katie!" Sue called out, and again there was a smattering of applause.

Katie waved away the compliment. "We've all worked hard and our increased budget for advertising has greatly enhanced our visibility."

"Do we want to just accept people who haven't paid but do buy a business?" Jordan asked with a pointed glance at the detective.

"I say yes," said Charlotte Booth, who owned the Square's jam and jelly shop. "Dennis paid for the year—and Wood U is—or will be again—a going concern. Anyone taking over such a business has a lot of the same expenses a start-up would. Let the new guy pay when dues come due in January."

"I second that motion, and propose we change the charter to reflect that," Conrad said.

Katie looked around the table. "Those in agreement?" Seven hands shot into the air. "Those against?" Just two members—Nona and Jordan—voted no. Nick and Don abstained.

"We're too new to have an opinion," Nick said in explanation. "We'll wait until we've been a part of the group a little longer before we voice our views."

"I sure hope you won't wait too long," Katie said. "We need all the good ideas we can get to keep Victoria Square *the* place to shop in this portion of Monroe County."

Nick smiled shyly and nodded.

Katie banged her gavel against the table. "The vote's carried. Gilda, would you draft something for the charter for us to vote on at the next meeting?" Gilda nodded.

"Moving to the next item on the agenda, I'd like to remind everyone that there is no such thing as designated parking on Victoria Square," she said, leveling her gaze at Nona, who continued her oblivious routine. She picked up her wineglass and took a demure sip. "If anyone needs reminding, you'll find this covered in the group's charter under shared facilities, paragraph three. Does anyone have any questions?"

No one said a thing, although several other people had turned their attention to Nona as well.

Sue raised her hand. "There's an elephant in this dining room," she said in a quiet voice. "I think we all want to know what's going on with Dennis. Is he really dead or is he wanted for murder?"

All eyes turned to Davenport, who raised his hands in submission. "I'm no longer in charge of the investigation. However, if you have any information you feel is relevant, I encourage you to share it with Detective Hamilton of the Sheriff's Office."

"If you're not working on the case, can you tell us what's going on? I mean, a murder on the Square could adversely affect business for all of us," Francine said, sounding nervous.

"All I know is that someone killed a man and torched my new business. That's about it."

Katie knew better, but she also knew Davenport was going to have an uphill battle winning over the other members of the Association and decided to cut him some slack and said nothing.

"Our inn was broken into sometime between Friday and Monday mornings," Don said, addressing Davenport. "Should we be worried about a copycat fire?"

"The Sheriff's Office is looking at a person of interest in that matter."

Katie knew Davenport meant Andy's employee, Blake Taylor.

"They think they'll have that portion of the crime wrapped up in a matter of days," Davenport continued.

"Then there were two different crimes committed?" Charlotte asked.

"Possibly," Davenport said, hedging.

"And they still haven't identified the body?" Jordan asked.

Davenport shook his head, and Katie again thought about the Big Brown driver who'd suddenly retired. But it couldn't be him. What would he be doing on Victoria Square on a Saturday at that time of night? And then she remembered what Davenport had asked her the morning after the fire: Had Dennis and Abby had marital problems? Abby had said Dennis had disappointed her on a number of occasions. Gilda had mentioned that Jerry was a flirt. Abby had worked alone in the shop for most of the winter. Had she and Jerry developed a friendship when he made his deliveries? Had Dennis been jealous of that friendship?

Don't, Katie chided herself. *You're making assumptions based on nothing.* But she couldn't get the idea out of her head.

"Katie. Katie!" Sue called.

Katie shook herself.

"Shall we go on to the next item on the agenda?"

Katie looked down at the piece of paper in front

of her and bit her lip. She should tell Davenport her theory—even if he just pooh-poohed it, and he would.

"It's time to start brainstorming for this year's Dickens Festival. Any ideas?"

"Why don't we table that until after the big party on Saturday night at Artisans Alley—that way we can get your vendors' input, too," Gilda suggested.

Davenport looked up sharply. "You mean at my retirement party?" Everyone looked at him as though he were crazy.

"No—the Artisans Alley Christmas in July party," Gilda clarified.

"Your party is on Saturday?" Katie asked Davenport, aghast.

"It sure is. We've rented one of your empty stores at the front of Artisans Alley. You should have already received the check *and* an invitation."

"But I thought your party was on Friday!" Katie cried.

Davenport shook his head, looking agitated.

Katie heaved a big sigh. "Swell."

"But as long as there's going to be a lot of celebrating anyway, why don't we combine the parties? That way Katie's vendors can meet you and welcome you to the Square, too," Charlotte said.

"Great idea," Sue echoed. "I spoke to Rose

Nash just yesterday. There'll be a ton of food, and it'll be a great way to get word out about the shop reopening."

Davenport shrugged, but didn't look at all happy. "Sure. Sounds great."

"Katie, maybe you could put a sign out in the parking lot to let everyone know they should go inside to meet Ray," Gilda suggested.

"If this heat wave doesn't break, or it rains, we may *all* be inside the Alley."

"The more the merrier," Conrad said, proffering his wineglass.

"I'll be displaying some of my new inventory. I sure would like some input on whether you think it will sell," Davenport put in.

"Who are your suppliers?" Gilda asked.

Davenport looked confused. "I don't have any. I bought the stock from Wood U, although I'm not sure what's salvageable right now. But I've made a lot of products myself. And since the store won't reopen for a couple of months, I'll have time to make even more."

"You'd better find a supplier fast," Nona advised in rather a snide tone. "That is, if you don't want to find yourself with customers and no stock come December."

For the first time since Katie had known him, Davenport looked unsure of himself. He had a lot to learn about retail, and she was sure his fellow Association members would give him a crash

226

course—at least when it came to all the negative aspects of the profession.

The waitress arrived to clear the table, and Katie called the meeting back to order.

The rest of the items on the agenda went quickly. As they concerned regular Square maintenance, all the resolutions were passed without discussion. Nick and Don cast their first votes, and Nona abstained from all but one of the suggestions. Katie acted as if she didn't notice Nona's negativity. It wasn't worth it. The meeting broke up by eight o'clock with the scraping of the wooden chairs on the ceramic-tiled floor.

Katie intercepted Davenport before he could leave. "I'm so sorry about the mix-up. I honestly thought your party was slated for Friday."

"Yes, well. We'll have to make the best of it, won't we?"

"There's plenty of parking, and as Gilda suggested, we'll put a sign out to direct your friends to your party. And if they end up mingling with us, it won't be a problem. There's always more food than we could ever eat."

"Good night, Mrs. Bonner."

"Katie," she reminded him.

All but Katie and Sue had left. Sue hefted her purse and a canvas bag. In her hand she held the steno pad she'd used to take notes on the meeting. "Katie, we seem to have a sticky situation. One of the members didn't pay for her dinner tonight."

Katie frowned. "Let me guess—Nona Fiske."

"How did you know?"

"Lucky guess."

"What shall we do about it?"

Katie sighed. "Could you give her a call in the morning and remind her? If she doesn't pay by next meeting, she'll have to reimburse the Association before she can order again. If she doesn't order, we'll add it to her dues for next year."

"And if she doesn't re-up?"

Katie sighed. Was there no end to the situation with Nona? "We'll have to eat it."

Sue looked startled for a moment, and then laughed. "Oh, I get it. A pun. We'll have to *eat* it!" She laughed again. "Oh, Katie, you *are* funny."

She hadn't meant to be.

The women walked out together. The sun was only just beginning its downward trajectory, and the day's heat and humidity slammed them as they stepped from the diner into the parking lot. Sue sighed. "I can't wait until the cooler weather arrives. This humidity plays havoc with my hard candies."

"And I've got thirty-five thousand square feet of retail space and only about twenty percent of it is air-conditioned. It's like an oven at the Alley."

"Can't you do something about it?" Sue asked.

"I'm afraid I'm going to have to," Katie said.

"I've got a date with my TV and a fan and I'd better get going before I melt," Sue said and headed for her car. Katie had walked to the diner and she gave a wave before she set off for home, wishing she had more than a TV and a fan to go home to. And, in fact, she had no intention of going straight home. Or at least she had one more stop to make before she climbed the stairs to her sweltering apartment.

Sixteen

"I am in deep doo-doo," Katie admitted, accepting the can of Coca-Cola that Andy handed her.

"How could you make such an obvious blunder?" he asked as he shut the cooler door and donned a new pair of plastic gloves before he turned back to his work surface and began adding toppings to the round of pizza dough before him.

"The dates were similar," she said and popped the can's tab, taking a deep gulp. "I mean, they both started with a one in front of them."

"So what's the big deal anyway? The Artisans Alley party is outside and the retirement party is inside. You can always move your party down the Square a bit. Hold it in front of some of the other stores. As long as there's no trash cluttering things up in the morning, why would anyone object?"

"I'm worried about the weather. What if it's still in the nineties? Some of my vendors are elderly. They could collapse from the heat."

"So have a few fans available for them to sit by."

Katie glared at him. "That would just be blowing hot air on them. The paper said it might rain, too. I was thinking of moving the party inside to the lobby. At least it would be ten or more degrees cooler than outside. It's one of the few places inside the building that actually *gets* cool."

"So, why can't Davenport have his party in the shop and you have yours in the lobby? Correct me if I'm wrong, but there is a wall and door separating the spaces, isn't there?"

"I suppose we could," Katie said, resting the cold sweating can against her cheek.

"And like you said, as long as you have a bunch of signs outside and in the entryway, it shouldn't matter. And if Davenport is going to be part of the Square anyway, can't you make it a welcome-to-the-neighborhood party, too? You were inviting the rest of the Merchants Association, right?"

"I suppose I could." She gave Andy a grin. "You have good ideas. You ought to try to make it to more of our Merchants Association meetings."

"And you ought to hold a breakfast meeting once in a while so that I *could* come."

"Another good suggestion," Katie agreed. "We might actually get more work done and spend less time socializing."

Andy finished up his pizza and handed it to his assistant, Keith, who popped it into the oven. Andy started on another pizza just as the phone rang. "You wanna get that?" he asked Katie.

She stepped over to the wall phone and picked it up. "Angelo's Pizzeria." But instead of it being a customer, it was the voice of a frightened young man on the line. "Is Andy there? Tell him it's Blake. I have to talk to him. Now. It's really important."

Katie rested the phone against her chest. "Andy, it's Blake. He says he has to talk to you and that it's important."

Andy's face darkened as he stripped off his gloves and accepted the call.

Katie took her place on the other side of the counter and sipped her Coke.

"What the hell?" Andy said. "Did you call your parents?" Katie could see Andy's shoulders had tensed. "No, I'll come. Don't say *anything*. Yeah, I won't call them now, but you know I'll have to later." This didn't sound good. "Hang tight. I'll be there soon." He hung up the phone and swore. Then he removed the dishtowel tucked into his jeans that served as a makeshift apron, and tossed it under the counter.

"Is Blake in trouble?" Katie asked, although she suspected she knew the answer.

Andy nodded, and she could see by the set of his jaw that he was upset. "He's been arrested for arson."

"For the fire at Wood U?"

He shook his head. "A construction site over in Greece." The Rochester suburb next to McKinlay Mill, where Katie had grown up. "I'd hate to have to call in one of the other kids this late at night. Can you help out until I get back?"

"Sure." Katie had done it a number of times when Andy was shorthanded. She could take phone orders and make pizzas as well as any of his employees. And besides, it was slightly cooler and a whole lot less humid in the pizzeria than it was in her apartment. He was actually doing her a favor by inviting her to stay there for several hours.

Andy scooted around the counter, gave Katie a quick kiss, and bounded out the door.

Katie and Keith watched him get into his car and pull out of the lot. She met the boy's gaze. "Looks like it's just us," she said as the phone rang again.

Keith grabbed it. "Angelo's Pizzeria." He listened and didn't take notes. "Yeah, she's here."

He handed Katie the phone. Would it be

Davenport? Was he going to berate her about the mix-up in the party spaces for Saturday night? "Hello?"

"Katie, it's Nick Farrell."

"Oh." She laughed. "You're the last person I expected to hear from. And I'm sorry, but I really can't tie up the pizzeria's line. Can we talk tomorrow?"

"That's why I'm calling now. We heard you have a storage unit full of antiques you might like to unload, and we've got a house that needs filling."

Katie found herself gritting her teeth. Had Seth let it slip? She did *not* want to part with her treasures. "I do have some items, but I'm not interested in selling them."

"Are you sure? I understand Artisans Alley is in need of cash to fix the HVAC system."

And who told him that? Seth again?

"I really need to get off the phone," Katie said, stalling.

"Right. I can come over to the Alley tomorrow morning and we can chat. Is that okay?"

"Sure," she said, trying not to sound at all angry.

"Great. I'll be there about nine. See you then."

Katie hung up the phone, which immediately started to ring again. She grabbed the receiver. "Angelo's Pizzeria."

"Yeah, I'd like to order a medium with cheese,

pepperoni, and onions. How long will it take?"

Katie hesitated, still angry that someone had told Nick about her antiques. "Uh . . . twenty minutes pickup. An hour if you want it delivered."

"Wow, that's a long time. I'll pick it up." Katie took down the order, then the name and phone number of the customer. She hung up and donned fresh gloves to make the pizza. Seth wouldn't tell her who'd bought Wood U, but would he have told his high school buddy that she had all those antiques that were perfect for Sassy Sally's?

The phone kept ringing and the pizza orders kept coming. There was no way Katie could call Seth to ask.

She'd just have to seethe in silence until the next morning.

Andy finally called just as Keith left and Katie locked up the pizzeria for the night. "I'm sorry I didn't call earlier. It's been a nightmare kind of evening," he admitted.

"How did things go with Blake?"

"Not good. It looks like he was caught red-handed. They've got video of the crime. And it's only a matter of time before the Sheriff's Office arrests him on the Wood U fire. He admitted to me that he did that, too."

"But why?" Katie asked. "Blake graduated from

school. Dennis retired. Blake never would've had to interact with Dennis again."

"Revenge, plain and simple. And setting fire to something gives the kid a thrill," he said bitterly. "Why couldn't he just play Xbox and be a kid for just a little while longer?"

"Andy, you said yourself this wasn't the first time he's torched something. The boy needs help."

"Unfortunately, they're going to toss him in jail and let him rot there for a very long, long time."

"I'm so sorry," Katie said, not knowing what else to say. She turned to practical matters. "Do you want me to leave the receipts in the register, or should I just take them up to my apartment?"

"Lock them in the register and put the key in the usual place. I'll stop by on my way home and pick them up. I've still got to make the dough for tomorrow's cinnamon buns. Damn Danny for taking this week off."

"Do you want to come up for a nightcap?" Katie offered.

"I would, but you've had two late nights in a row. You've got to be at the Alley in less than seven hours. You need your sleep."

Thank you, she silently agreed.

"Thanks for pitching in again tonight," Andy said.

"Hey, you'd do the same for me."

"I wouldn't, and you know it. Making a pizza

and taking orders isn't like managing a business as complicated as Artisans Alley. And you must've been bushed after the day you put in, not to mention dealing with the Merchants Association."

"Stop! You're making me feel even more tired," she joked. "However, I will allow you to repay me with breakfast tomorrow morning. How about two cinnamon rolls?"

"You got it! Thanks again. See you in the morning."

"Good night."

Katie hung up the phone. She switched off the lights and locked up, then trudged up the outside set of stairs to her apartment. For safety's sake, after she'd rented it, Andy had blocked off the stairs inside the pizzeria that led to the apartment. She was glad one of the Square's big parking lot lamps illuminated the staircase. After what she'd been through the evening before, she was almost as nervous as Francine Barnett.

Katie entered her apartment and was welcomed by two sleepy cats, who informed her that they could sure use a snack. She filled their bowls with treats and then switched off the kitchen light. The same light that lit her staircase made a useful night light. She moved to take one last look at Victoria Square.

Just as she was about to turn away she heard the sound of a car engine, and headlights cut through the darkness at the far end of the parking lot, near Wood U. Who would be on the Square at this time of night? She was the only one who actually lived there. Could it be Dennis Wheeler? Did the killer always return to the scene of the crime? Odd as it seemed, Abby hadn't come to fetch her husband's car and the last Katie had looked, it was still sitting in the back lot. Could he have claimed it? She couldn't see from her current vantage point, and wasn't about to go poking around outside alone at that time of night. But the thought of Dennis Wheeler hanging around Victoria Square—a man she'd never feared in the past—truly did frighten her.

And she didn't like feeling that way.

Not one damn bit.

Seventeen

The sound of a roaring engine pulling into Victoria Square caused Katie to stop sipping her English breakfast tea and glance out the window in time to see the back end of Vance's pickup truck zoom buy. She glanced at her clock. She wasn't due to open Artisans Alley for another fifteen minutes. Seconds later, another familiar car pulled into the lot. It belonged to Ida Mitchell. Would she never tire of her protest?

Katie poured the rest of her tea down the sink, grabbed her keys, and locked the apartment.

Vance was assembling the EZ-UP while an impatient Ida stood nearby, tapping her foot.

"What's going on?" Katie inquired politely, squelching the urge to make a more vehement demand. "When you took down your canopy yesterday, I figured that would be the end of this ridiculous campaign of terror."

The corners of Vance's mouth quirked upward, but he didn't pause. "We can't let Ida fry out here, now can we?" he said reasonably.

"And we don't have to encourage her either," Katie said under her breath.

"She'll get tired of it in a few days. And when I take it down tonight, I'll tell her I can't bring it back tomorrow. I only brought it today because she cornered me yesterday when I was hot and vulnerable," he muttered.

"Are you two talking about me?" Ida demanded. "Because if you are, I want you to stop it right now!"

Katie's fists clenched. "I would love to stop talking about you—forever." She wagged a finger in Vance's face. "This is the last day I'm going to put up with this."

"What are you gonna do?" Ida whined, sounding like a spoiled child. "Arrest me?"

"That's an option," Katie said. "Technically you are trespassing. If they don't throw you in jail, they could make you pay a big fine."

Ida blinked in surprise. She didn't have any money at her disposal, and the threat to her pocketbook actually seemed to take some of the steam out of her.

Katie wasn't about to debate the subject any longer. She turned and stomped toward the vendors' entrance and opened the door, letting it slam shut behind her.

True to his word, Nick Farrell showed up at Artisans Alley at precisely nine o'clock holding two tall cups, both of them bearing domed plastic lids. "Are you busy?" he asked.

"Always. But not too busy to chat with a member of the Merchants Association—and a new friend. Come on in," Katie said and gestured to her guest chair. Thank goodness she'd had an hour to cool down after her latest altercation with Ida, the term cool being relative. "Sorry it's so hot in here." She turned the fan to its lowest setting, which was still almost as loud as a lawnmower.

"This ought to cool you off," Nick said, handing Katie one of the cups.

"Thanks." She inspected the offering. A mocha frappe with a drizzle of caramel on the whipped cream. He handed her a straw.

"Is this a bribe?" Katie asked, and removed the paper wrapper from her straw, inserting it into the drink.

"Maybe," Nick admitted and smiled. He had dazzling white teeth. He must have bleached them on a regular basis.

"Let's not get into the subject of my treasures just yet. I want to enjoy at least some of this," Katie said and took a sip. *Mmm . . . nice.* "What did you think about the meeting last night?"

"It was great."

"I hope you didn't feel intimidated, what with being the new guys in town. You really can make any suggestions you want. That's what the Association is all about."

"Don't worry, we talked about it last night and we have a lot of ideas. We're going to have a brochure stand in our reception area, and we want to include everyone on the Square. And we want to talk about partnering with other merchants for special offers for our guests."

"Some of the merchants are already doing that. You'll find an enthusiastic audience. Give me a call before the next meeting so I can put your ideas on the agenda."

"I'll do that," Nick said, and took a sip of his own drink. "I was surprised to find out the former owner of Wood U was none other than Mr. Wheeler from my high school shop class."

"You knew him?"

"Oh yeah," Nick said, and the set of his mouth told her it hadn't been a pleasant experience.

"It seems like he had a reputation for picking on some of his students," Katie ventured.

"Tell me about it. I was one of them. I guess I just looked gay, and in those days, it didn't take much to bring out the bully not only in Old Man Wheeler, but in the other testosterone-soaked jocks that were my classmates. I was lucky Seth jumped in to save me."

"No one suspected he was gay?" Katie asked. Dumb question. She hadn't suspected it. Andy had had to clue her in.

Nick shook his head. "Not a chance. He was the quarterback on the football team. Luckily for me, the guys respected him enough to listen when he told them not to pick on me. Funny—the kids laid off, but not Wheeler," he said bitterly.

Good grief. How many of Dennis's former students on Victoria Square held a grudge?

"Were you the only one in the class that got picked on?"

"Most of the time. It seemed like he singled out one kid in every one of his classes. Lucky me, huh?" He took a long sip on his frappe.

"When you and Don bought the Webster mansion, did you know Dennis had a shop on Victoria Square?"

Nick nodded. "Seth mentioned it when he first told us about the property. He knew if we bought the house, we'd run into Wheeler at the Merchants Association meetings."

"Did the idea bother you?"

"A little. But my dealings with the man happened twenty years ago. I was hoping the jerk had at least learned to hide his homophobia." He sighed. "But talking about Wheeler is not why I came to see you this morning."

"Aha! Now for the *real* reason for your visit," Katie prompted, just as glad to drop the former subject.

Nick hesitated then smiled, flashing those dazzling teeth again. "I'd love to hear about your storage unit filled with goodies."

Every muscle in Katie's body tensed. "Yes. I do have quite an inventory."

"I wonder if there's anything in there you'd be willing to part with?"

"To tell you the truth, I haven't thought about it."

Liar!

"I know we're not in a position to take possession of anything quite yet, but I did want to broach the idea with you. And maybe you could tell me about what you'd planned for the inn."

"I'd planned to furnish it with antiques and collectibles, just like you."

"I've already made up a list of tentative items. Don and I both love brass beds, and we're hoping to find some great-looking full beds and convert them to queen size."

"That was on my agenda, too," Katie admitted.

She could feel the sweat beading in her hair, despite the fan. She wouldn't have to swelter in this sauna of an office if she could upgrade the HVAC systems. To do that, she needed at least fifteen thousand dollars—probably more like twenty to do the job properly. Selling off her antiques wouldn't pay for it. It just wouldn't.

"I love old oak—golden oak," Nick corrected himself. "And it's appropriate for the house. I've been looking for a commode with a marble top, too."

And I have a gorgeous one in mint condition in the storage unit.

"Shopping at online galleries is fun, but it's so expensive," Nick went on.

"I haven't had a chance to gather that list I promised you. But I will. Have you tried craigslist?" Katie asked.

Nick took another sip and nodded. "I'm searching every day."

Katie wouldn't meet his eyes. He had brown puppy-dog eyes. Eyes that could melt your resolve. If she dared look, she'd be *giving* him the stuff for a song.

"Do you have pictures?" Nick prodded.

"I took a few," she admitted.

"I don't suppose they're on your hard drive," he said, nodding in that direction.

"As a matter of fact . . ." *Go ahead, tell him NO!* "I do."

"Could I see them? Not all of them. Just a few." He smiled and laughed. "Go ahead—tease me."

If you open that file, he's going to wheedle at you until you cave, the voice said.

"Sure." She reached for her mouse and gave the right button a double click, awakening the slumbering computer. She didn't have to search for the file because she'd moved it to her desktop and kept it in the right-hand corner for easy access. And she'd found herself accessing it a lot in the past couple of days.

She clicked open the folder and ten subfolders appeared. "What did you want to see? Bedroom furniture? Dining room? Linens? Lighting? Dishes and silverware?"

"Bedroom furniture," Nick said, and there was a hungry set to his eyes.

Katie clicked on the file marked BEDROOMS, and eighteen or twenty thumbnails appeared on the screen in tidy rows. She clicked on one of them and a brass headboard appeared. Because of its shape, it reminded Katie of a piece of commercially made bread—rounded on the top with little indents on each side, and a series of spindles of different lengths running under the top rail.

"Oh wow," Nick breathed, leaning in to study the photo. Katie had stood the headboard on the side of the storage unit before she'd wrapped a mover's blanket over the top to protect it from . . .

she wasn't sure. Just to keep it safe, because she loved it so much.

"I've seen something similar in a reproduction catalog," she said.

"I know the one. They call this a rainbow bed. The catalog wanted over two grand for a queen-size model. How much did you pay for this?"

Katie sighed. "Two hundred dollars."

"With a matching footboard?" he asked. Katie nodded. "Omigod!"

Katie clicked on another view—a close-up of one of the spindles.

"It sure would look nice all polished and shiny," Nick said wistfully.

Katie clicked on another photo. The twin headboard had been painted red at one time, but it was peeling and in need of some serious TLC. It was probably lead paint, which meant it would need careful restoration, too. "I have two of these, with footboards. They're kind of pretty," she said without enthusiasm, much as she wanted to gush. Heck, they were *gorgeous!*

"We're going for down duvets with high-thread-count covers. Some matching shams and accent pillows would look divine."

Katie looked at him askance. "Have you been reading my mind?"

Nick laughed. "I have been accused of that in the past—at least when it comes to plans for Sassy Sally's."

The name still made Katie cringe. "Have you planned to open a B and B for a long time?" she asked.

"Ever since I graduated from Cornell's School of Hotel Administration—just about twenty years. I've worked all over the hotel industry. As a night manager in a mom-and-pop operation, assistant manager at a Holiday Inn Express, concierge at a Marriott in San Francisco, and I've done a couple of stints managing small bed-and-breakfast operations. I liked them best, but of course they didn't belong to me. This is my first opportunity to do it all—and this time make it *all* mine." He laughed. "And a little of it will be Don's, too."

"I'm impressed with your résumé. Makes me feel like I haven't done my homework."

"I'll bet you have. How long have you had the innkeeping bug?"

"Ever since my college days when I worked a summer job as a maid in a small inn. It was hard work—but I knew from that first day that it was what I wanted to do for the rest of my life. Of course, I took time out to get my master's in business administration—I figured it couldn't hurt when it came to running my own business."

"I'll say," Nick agreed. "So how did you end up here?"

"It's a long story. But I think I'd rather tell it to

you over a glass of wine and in a much nicer location."

"I'd love to take you to lunch sometime."

Katie smiled. "I'd love to go."

"I'll call you in a few days. That'll give you time to get used to the idea of parting with your stuff."

"I can't promise my answer will make you happy."

"Nothing in life is certain," Nick said and rose from his seat. He dumped his empty frappe container in Katie's trash.

"Maybe when you're ready to decorate, you might want to take a walk around Artisans Alley. We have a lot of lovely things for sale."

"I'll do that."

Katie walked him to the front door. "I'll call you in a couple of days," Nick promised, and leaned forward to give her an air kiss. He pulled back, gave a wave, and headed out the door, passing the Big Brown deliveryman, who was on his way in.

"Hey, Greg. Need help with those boxes?" Katie asked.

The deliveryman hefted three of them, his arms extended to their full length, holding them steady by tucking the top one under his chin. "No, thanks," he said and tipped them up and onto the empty cash desk.

"Still enjoying the route?" Katie asked.

"I sure am. Jerry Murphy always called it a plum assignment. Said the people were really friendly. He was right, too."

"I was wondering, have you heard anything from Jerry since he retired?"

He shook his head. "Didn't expect to. But I was hoping he might part with his wheels."

"I beg your pardon?"

"Jerry restores old cars. He's been working on a '57 Chevy for the past year. I was hoping he'd sell it to me. I mean, he was going to retire to open a shop and restore cars full-time. What's he need with a finished car?"

"Yeah," Katie muttered.

"Gotta go. The route calls," Greg said and headed out the door.

Katie bit her lip and started back for her office. It bothered her that Jerry had just dropped out of sight. It was crazy to think that he could've been the body at Wood U. After all, she thought once more, what would he be doing there on a Saturday night?

"He's a flirt," Gilda had said. Had he flirted with Abby Wheeler and Dennis was jealous? Jealous enough to kill the guy?

That didn't make sense. And there was no proof the dead man was Jerry Murphy or even that it was Dennis Wheeler. And why would Jerry want to kill Dennis anyway?

And there were others who held grudges against

Dennis Wheeler. Blake Taylor had set the fire at Wood U as an act of revenge. Nick had only recently returned to McKinlay Mill, and there was no denying he hadn't gotten over being the brunt of Dennis's so-called jokes. But the idea of such a nice man—a man who Seth admired enough to participate in his wedding—killing Dennis Wheeler was impossible.

And yet . . . nothing felt right about that death. The fact that the deceased's face had been blown apart so that identification would be difficult. Not impossible, but such a delay would give the perpetrator enough time to come up with an alibi, or to make a contingency escape plan. That would explain the intruder hiding at Artisans Alley.

But something was missing from that equation, and what that was, Katie had no idea. Davenport didn't seem to have a clue either. Maybe it would take Detective Hamilton a year or more to figure it out, because right now the task seemed insurmountable. Maybe they'd never know the whole truth. Maybe there'd never be closure—for Abby, for Davenport—for anyone on Victoria Square. That thought depressed Katie. But then, if she was honest with herself, it really wasn't her problem.

But it seemed like it should be.

Katie hadn't been back at her desk for even five minutes before a knock on the doorjamb caused her to look up from her computer screen. Liz Meier, the stained glass artist, stood in the doorway, and Katie could see a couple of blonde-haired beauties standing behind her.

"Katie, there're some people here to clean one of the shops out front," Liz said, sounding uncertain.

"Oh, yes. They must be Detective Davenport's daughters." Liz stepped aside and the tallest of the young women fingered a wave. "Ms. Bonner? My name is Sophie Davenport. Mr. Cunningham said it would be all right if my sisters and I cleaned the space for our dad's party."

Katie stood. "Yes. And please, call me Katie."

Sophie giggled. "Thanks. These are my sisters, Sasha and Sadie." The other two young women waved. They looked like identical twins, from their blonde tresses and dimpled smiles down to their matching tops, jeans, and sneakered feet. How did grumpy old Detective Davenport ever produce such beautiful children?

"I'm afraid it's pretty dusty," Katie admitted. "It hasn't been rented out in quite some time. Do you need some cleaning products?"

"We brought everything we thought we'd need, but we can probably use a bucket or two of water, and a place to dump it."

"Sure." Katie grabbed her keys from the cup hook that hung on the wall near her desk. "I'll open it up for you."

The girls backed up, giving Katie room to sidle past them. Katie led them through Artisans Alley and into the lobby. As Sophie had said, outside the locked storefront were several cartons filled with paper towels, buckets, soap, and other cleaning materials, along with a couple of brooms, mops, and dustpans.

Katie inserted the key in the lock and opened the door to the shop. The air smelled stale. She didn't envy the girls' task, but they didn't seem deterred.

"Wow, what a great space," Sophie said, admiring the size of the shop, which despite all Fred's efforts these past few months, had not been rented. "We'd like to put up some decorations. Would it be okay if we put up streamers and a banner?" Sophie asked.

"Sure," Katie said. "Don't worry about using tape or tacks. These walls will need to be patched before the next tenant takes over."

"Thanks." Sophie leveled a serious stare at her sisters. "Ladies, hop to it. Sasha, you start sweeping. Sadie, follow Ms. Bonner to fill the bucket with hot water."

Both girls giggled, and saluted their older sister. "Aye-aye, Captain," they said in unison.

"Let me know if you need anything," Katie told Sophie as Sadie gathered up the bucket. She led her back to the washroom, where Sadie filled the bucket partway, gave her thanks, and headed back to join her sisters.

What nice girls. Davenport and his wife had obviously been stellar parents to have raised such lovely daughters, who not only seemed to get along, but loved their dad unconditionally.

Katie sighed, wishing she could remember her father. If it weren't for old pictures, she'd have no recollection of his face at all.

The phone rang, and Katie grabbed it. "Artisans Alley, Katie speaking. How may I help you?"

"It's Ray Davenport."

"What a coincidence. I just met your daughters. They came to clean the room for your retirement party. They're lovely girls."

"Yeah, I'm pretty proud of them. Their mom was, too."

Was there a catch in his voice?

He cleared his throat. "But that's not why I called. I wanted to let you know the Taylor kid confessed to setting the fire at Wood U."

"I knew he'd been arrested," she said sadly.

"The kid agreed to plead guilty to that charge, but not to the murder. He swears he didn't know there was anyone in the building at the time he set the blaze."

"But we all know Dennis Wheeler's car was parked out back."

"Yeah, we do. The kid swears he's never handled a gun. Yada, yada, yada. But get this, his father owns a Magnum."

The kind of gun that killed the person at Wood U.

"Can they test to see if it's the same gun? I mean, did they recover a slug at the scene?"

"A slug?" Davenport repeated. "You've been watching too many TV shows, Mrs. Bonner."

"That's Katie," she reminded him.

"Yes. Katie. It's going to take some time to get used to calling you that." No more than for her to get used to calling him Ray. "Anyway, what I'm getting these days is just secondhand info. I'm not sure what evidence may have been collected since I worked the case." He didn't sound at all hopeful.

"What happens next?"

"They keep investigating."

They, not him. That had to gall him.

"Dennis Wheeler is still the chief suspect," Davenport said, "and finding him is their top priority right now."

"Do you think they're going to find him?"

"Yeah—one way or another."

That could take weeks. Time to spring her other theory on him. "What if you wanted to find out other stuff? Do you still have access to DMV records and the like?"

"Why?" he asked suspiciously.

"The Big Brown delivery guy who served Victoria Square seems to have disappeared."

"What do you mean?"

"The man suddenly retired. No one seems to have heard from him." Nobody on Victoria

Square, at least. "I want to find out about Jerry Murphy's car. It seems he restores old cars and he has a 1957 Chevy."

"So?"

"So . . . if you knew his address, we could call him and find out the story about his so-called retirement."

"And why would I care?"

"Because you told me I could come to you with anything."

"I did, didn't I?" he said, and didn't sound happy about it.

"Well, I think there's a possibility the dead guy from Wood U is Jerry Murphy."

"Are you out of your mind?"

"I'm serious."

"What's your evidence?"

"Gut feeling."

"Gut feeling doesn't cut it in a court of law."

"Who said anything about court . . . yet? Could you just go look up the information, as well as call his former employer to see how he tendered his resignation?"

"How is that relevant?"

"It sure would look suspicious if he didn't do it in person, wouldn't it?" The silence on the other end of the line wasn't promising. Time to pull out the big guns and beg. "Please—as a favor to me?"

He sighed. "Passing myself off as someone

working this murder case could get me in trouble. Big trouble."

"Who says you're working on the Wood U murder? And aren't you still officially a member of the Sheriff's Office until Friday?"

"Technically," he admitted.

"Then you'd just be looking into why the guy suddenly quit his job."

"Why am I supposed to tell them I'm calling?"

"Because . . . a family member is worried? Because his car was illegally parked? I don't know. You're the one who's made cold calls on people for the last thirty-odd years. Use your imagination." Hadn't he told her the same thing when he'd wanted her to speak to Abby Wheeler?

She heard him sigh again—heavily. "If I find the time."

"Thank you for telling me about Blake."

"Yeah—yeah," Davenport grumbled.

"But you know, if I'm wrong about Jerry . . . there are a lot of Dennis Wheeler's former students still in the area. Students who did not like the man—and with reason."

"Wait a minute. Are you switching sides again? You just told me you thought the victim was Jerry Murphy. Now you think it's Wheeler? Lady, make up your mind."

"I'm trying to keep an open one—at least until the medical examiner actually makes a formal identification."

"That isn't going to happen until they can get a DNA match and can rule Wheeler out. Until then . . . it's open season."

"With Jerry Murphy as a suspect?"

"Only to you. Which one of his former students do you think did the deed?"

"I'm not saying I have a suspect. But I've heard from at least two of his former students who were picked on by the man."

"Are you counting your boyfriend among them?"

"Andy's no killer."

"So you say. Who's the other?"

"I'm not going to say. You're ready to blow off my ideas once again and I'm not going to give you more bait."

"I've been listening," he said, but she wondered if he'd been rolling his eyes, too.

"Listen, I gotta go. I'll think about what you said and I'll talk to you later." Davenport cut the connection.

Katie hung up the phone. Well, at least he hadn't just told her to mind her own business. She had to admit he *was* actively listening to her and not entirely dismissing her ideas out of hand.

She sighed. It was too bad about Blake. Andy wasn't going to get over this anytime soon. Maybe she should make him dinner once again. If he could get away for even fifteen minutes, it might help him feel better.

She quickly dialed Andy's cell phone, since she knew the shop was closed and he wasn't likely to answer that phone.

"Hey, Katie, what's up?" Andy asked. Katie could hear the whirr of the dough mixer in the background.

"I just thought about you and wanted to hear the sound of your voice. Is that okay?"

"That's always fine with me," he said, and she could hear the smile in his voice.

She wasn't about to mention Blake to spoil that good mood. "I'll probably drop in later to see you."

He laughed. "You do every night anyway."

"I know, but . . . I miss you."

"I miss you, too. But I gotta get this dough ready for tonight. Okay?"

"I'm sorry. With all the interruptions I get, I sometimes forget other people are on tight schedules."

"Thanks for understanding. I'll see you later."

"Bye." She hung up.

Katie heard voices in the vendors' lounge.

"Are you sure you're okay?" Was that Vance? He sounded worried.

Katie heard the murmur of a soft voice answer him. She got up from her chair and entered the vendors' lounge. She found Vance standing over Gwen Hardy, who sat hunched over at the table, her head resting in her hands. "Is anything wrong?" she asked, concerned.

"I found Gwen lying on the fainting couch in her booth," Vance said. "Looks like she passed out."

"Wasn't it lucky I had the appropriate furniture just waiting for that to happen," Gwen said, her voice sounding weak.

"Do you want me to call nine-one-one?" Katie asked, concerned.

Gwen shook her head, looked like she regretted it, and winced. "I was walking security and it was so hot I thought I was going to keel over. My booth was nearby so I went to sit down before I fell down."

"Would you like a glass of cold water?" Katie asked.

Gwen looked up and nodded, her hazel eyes looking dark against her pale skin.

Katie hurried to the fridge. Luckily the jug was still full, and she grabbed a clean coffee mug from the rack and filled it. She handed the water to Gwen, who gratefully drank it.

"I'm so sorry this happened, Gwen. But you've at least convinced me that whether we can afford it or not, that new HVAC system has got to be installed—ASAP. I can't have customers and vendors dropping like flies on me. It's time to do something drastic."

"I hate to say it, but I've been waiting weeks for you to come to that decision," Vance said.

"I'll call the heating and cooling company and

have them come out as soon as they can to fix that air-conditioning once and for all."

"But how will you pay for it?" Gwen asked, sounding worried.

Katie sighed. "I'll find the money. Somehow. Will you be all right, Gwen?" she asked, truly concerned.

Gwen nodded. "Katie, please don't go into hock just because of me."

She patted the woman's shoulder. "It's not just for you—it's for all of us."

Katie stormed off for her office and grabbed the phone, but didn't call the heating company. Instead she dialed another number. "Nick? Hi, it's Katie. I think I'm ready to part with some of my treasures. When can we talk?"

Eighteen

The scheduler at Beltram Heating and Cooling said they could be out as early as Monday to start work on replacing Artisans Alley's HVAC systems. Katie had hoped for sooner, but with this heat wave, she was glad they could begin the job even that soon. Next up, she printed out an inventory of what was stockpiled in her storage unit, as well as color photos of the bigger pieces. She had an appointment with Nick in half an hour at the unit and hoped they could come to an equitable price on the whole lot.

She slid the papers into a kraft envelope, grabbed her keys and purse, and headed out of her office. Vance was searching the vendors' lounge fridge, quietly swearing under his breath.

"Now what's missing?" Katie asked.

"My brand-new bottle of iced tea. Unsweetened, with lemon," he groused. He slammed the door. Katie's warning sign was also missing.

"Sorry about that, but I was just about to have you paged anyway. I need to run an errand. Can you watch over the Alley for a couple of hours? I promise I'll be back well before closing."

"Sure. Although I may send one of the walkers out to get me another iced tea."

"I'll bring you a gallon jug when I get back."

"Sounds like a worthy trade-off," Vance said, his eyes crinkling behind his gold-tone wire glasses. "In the meantime, I guess I can drink—yuck—water."

"If nothing else, it does quench your thirst."

Katie took off, heading for the front entrance, but before she could leave the building, she ran into Edie Silver. "Hey, stranger, I've been waiting to hear your potluck report for days."

Edie blushed, almost the color of her tomato-colored polyester top and slacks. "Sorry, my daughter-in-law planned my grandson's graduation party for last weekend. I helped with the food and got so busy with them I didn't even have a chance to come in and tidy my booth, and then I had a bunch of appointments this week. I had to wait almost two hours at the doctor's office yesterday." She paused to take a breath. "I couldn't even make it in to pick up my check until today, but that doesn't mean I've been slacking off. Thank goodness for the telephone, because I was able to call everyone on my list and I've got everything lined up for Saturday. The tent, the chafing dishes, and plenty of ice and coolers."

"Great. Thanks, Edie. You and Rose deserve all the credit for this potluck. I'm sure the vendors and the merchants are going to have a wonderful time because of your hard work."

Edie smiled, her wrinkled cheeks coloring once again. She shook her head, embarrassed. "I see a lot has been happening on the Square and at the Alley since I've been gone."

"Way too much," Katie admitted.

Edie shook her head. "Poor Mr. Wheeler. His poor wife. And I heard there was a burglar here at the Alley."

"The only thing missing was the food in the vendors' lounge refrigerator, but it really shook me up to know that someone had been staying here in the Alley for days at a time. I'm often here after closing—all alone for hours on end."

Edie shook her head with grandmotherly

concern. "Haven't I warned you about that in the past?"

"You warned me about walking into the darkened parking lot—which I admit, can be scary, but I shouldn't have to worry about trespassers. And Andy's right next door if I need him. This time I just called nine-one-one and hid under my desk until someone arrived."

"Good girl." Edie's expression turned even more serious. "I understand you've ousted Ida."

"It wasn't without provocation," Katie said, sensing a lecture was about to commence.

Edie shook her head. "I know Ida is probably the biggest pain in the neck that ever lived, but I feel sorry for the poor old thing. After all that she's been through these last few months."

Old thing? Edie had to be at least ten years older than Ida. "Oh?" Katie asked warily.

Edie nodded. "Her sister—bless her heart—died back in early May, just after the two of them returned from wintering in Florida."

"Oh dear. I had no idea," Katie said.

"That's when Ida's lawyer became her guardian. He knew she couldn't cope on her own and moved her right into an assisted senior living facility."

"Isn't that terribly expensive?" Katie asked. Ida had been crying poverty since the day Katie met her. She hadn't paid her booth rent to Ezra Hilton in years, and had said she had no means to make up for that shortfall.

"Ida comes from money," Edie assured her. "*Big* money."

Katie fought to control the sudden anger that coursed through her. She swallowed and forced herself to think the best. If Ida had caretakers, chances were she didn't have control over her finances and perhaps her sister had held the purse strings—and now her lawyer did the same. "If Ida needs to be in an assisted living facility, should she even be driving?"

"She's fine to drive, but she needs help with other things. She never learned to cook—and she can take her meals in the dining room with the other residents. The facility also provides cleaning and laundry services."

"How do you know all this?" Katie asked.

"Well," she started with an air of superiority, "I cared enough to ask her."

Katie frowned. She believed Edie, but she wasn't sure she believed Ida. Then again, was Ida creative enough to lie or at least embellish the truth?

"I'm about at the end of my rope dealing with her. Now I want her out of my parking lot."

"Her problem is she gets fixated on one thing at a time and can't focus on anything else. She needs to break out of her shell and try something new. But that isn't easy for people like Ida."

"Don't I know it." Katie glanced at her watch. "I'd love to chat some more, but I've got an appointment in ten minutes. I'd better get moving."

"I'll be around for a couple of hours. If you get back before I leave, maybe we can talk some more about the potluck."

"Sounds like a plan. Talk to you later," Katie said and hurried for the door.

She exited the Alley via the front entrance and paused to look to her right. Sure enough, Ida still sat under Vance's awning on a white wicker chair outfitted with an overstuffed cushion. On the small table beside her was a plate of what looked like homemade cookies. Ida wore dark glasses and sipped an expensive iced coffee, looking haughty and regal. Worse, she seemed to have gained several attendants—older ladies dressed in Bermuda shorts and shell tops, wearing tennis shoes and unfriendly expressions. Katie didn't recognize any of them. Were they Ida's friends from the senior living complex?

"Look, it's that mean woman who took Ida's job away," one of them shouted, pointing at Katie.

All eyes turned to glare at her, and they began to chant. "Unfair, unfair, unfair!"

Katie turned and hightailed it for her car. She couldn't deal with Ida then and there, but she'd have to come up with something to get her out of her parking lot and away from Artisans Alley. Did Detective Davenport know a hit man out on parole?

She could but hope.

Nick Farrell had made it to the McKinlay Mill Self-Store facility before Katie. She hadn't expected him to be alone—figuring that his partner, Don, would accompany him—but instead it was an older woman who sat in the passenger seat of Nick's car. Katie got out of her Focus and approached Nick's Explorer, which was still running with the air-conditioning on full blast. He hit the power button and his window rolled down.

"Hi, Katie. I'd like you to meet my aunt, Sally Casey."

Sally leaned forward and gave a wave. She was dressed all in pink—pink slacks, pink T-shirt covered by a pink jacket. She also wore dangly pink flamingo earrings and a pink sequined hat with a faux blonde ponytail sticking out the back, which did not hide the fact that she'd lost all her own hair, as well as her eyebrows and lashes. She had to be the sick relative Nick had come back to McKinlay Mill to take care of.

Katie gave her a smile. "Nice to meet you."

"Nice to meet you, honey," Sally said with the hint of a Southern drawl and what Katie's aunt Lizzie would've said was a whiskey voice, although Katie would've bet the huskiness came from too many cigarettes, not an overindulgence in liquor. "After what I've been through, I'm thrilled to meet anybody and everybody." She laughed. "You better open that storage unit before my nephew here pops a rod with excitement. All he's done for the last few hours is speculate about your stash of goodies. Open that door so he'll shut the hell up."

She was Sassy Sally, all right, but Katie had a feeling she would like the old gal.

"I have not," Nick said in defense, but his ears were going pink.

"Yes, ma'am," Katie said, and crossed over to the locked entrance. She swiped her key card through the scanner and the gate obligingly opened. She waved Nick through and got back in her own car, scooting through just before the electronic gateway swung shut once again. Inching her car past his, she drove down the narrow strip of asphalt until she came to her own garage door.

The sun beat down on her as she unlocked the unit, pushing the door up to reveal the contents. Nick hit the control that rolled down all the windows in his car before turning off the engine. "Are you sure you won't get too hot, Aunt Sally?"

"Honey, this heat wave has been a godsend for me. I've been freezing my patootie off for weeks. Now get out of this car and satisfy your curiosity before you have a stroke."

It didn't take any more encouragement for Nick to hop out of the car, excited as a kid on Christmas morning. His fists were balled, no doubt in an effort to keep from wringing them, and he failed to keep the excitement out of his voice as he asked Katie, "Where do we start?"

She waved a hand in the direction of the open garage. "Go at it. Feel free to bring the stuff out in the open for a better look, if you like."

Nick practically leapt into the unit and Katie circled around to stand by his car.

Sally shook her head and tut-tutted. "Pitiful, isn't he?"

"I think it's rather cute. I felt the same way when I collected all this stuff."

"You poor little thing. Nick told me a little about your situation. It must break your heart to have to part with all your booty."

Katie managed a halfhearted laugh. "You don't know the half of it. But . . . I can't use it and Nick and Don can. Maybe we'll all be happy. I did choose it all to fill that house. That's where it belongs."

Both women looked up as Nick hollered, "Ye-ha!" from inside the unit.

Again Sally shook her head. "Pathetic."

Katie laughed.

"Honey, why don't you come and get out of the sun and sit in the backseat. I've got a feeling that boy is going to be in there for a while. I wouldn't want you to keel over from heat-stroke."

"Gladly," Katie agreed, then opened the door and hopped inside the car.

There was something about Sally that looked familiar. "Have we met before?" Katie asked.

Sally shook her head, her faux ponytail bouncing. "I don't think so. But I visit Victoria Square quite a bit, including Artisans Alley. Great place to find unique Christmas gifts."

It was then Katie remembered where she'd seen Sally. The Carol Channing look-alike at Gilda's Gourmet Baskets on Monday afternoon.

"From the sound of your voice, I take it you're not from around here."

Sally shook her head. "I'm originally from bluegrass country. My sister married Nicholas's Yankee daddy and I wasn't about to let her come up here all on her lonesome, so I jumped on a Greyhound and . . . well, I just never left—even after Lucy died." She sighed, her mouth drooping.

"Are you sorry now?" Katie asked.

"Hell, no. And I'm tickled pink"—she plucked at the shoulder of her T-shirt—"that Nicholas and Don decided to come back to McKinlay Mill. I'm just sorry they had to come back to take care of me." She shrugged. "Nicholas assured me he was sick of the big city—and who could blame him? So . . . I'm pretending it was the idea of opening the inn that lured him back, not my lung cancer."

So that was her problem.

"I understand you and Seth Landers are friends," Sally said. "What a good boy he is. Like a member of our family. His daddy was my lawyer, and now he is, too."

"I like to think of him as the big brother I never had," Katie agreed.

Sally looked toward the storage unit as another *whoop* of joy burst forth. She shook her head yet again, beaming with pride. "I don't know what I would have done these last couple of months without Nicholas and Don. Nicholas is like my own kid, and it didn't take much for Don to worm his way into my heart either."

"You're lucky to have a great family."

"And friends," she added. "Seth made sure my driveway was plowed in the winter and even came over and cut the grass himself a few times. I've been pretty sick for a while. Without my boys and Meals on Wheels, I'd have been in a real pickle. I just wasn't in a position to cook for myself, and they delivered five meals a week. It made a big difference. Of course, now dear Nicholas and Don are here and have been taking care of me for the past two months and cooking up a storm. I feel positively spoiled."

Meals on Wheels? The words sparked an idea.

"I've got a"—Katie hesitated to say the word—"friend who needs to feel useful. Does Meals on Wheels need any volunteers?"

"Heavens, yes. They're always looking for people to help out. Can your friend drive?"

Katie nodded.

"As long as she's got a good driving record, they'd probably welcome her with open arms."

"This friend is in her sixties. Would they think she's too old to be out there driving meals to seniors?"

"Heavens, no. Most of their volunteers are the able-bodied elderly who want to help out those less fortunate."

"That's good to know."

"The woman who used to visit me said the program has been active in this county since the late 1950s. They were pioneers in delivering food to what they used to call shut-ins."

"I had no idea," Katie said.

"Why don't you ask your friend if she'd be interested in helping out. They really could use her."

And it would get Ida out of my hair during the week.

Katie laughed. "I just might do that. How do I get in contact with them?"

"You could go online. I know Google is my best friend—except for my darlings, Nicholas and Don," Sally said and laughed.

Their attention was diverted as Nick dragged out a big, clear, and very dusty plastic tote filled with wrapped items. "I want everything," he said with delight.

"Are you sure?" Katie asked. "You've only been in there five minutes."

"I know what I like, and so far I've liked everything I've seen. Now we just have to come to some kind of financial agreement. Will you take fifty?"

Katie blinked. "Dollars?"

"No, grand."

Katie started. "Are you kidding?"

"No, I'm not."

"No," Katie blurted. "That's far too much."

"Not if everything else is the same quality as what I've already seen."

Katie shook her head. "I've got a complete inventory and a bunch of pictures in an envelope in my car. You take them home tonight and study them. Then tomorrow call me and give me a more realistic bid."

Sally turned around to give Katie a once-over. "Honey, you have to be the worst businesswoman on the face of the planet. Or perhaps the only honest one. Take the money and run," she advised.

"Not if I want to live with myself," Katie countered.

"Okay," Nick agreed. "I'll come up with a more reasonable offer. But you have to let me repay you for what you've spent on the storage of this stuff for the past few years."

"I might be persuaded to do that," Katie agreed.

"Can I take this box home with me?" he asked eagerly.

"Sure, why not," Katie said. It would be better if she didn't peek at any of the crystal or linens, lest she change her mind and call the whole deal off.

She got out of the car and went back to her own to grab the envelope with the inventory and pictures, handing it over to Nick as soon as he'd lugged the tote into the backseat of his car.

"I'll study this and call you in the morning, okay?"

"Believe me, I'll be waiting for the phone to ring."

Nick's grin was nearly ear to ear. "If we strike a deal, I'll have a cashier's check for you before the end of tomorrow."

"My customers and vendors will be eternally grateful for the new air conditioner. Just let me close and lock the unit and we'll head on out."

She pulled the garage door down, locked it, and then got in her car and started for the exit, surprised she hadn't been overcome with an overpowering feeling of sadness. It would be freeing to be rid of all that furniture and bric-a-brac—as well as the monthly rental on the storage unit. She could apply that money to the last outstanding loan and maybe have it repaid by the end of the year. And then she could once again start saving for her English Ivy Inn.

"Saft in the head," Aunt Lizzie would say about her obsession with that dream.

Saft or not, Katie was determined. And isn't that what a Scot like Aunt Lizzie would expect?

Nineteen

By the time Katie had stopped at the grocery store to buy a jug of iced tea for Vance, and returned to Artisans Alley, Ida and her friends had given up their protest—at least for that day. Katie was sure Ida would return the next morning. She was also sure if she looked up the word "stubborn" in the dictionary that she'd find Ida's picture there.

Upon entering the Alley, she spied Vance helping a customer, brandished the bottle, and mimed she'd put it in the vendors' lounge fridge. He nodded, and went back to his work.

Once back in her office, Katie went straight to her computer and Googled "Meals on Wheels," found a local number, and picked up the phone. In a matter of minutes, she knew everything she needed to know to give her pitch to Ida. Now to convince the woman that the work would be far more fulfilling and necessary than taping down sales tags—something Katie hadn't been able to do in the past.

No sooner had she put the receiver back in its cradle than the phone rang again. She picked it up. "Artisans Alley. This is Katie. How can I help you?"

"If you can don an apron and grab a paring knife, you can help me with dinner tomorrow night."

"Seth, is that you?"

"Of course. We talked about cooking together this week and I was hoping you were free tomorrow night."

"Let me check my calendar." She gazed over the whiteboard calendar that hung on the back wall of her office. It was filled with Artisans Alley's goings-on, but nothing of a personal nature. "It just so happens I do have a few hours free. Shall I pencil you in?"

"If you would," he said with amusement in his voice.

"What are we having? Can I bring anything?"

"You don't have to bring anything, and it'll be a surprise. It'll be a surprise because I haven't figured out what I'm going to throw on the grill yet. But it will be meat."

"Ooh, you sure know how to impress a girl. Meat. Hmm. Will you be inviting Nick and Don?"

"Maybe another time. This night is just for us."

"And you make me feel special, too."

"What are big brothers for?"

"Well, don't plan any dessert. I'll bring something."

"Sounds good to me. Come on over around six."

"See you then." They hung up.

Katie sat back in her chair. Seth was a pie lover, and the local orchard had had a bumper crop of cherries this year. She'd buy some and make a cherry pie from scratch. It was a lot of work to stone the cherries, but what else did she have to do that evening? She'd bake the pie in the morning before it got too hot, and put it in her fridge after it cooled. She'd take it out just before she left and was sure it would be room temperature by the time she drove over to Seth's place.

With that decision made, Katie decided it was time to do some real work. But as usual, before she could pull out the stack of bills that needed to be paid, someone else knocked on her doorjamb. "Katie?"

It was silver-haired Joan McDonald, a woman of about sixty who made and sold primitive-looking figurines of clay. Her booth was up in the loft, the hottest place in all of Artisans Alley.

"I know what you're going to say. That it's very hot up in the loft."

"Yes, it is. Rose told me there's not much you can do about it without a big influx of money.

But that's not why I'm here. It's . . . the smell."

"Smell?" Katie asked. She didn't like the sound of this. Joan nodded. "Any idea what's causing this odor?" *Please, don't let it be a rat that burrowed in and died in one of the walls,* Katie pleaded to herself. She couldn't deal with that, although maybe Vance could. He was usually willing to take on whatever dirty work Katie couldn't handle herself.

"Not what," Joan said, "who." She wrinkled her brow for a moment. "Or should that be whom?" She shrugged. "It's Godfrey. The man positively reeks."

Katie wasn't sure how to answer. "I believe he has a medical condition that makes him sweat profusely," she said as tactfully as possible.

"Sweat may be a part of it, but I don't think he's changed his clothes in several days."

Katie glanced at the worker schedule she'd drawn up at the end of the previous month. "That's funny, I don't see him as listed to work this week, and yet I think I've seen him here every day of late."

"It's one thing if he'd take his stinkiness with him, but once he's left the area, the odor lingers. Between that and the heat, I haven't had a sale all week. Will you please speak to him?"

Doing so was not the top item on Katie's list of things to do. But she guessed she'd have to make it so. She sighed. "Yes. Is he here now?"

"He was around a few minutes ago. If you go up to the loft, maybe you can catch him. In the meantime, you might want to dig around in your tool drawer to see if you have one of those disposable dust masks. You'll need something to cover your nose and keep the worst of the smell out."

"Duly noted. Will you be at the potluck on Saturday?"

"I wouldn't miss it for the world. I've already made and decorated five-dozen cutout cookies. I just have to hope my husband doesn't find them hidden in the freezer and eat them all before the party."

Katie remembered that Joan had brought some in during the holidays. She'd used anise instead of vanilla extract. They were damn fine cookies. "I'm looking forward to them."

"See you there," Joan said with a wave, and turned to leave.

Katie stood. She'd better go upstairs and try to find Godfrey. But surely the smell couldn't be as bad as Joan described.

She'd been wrong. To say the stench took her breath away was putting it mildly. Waving a hand in front of her nose did nothing to drive away the smell. Too bad the windows had been painted shut many years before. Gasping, Katie hurried for the next room, her chest heaving as she tried to breathe in untainted air.

Joan was right. This was a serious problem.

Katie wandered through the aisles to the balcony that overlooked Artisans Alley's main sales floor. At the top of the stairs was a phone. She punched in the code for the intercom. "If Godfrey Foster is in the building, please come to the manager's office. Godfrey Foster, please report to the manager's office." She replaced the receiver and headed toward the back of the building, hoping to run into him on the way, but had no such luck.

Katie impatiently waited in the vendors' lounge for a good ten minutes, using the time to tidy up where vendors had left crumbs on the table and well-read copies of not only the Rochester *Democrat and Chronicle*, but *USA Today*. The place was shipshape in no time, but Godfrey never showed up. He'd probably already left the building, which was fortunate for her vendors and their customers, but not for Godfrey's future visits—that is, if he didn't clean up his act, and specifically his body odor.

Katie returned to her office, checked her Rolodex of vendor numbers, and called Godfrey's home. His phone rang and rang—eight, nine times. No answering machine kicked in, and neither did voice mail. She hung up her phone. Now she'd have to be on the lookout for him.

Swell. Just swell.

Katie glanced at the clock on her wall. They'd

be closing in a little over an hour. How had the day gotten away from her? Before she had a chance to start anything, Joan reappeared in her office doorway. "He's outside! He's outside!" she called. "Go catch him."

"Where?"

"In the parking lot. I was helping a customer carry something to her car and saw him sitting on the hood of his car. He's got it parked in the shade over by The Angel Shop."

Katie practically jumped out of her chair and headed for the back door. In moments, she'd jogged across the hot parking lot. Joan hadn't been kidding. She could smell Godfrey from a good five yards away.

"Godfrey, I need to speak to you," Katie said, and halted, staying downwind.

Godfrey looked more than a little rumpled, his hangdog expression reinforcing the air of depression that seemed to surround him. "I suppose you're going to yell at me."

"Not yell, but I must ask that you stay away from the Alley until you bathe and change your clothes. I've had complaints from other vendors."

"I know, I know," he said and seemed to slump even lower. "But I—I can't," he stammered.

"This isn't like you, Godfrey. Something's going on. Why don't you tell me about it," Katie said impatiently.

The man sighed, looking thoroughly miserable.

"I don't have a home. At least not right now. For the past couple of days I've been living in my car."

"In your car?"

"And before that . . . I was staying over in the Alley," he nodded toward the old building. "That is, until you and the cop chased me off."

Godfrey was the owner of the suitcase with the ladies' pink disposable razor?

"Godfrey, what on earth were you doing hiding here in Artisans Alley?" she demanded.

"It's a long story," Godfrey said, his face turning an unattractive shade of red. It seemed to cause his sweat glands to shift into overdrive. Rivulets of perspiration ran down his temples onto his cheeks and dripped from his chin. Was it the heat or his confession that made him look like he'd just stepped out of the shower—which was where he needed to go immediately.

"I've got plenty of time to listen, although I'm not sure I can stand the stench," Katie admitted.

Godfrey sighed, seemed like he was going to say something, and then sighed again, maintaining his silence.

Katie had plenty to say. "You are guilty of trespassing. You're guilty of stealing food from the vendors' lounge's refrigerator, and you're guilty of scaring the heck out of me! If you don't give me a reasonable explanation, I'm going to hand-feed you to the Sheriff's Office."

"No, no—please! I can explain everything."

Katie crossed her arms and waited.

Godfrey looked away and bit his lip.

"I'm waiting," Katie reminded him.

Godfrey let out an exasperated breath. "Last Saturday my wife went to Syracuse to visit her sick mother for the week."

"What's that got to do with you squatting here at Artisans Alley?"

"I kind of had the boys over for a poker party that night and things got a little out of hand."

Katie frowned. "In what way?"

"One of the guys ate more than his fair share of the pizzas and washed it all down with a little too much beer. Then he had an intestinal problem and had to use the facilities, which are upstairs in my house."

And where was this story leading?

"Suffice it to say, I had a little water problem." He paused and thought that over. "Actually, I had a really big water problem. Ya see, we were all in the garage 'cause my wife would give me hell if they made a mess in the house and . . . well, we were out there for a long time before we heard this big crash. We went running inside and, well, the bathroom and bedroom floors were sitting in the living room and kitchen, and Niagara Falls was running down all the walls. All we can figure is the toilet overflowed for more than an hour."

"And it caused all that damage?"

Godfrey rolled his eyes. "Mike thinks he mighta left the water running full force in the bathroom sink, too. He was kind of drunk."

"Don't tell me. You're trying to get it all fixed so that when your wife comes home, she won't even notice."

"Oh, she's going to notice all right, but . . . yeah, I want it fixed and I had to move out. This is gonna cost me a small fortune. I don't have the money to stay at a hotel, too."

"Why couldn't you just stay with the buddy who caused all these problems?" Katie asked reasonably.

Godfrey shook his head. "His wife isn't happy with me. My buddy fell asleep in the chaise lounge and got eaten alive by mosquitoes. He didn't go home until almost six the next morning. She already threatened to throw *him* out, so she wasn't about to let *me* stay there."

"What about the other guys that came to your party?"

"Their wives don't want a houseguest either," he said glumly.

"So you just decided to park your carcass in my building, breaking all kinds of occupancy laws that could shut down Artisans Alley, as well as inconvenience all my other tenants in the building."

"I didn't know that," Godfrey said, sounding like a contrite little boy.

"Did you also break into the Webster mansion and squat there for a day?"

"What a nightmare," Godfrey admitted. "No plumbing, no electricity. I couldn't even run a fan."

Katie shook her head, thoroughly sick of dealing with the little twerp. "Godfrey, you're done. Not only staying here, but you're done as a vendor. I want your booth vacated by tomorrow afternoon."

"Please, Katie, don't throw me out. No other gallery in the area will let me show my stuff. They said it's not good enough."

"So now you insult me by saying the arts and crafts displayed at Artisans Alley are pure junk?"

"I didn't mean that," he said, waving his hands in the air as though to erase his previous words. "But those galleries are juried—you have to jump through loads of hoops just to get in—and Artisans Alley lets just about anybody in."

Katie sighed. "No, I don't suppose a *real* gallery, like the Dawson, would *let* you sell your dryer lint art," she said with mild reproach.

"You know my stuff sells. I make more than double my rent every month."

Katie had to admit he was right. As the one who cut the weekly checks, she knew who made their rent—and a profit—and who didn't. Godfrey had been doing better than the average vendor even if his lint art did look tacky. There was no accounting for his customers' tastes.

"I'm sorry. I know I shouldn't have done it, but I'm going to need every cent I make here at Artisans Alley to help me pay for the repairs on my house. Please—please don't make me leave or report me to the cops," Godfrey begged. Was it sweat or tears pooling in his eyes?

Katie felt her resolve melting. Again her aunt Lizzie, in her thickest Scottish accent, would've said she had "saft" written across her forehead for everyone to see.

"All right. I won't turn you in. But I want you to apologize to everyone whose food or drink you took from the vendors' refrigerator *and* make restitution."

"But I already told you I need the money I make here to—"

Katie held out a hand to stop his gush of words. "I'm sorry, but your actions caused stress for a lot of people—me included. Apologizing and making things right is the very least you can do."

Godfrey hung his head, looking thoroughly miserable. "All right. I'll do it."

"Good. And you can start by giving me back my pretty rose plate. The one that had the peanut butter buckeyes on it. I didn't notice it stashed in Chad's Pad along with all the other stuff you pilfered."

"Uh . . . I kind of had an accident with it."

Katie felt her blood pressure start to rise again.

"I was so hungry, and in such a hurry to get that candy out of the vendors' lounge and up the stairs . . ." The very narrow stairs with steep treads that were easy to trip on. "That I kind of fell and . . . broke it."

Not only had Katie lost her trove of treasures in the storage unit, now she'd lost one of her favorite vintage plates. That would teach her to bring in treats in anything other than throwaway plastic containers.

"Where are you staying now?"

"In my car," he said, refusing to meet her gaze.

"When will the work be done at your house?"

"Saturday—and hopefully before my wife gets back into town."

Katie frowned. She couldn't let him stay in his car, but she also couldn't risk having the Alley shut down by letting him stay there. The man had not ingratiated himself with the other vendors, so it wasn't likely any of them would take him in. She certainly had no room in her apartment for a visitor—and he was the last person on the planet she would want as a guest. Maybe she could ask Andy . . .

If nothing else, though, she could offer him the use of her shower, and told him so.

"Thank you, Katie. You have no idea how terrible it feels to wear the same clothes for days.

Not to be able to shower. I don't know if you've noticed, but I sweat a lot."

No kidding.

"Do you have clean clothes?"

"No. Everything I brought with me was in the storeroom upstairs."

"It's your lucky day, then. The Sheriff's Office has decided they're done investigating. You can go up there and retrieve your stuff and then I'll walk you over to my apartment so you can shower. I'll also see if I can rustle you up a place to stay until you can go back home."

"I don't know how to thank you, Katie."

"Don't cause me any trouble ever again."

"I won't," he promised.

They walked back to Artisans Alley. Katie gave Godfrey the key to Chad's Pad and told him to meet her outside in five minutes, then she called Andy.

"No!" he said emphatically. "You've already told me this guy is a major pain in the ass. I don't want him as a houseguest—especially as I couldn't be there to supervise things. I don't want my house wrecked, too."

"It was a buddy who ruined his house," she said, wondering why she was defending the jerk.

"No." The silence lengthened between them. "Are you mad at me?" he asked.

"No. I wouldn't want the guy as a houseguest either. But I figured I should make the effort—

before he's arrested for vagrancy or something for living in his car."

"All right. Well, I'll see you later, then," Andy said, and cut the connection.

Katie put down the phone and headed for the front exit. She passed several vendors on the way, but didn't know any of them well enough to ask if Godfrey could bunk with them for a few days. She paused at the register. Rose was reading a romance novel. She placed a bookmark between the pages and closed the book. "You look like a woman with a problem," Rose said.

"Yes, and his name is Godfrey Foster." Should she ask Rose to let the man stay with her? She was a widow with a big empty house . . . Then again, she didn't want to lose Rose's friendship either. Still, Rose was good at problem solving.

"What's wrong with Godfrey—besides the fact that he smells?" Rose asked.

"Seems he's got a contractor working in his house and has been ousted for the next few days. Thanks to the damage—he had a flood—he hasn't got the cash to stay in a motel."

"Don't tell me he was the one in Chad's Pad."

"I won't then."

Rose shook her head.

"Since Tuesday night, he's been staying in his car."

"That's not good." Rose pursed her lips. "Let me make a few calls. My church has an emergency fund for situations like this. Pastor Anderson may be able to come up with something to help Godfrey."

"That would be wonderful. Thank you. I'm taking him over to my place right now to let him take a shower. We should be back in about half an hour."

Rose nodded. "I'll see what I can do." She set her novel aside and pulled out her purse, retrieving her cell phone. Godfrey trudged down the main staircase holding an armful of rumpled clothing. She could smell him before he came within ten feet. Would she need to fumigate the Alley and her apartment?

"Hurry," Katie said, and led the way out the door. Several customers turned their heads sharply as they passed. "It's not me," Katie whispered, much to Godfrey's chagrin.

A hot breeze assaulted them as they exited the building. Katie found herself looking at the clothes Godfrey held. "The Sheriff's Office took one of your shirts. At the time we thought Dennis Wheeler might be hiding out in the loft."

"I guess I can't ask them for it back—not if I don't want to be arrested," Godfrey grumbled as they approached the stairs that led to Katie's apartment.

No, he couldn't. But then . . . Abby Wheeler had positively identified the shirt as belonging to her husband. Hundreds of the same shirt could have been sold in the greater Rochester area. She was probably just mistaken.

Wasn't she?

Rose's pastor did come through, and found a family willing to host Godfrey for the next couple of days. Of course, that wasn't the end of his problems. He admitted he hadn't even warned his wife of the destruction in their home. Katie was glad she would not be around when they began that discussion.

With Godfrey taken care of, Katie turned her attention to more pressing matters—closing the Alley and heading out to buy the cherries for Seth's pie.

After she and Joan walked through the building to check that everyone was out, Katie headed for her office to shut down her computer for the day. She walked through the main showroom to the light panel in the front of the store, threw the switches, and locked the French doors.

The dance studio was still open and Katie peeked through the glass door to see a line of little girls in black leotards scuffing across the wooden floor in their ballet slippers. The sight never failed to delight her.

Next she passed the unrented storefront the Davenport girls had tidied earlier in the day. She unlocked the door, stepped inside, hit the lights—and did a double take. The space was transformed. It sparkled. Not a speck of dust remained on the floor, and it looked as though the dingy walls had been washed. In addition to the streamers, they hung a banner that said, HAPPY RETIREMENT, DETECTIVE DAVENPORT. It looked professionally made, with a rainbow of vinyl letters and balloons. The girls had also set up tables, chairs, a buffet table, and another empty table. A small note sat on the center of the dark tablecloth. It said, "Dad's Stuff."

Katie frowned. *Stuff?*

Had the detective won a number of awards over the years? Trophies, plaques? Were the girls going to display it to Davenport's fellow officers and cronies?

Katie withdrew the cell phone from her pocket and hit autodial for Fred Cunningham. It immediately went to his voice mail. "Hi, Fred, it's Katie Bonner. Thank you for renting my storefront to the Davenports for their party. They came in today to clean and now the room positively shines. After the party Saturday night, you may want to come over and take pictures to update the listing on your website. We might finally be able to move it. Thanks. Talk to you later."

And why hadn't she thought to clean it herself? Who wanted to rent a messy place? Now if only she had the time to do everything else that needed to be done in the building . . .

Once she'd locked the door, she paused before heading for her car, and looked toward the Webster mansion. She could see debris jutting out of the Dumpster in front and wondered how much of the demo had been completed in the past two days.

Should she look?

Why not? The farm stand didn't close until six. She had plenty of time.

The asphalt under her feet was hot enough to sauté onions, and Katie was glad she wore thick-soled sneakers. Would this heat wave never end? The forecast didn't call for anything but ninety-plus temperatures for at least another five or six days.

Victoria Square's parking lot was virtually empty, with just the cars of the shop owners dotting the area. The heat shimmered around her as she approached the large rectangular Dumpster. She struggled to see over the top. As Nick and Don had said, the work crew had attacked the drywall that needed removal, but they'd also cleaned up the yard. The rickety picket fence was gone, and so was all the rest of the detritus that had accumulated over the past decade. Someone had run a lawnmower over the overgrown grass and had taken a weed whacker to the rest. What a difference that small amount of work had made to the home's appearance. It almost looked welcoming.

It'll never be yours, that voice inside Katie taunted.

"But it will be pretty," she murmured aloud and actually smiled. She was making progress.

Katie scooted around the Dumpster and mounted the creaky porch steps. She rubbed a clear spot on one of the filthy windows and peeked inside. The entryway had been cleared of non-load-bearing walls, and the bones of what had once been a showplace home were now visible once again. Would they start restoring the woodwork next? Even if she couldn't be a part of the restoration, seeing incremental progress was nonetheless exciting.

She turned around and immediately caught sight of Wood U, looking forlorn with the yellow crime tape still attached to the front of the building, and all the windows and entrance covered in fresh plywood. What an eyesore, but then hopefully by the time Sassy Sally's was renovated, Wood U would see a rebirth with its new owner.

Katie took a moment and sat down on the top porch step, still staring at the singed storefront next door. It might have been awkward for Nick Farrell to have to see, let alone interact, with such a demon from his past. And yet, conveniently, Dennis might now be dead. Had Nick heaved a sigh of relief when he heard about the fire on Sunday? He'd certainly been in good spirits Monday morning when Katie first met him.

Could she really consider him a suspect? Blake had started the fire, but someone had killed Dennis . . . or Jerry Murphy? . . . first.

All this uncertainty was damned aggravating.

And did she really want Nick to be implicated in Dennis's death or disappearance? She liked him. He seemed like a nice guy. He'd been Seth's friend for over twenty years. His aunt thought the world of him. Katie wasn't *really* suspicious of him.

Was she?

Twenty

Katie arrived at the fruit stand just as they were about to close, and even though the hour was late, the produce was still in good condition—not just the picked-over remains of the day. She bought three quarts of cherries, since Andy liked them, too. She'd stone two quarts for the pie she intended to make for Seth and one for Andy and his crew. They'd appreciate a treat, and by removing the pits, it would solve the problem of what to do with them. It would be disgusting, not to mention unsanitary, for the guys to be spitting cherry stems and stones around the pizzeria.

No sooner had she set to work than the landline rang. She was glad the phone that came with the apartment belonged to another generation. Not only did it have a long cord, but she could rest it on her shoulder and hold it against her cheek and talk while she worked—not like the smaller wireless one she'd had in her former apartment. She picked it up and resumed her seat. "Hello?"

"Hi. It's Ray Davenport."

"Why, Ray, you're calling so often, people are going to start talking," Katie said and smiled.

"Let 'em," he grumbled. "It might improve my reputation. Listen, I'm beginning to think you're psychic, Mrs. Bonner."

"I thought we were calling each other by our first names," she said, and pushed another pit from a fat, ripe cherry.

"Okay then, Katie. I did some checking on your Big Brown pal and learned his beautifully restored Chevy was found in the bottom of the Erie Canal. It was hit by a barge late last night. Two people were hurt."

Katie's heart skipped a beat. "Were they hurt bad?"

"Bumps and bruises only."

Whew! "And the car?" she asked and went back to her work.

"No longer a shining example of his restoration skills, I'm afraid. The plates had been stripped. They got the ID from the VIN number."

"Strange place to put your car if you've just retired," Katie commented.

"Retired, my ass," Davenport said. "The guy never showed up for work on Monday morning. The receptionist said they'd received an e-mail from Murphy's home account instructing them that he was retiring and to send his last check to his home, as well as any other paperwork that needed to be filled out."

"Isn't it a little unusual, let alone suspicious, to quit your job via e-mail?" she asked.

"It sure is."

"Could you do a little more pushing to find out more?"

He sighed. "I can try."

"Great. Any chance you can go and check the guy's house out, too? See if he's been back there? Maybe you could check his credit card report to see if there's been any action since he went missing on Saturday."

"Has anyone ever told you you're bossy?" Davenport asked.

"It may have come up once or twice during my life," she admitted, amused. "But honestly, Ray, this could be a big break in the case." *And what else have you got to do?* she felt like asking, but decided it wouldn't be in her best interests.

"Yeah, yeah," he said, but he didn't sound convinced. "I'll call you back if I have any news."

"Thanks, Detective—er, I mean Ray." She hung up.

With the cherries now pitted, Katie decided to see what she could rustle up for her dinner. She inspected the contents of the refrigerator. A half-empty box of Bisquick, bran flour, all-purpose flour, half a carton of milk, its expiration date growing near, and one egg. She'd need that for the glaze on Seth's pie. The freezer compartment held an assortment of frozen dinners, but none of them appealed to her.

One good thing about living over a pizzeria—she might be sick of the fare, but there was always something freshly cooked to eat. She took her plastic bowl of washed and pitted cherries downstairs and entered the shop.

"Hey, Katie," Andy called, just as the phone rang. He hadn't sounded too cheerful. Had he heard more news about Blake?

When Andy finished taking the order, he hung up the phone and turned to Katie, noticing the bowl of cherries on the counter. "Are you trying to tell me something?"

She looked down and laughed. "Yes, I guess I am."

"Tell you what?" Keith asked from behind Andy as he checked on the progress of the pies in the oven.

"That life is just a bowl of cherries."

"Is it? I never knew what that meant," Keith said.

"Me either," Katie admitted. "But I thought you guys might like to snack on something healthy for once. I already pitted them, too."

"Even better," Andy said, then grabbed a couple and tossed them into his mouth.

"Sweet, aren't they?" Katie asked.

He nodded.

Keith moseyed over and grabbed a handful. "Thanks, Katie. There's a lot here."

"I thought the guys might like to grab some in between deliveries."

"Thoughtful of you," Andy said and smiled wanly. Something was definitely up.

Keith went back to his work while Andy donned his gloves once again and concentrated on the pizza he was constructing. "Did you want something to eat?"

"Just a slice if you've got one available."

"Coming right up," Keith said.

Katie leaned over the counter. "Is something the matter?"

Andy nodded. "Not much escapes you."

"I'm just a nosy busybody. Is it anything you can talk about?"

"Blake."

"I thought as much."

Keith handed Katie a slice of pizza on a paper plate. "Thanks," she said. He grabbed a few more cherries and retreated back to his oven. Katie grabbed a couple of napkins before she helped herself to a Coke from the cooler. "Are you going to tell me about it?" she asked Andy.

"There's not much to tell. The DA wouldn't cut him any slack. They offered a plea bargain, and he took it."

"Jail time?" Katie asked.

Andy nodded. "They said they'd cut the time if he admitted he set the Wood U fire, too."

"How long will he get?"

"Five years."

Katie winced. An eternity—at least to an eighteen-year-old boy.

"At least they'll send him to a minimum-security prison. I'd hate to think of what would happen to him in a place like Attica."

"Small comfort, though," she said and took a bite of pizza.

He nodded grimly.

She swallowed. "I'm so sorry, Andy."

He shook his head and transferred the pizza to a wooden paddle, handing it to Keith. He started on the next pizza. "It's always kind of bittersweet when my kids go off to college. I miss them, but I know they're on the right track and will make something of themselves. That they'll make me proud. It feels like I failed with Blake."

"You didn't fail him, Andy. He failed himself—and his parents."

"They're heartbroken," Andy admitted. "He's their only child."

Katie took another bite of pizza and chewed slowly. It was inevitable that not all his charges would straighten up and become model citizens, but this first failure seemed to have hit Andy particularly hard.

She looked over at Keith, who was one of Andy's stars. The kid had worked at the shop for almost two years. He'd been accepted at Brockport State College, where he intended to study business administration. He thought he might want to open his own pizza parlor one day. In another month, he'd be gone, although Andy had assured him he could work anytime he wanted—on school breaks and weekends. Did Andy already have a recruit to man the ovens or would he wait until the school year started and the principal offered him another batch of troublemakers to mentor?

The phone rang, and Andy abandoned his pizza, stripping off his plastic gloves to answer it. He took down the order, hung up, and returned to his work. "I meant to ask you, what was Detective Davenport doing in your apartment the other day?"

"Oh, you saw him?" Katie asked, her voice sounding higher than usual. "We were talking about Abby Wheeler. I'd gone to visit and took her a box of cupcakes from Tanner's."

"I suppose he grilled you."

"Pretty much."

"I'll be glad when he's retired and we won't have to see him here on the Square anymore."

"Um . . . haven't you heard?"

"Heard what?"

"Davenport is the new owner of Wood U."

Andy stopped what he was doing and leveled an annoyed glance at Katie. "I guess it must've slipped your mind."

Katie laughed nervously. "I'm afraid he'll soon be a fixture around here. Or at least as soon as he can reopen the shop. He's still waiting to hear from his insurance company."

"Why did he want to know what you talked about with Abby Wheeler? I thought he was off the case," Andy said, and went back to work.

Katie shrugged. She wasn't about to admit she was helping the almost-former detective out. Andy would have a fit. "I guess you can take the detective out of the Sheriff's Office, but you can't take the need to detect out of the man. Or . . . something like that."

Katie ate the last bite of her pizza and figured now would be an excellent time to escape before he could interrogate her any more. He was almost as good at it as Davenport was. "I'd better get going."

"Do you want to take your bowl back now?"

"I'll get it tomorrow." She beckoned him closer and gave him a kiss. "I'll see you tomorrow."

"You better believe it," Andy said, and kissed her again.

"Smooch, smooch, smooch!" Keith teased from his station at the ovens, and plopped another pizza into a box.

"Get back to work, you," Andy said with chagrin, and Katie laughed.

"Do you want a kiss, too, Keith?"

"Ah, heck, no," the kid said, and flushed. "Andy would fire me."

"You said it," Andy said with mock indignation. At least he was smiling again, although Katie knew it would be short-lived.

"See you later," she said, and headed out the door, turned the corner, and started up the steps to her apartment. The phone was ringing when she entered the hot box known as her kitchen. She grabbed it. "Hello?"

"It's me again," Davenport said.

"Didn't I talk to you less than an hour ago?" Katie said as she stared at the cherries and wondered if she ought to bake the pie that evening. Lighting the stove wasn't going to make it much hotter than it already was.

"You did want me to keep you informed," he reminded her. "I'm only hearing stuff thirdhand these days, but I just got a call from a buddy of mine. You want an update on the freeloader at Artisans Alley?"

"Um, sure." Oh, dear. Had they figured out it was Godfrey?

"No fingerprints on file to match those found in

Chad's Pad, so whoever it is has no criminal record—as of yet. If we ever find the guy, you can always press for trespass."

"That's a comfort to know," she commented, and searched one of the bottom cupboards for her nine-inch pie pan. Since she'd promised she wouldn't turn Godfrey over to the deputies, pressing charges wasn't likely to happen.

"The thing is," Davenport continued, "nobody you suspect has fingerprints on file . . . your pal Jerry Murphy, nor Dennis Wheeler. And I did as you asked and looked into Murphy's credit report. His Visa card was last used last Wednesday, when he booked two Amtrak tickets going from Rochester to Miami."

"When were they for?" she asked, and opened the fridge to take out the flour and the shortening.

"Monday. Amtrak says they were never used."

"See, the evidence is mounting that your dead guy in the morgue *could* be Jerry," she said and took the measuring cups from the cupboard by the sink.

"You almost say that with glee. I thought you were friendly with this guy."

"I was. And if it is him lying there in a stainless steel drawer, I will be very sad. But if it *is* him, he deserves to be mourned by his friends and buried. Don't you agree?"

"Yeah, yeah," he muttered.

"What's the next step?" she asked, and pulled

out the silverware drawer, looking for her set of measuring spoons.

"To see if I can convince someone at the Sheriff's Office to buy into this theory of yours and dig up a relative for a DNA sample. Since the remains can't be identified by visual means, it's our only hope at this stage."

"I'm sorry I can't help you there. I only knew him casually. But some of the other merchants might have more information. I know he used to talk to Gilda Ringwald-Stratton quite often. He was in her shop every day. You might want to start there."

"Okay, okay."

"And will you call me if you find out anything else?"

"Haven't I been doing that on a regular basis already?" he asked wearily.

"Yes. Thank you."

"Talk to you later," Davenport said and cut the connection.

Katie hung up the phone. They were getting to be real pals, thanks to this murder case. She wasn't sure if she was entirely happy about that.

As she measured the flour into a mixing bowl, she wondered if what she told Andy was true. Would Davenport be able to keep his investigative nose out of things in the future? Would he really be content to stand behind a retail counter during the day and putter in his workshop at night?

Time would tell.

Meanwhile, her pie pan beckoned and she measured the shortening to add to the flour. Now if she could just stop being nosy and keep her mind on things related to Artisans Alley, the Merchants Association, and Andy, she'd be a lot better off herself. And yet without her, would anyone have made the connection to the abrupt disappearance of the Big Brown driver?

Dennis Wheeler hadn't been hiding in Chad's Pad. He hadn't shown up on anyone's radar since before the fire on Saturday night. He seemed to have annoyed plenty of people over the years, but was being annoying enough to get one killed?

She pondered that thought as she baked her pie. Dennis had to have killed Jerry Murphy and taken off. It was the only reasonable explanation. But until they could prove the body in the morgue was actually Jerry, no one was going to ask Abby Wheeler if she'd had a relationship with the (possibly) dead man.

Katie had a feeling Davenport wasn't going to be able to add one more solved case to his career résumé. Not, at least, in the next twenty or so hours before he was officially retired.

Twenty-one

Friday morning dawned and Katie woke up hungry. Very hungry. A few cherries and a slice of pizza weren't nearly enough food to keep a stomach busy during a twelve-hour period. Unfortunately, the breakfast options were just as limited as the dinner selections had been the night before. She'd spent a lot of money at the grocery store a few days before. What on earth had she bought, for there seemed to be nothing edible in the fridge or cupboards? She'd used her last egg to glaze the top crust of the pie she'd baked for Seth and she longed for an omelet. There was just one cure for that—breakfast at Del's Diner.

Overnight the temperature had dropped to a pleasant seventy-two, but the humidity still hovered at a sticky eighty percent. Del's would be cool and soothing and didn't she deserve to be comfortable for a crummy thirty minutes out of the day?

Katie walked the two blocks to Del's, enjoying the early morning peace. Except for the commuters heading for work in Rochester, McKinlay Mill looked like it could have subbed for Mayberry. It boasted no fishing hole, but she wouldn't have been surprised to see a small barefoot boy with a fishing rod running down the sidewalk. Ahh, thank goodness for TV Land reruns.

She arrived just before seven o'clock and found ten or twelve cars parked in the strip mall's lot, with an equal number parked in the McDonald's lot across the way. The senior citizens of McKinlay Mill were both establishments' best breakfast customers. Sure enough, when Katie entered the restaurant, she was the youngest patron by at least thirty years. However, she did see one familiar face among the crowd.

Sally Casey looked up from her menu, smiled, and waved to Katie. She waved back and Sally beckoned her to join her.

"You're up early," Sally said in greeting. "I don't think I've seen you here for breakfast before now."

"I ran out of eggs and got the urge for an omelet."

"This is the place. Will you join me?"

"I'd love to," Katie said and slipped into the booth's opposite seat.

Sandy, the morning waitress, arrived at the table. "What can I get you ladies?"

"More coffee, please. And then I'll have French toast, bacon, and a side of grits," Sally said.

"I'll have the western omelet, home fries, and white toast," Katie said. "And I'll take some of that coffee, too, please."

"You got it," Sandy said, and headed off toward the urn.

Seconds later, Katie was spilling a container of half-and-half into her cup. She looked up at her companion. "I know this is going to sound like a bad come-on line, but do you come here often?"

Sally laughed, her eyes crinkling with delight. "A couple of times a week. Even at the worst of my chemo treatment, I dragged myself in here, if only to eat a small bowl of yogurt and then go puke in the john. I needed to be with people." Her expression turned somber. "Don't ever get the big C, Katie, because people you thought were your friends will bail on you for fear they'll catch it—which is impossible. The scariest word in the English language has got to be 'cancer.'"

"I'm so sorry," Katie said, stirring her coffee. How could anyone abandon a friend at the time they most needed support? "But you said you're better now."

Sally frowned and shook her head. "I have to sound positive around my dear Nicholas to try to lift his spirits, but my oncologist has confirmed it. My days are numbered. So for the time I've got left, I'm going to do what I want to do, eat what I want to eat, drink what I want to drink, and if necessary, throw my middle finger at the world in general—and especially at my cancer."

"Oh, Sally, I'm so sorry," Katie said with a catch in her voice.

Sally reached across the table and touched Katie's hand. "Darlin', don't you be sad for me. I've had one hell of a good life, and I have no regrets. None at all." Something about her tone made Katie shiver. Or was it just the air-conditioning? Sally sighed and continued. "And when I die, I'll leave my sweetheart Nicholas a bit of money to help him get that inn of his on its feet. I'll die happy, knowing he's doing well, 'cause it wasn't always so."

"Oh?" Katie asked.

Sally shook her head. "My poor Nicholas. He was always a sensitive boy. Wouldn't step on an ant. But then something happened to him at a young age that . . . turned him."

Was she referring to Nick's homosexuality? Katie wasn't about to speculate aloud.

"When he was older, he came out to someone he thought of as a mentor. That was a big mistake. And when his daddy found out he was gay, he disowned him. My poor sister was forced to choose between her husband and her child. She was a fool, too."

"Oh, dear," Katie said sympathetically.

"From that day on, Nicholas became my boy. He lived with me and I put him through college, but those years weren't easy either. There was even a time when I thought Nicholas might kill himself, he was so distraught. Nobody should have to go through that kind of hell. Nobody," she said, her mouth quivering, her expression going blank.

Katie wasn't sure what to say, or even *if* she should say anything in response.

Suddenly the noise in the busy diner seemed to magnify by a factor of ten. Silverware rattled, the voices around them seemed more dissonant, and somewhere in the kitchen came the sound of breaking china.

Sally seemed to shake herself, and reached for her coffee cup. She took a gulp, leaving a pink lipstick smear on the rim. She sighed. "There wasn't anything I wouldn't have done to save Nicholas from any kind of heartache. And now I'll have to leave him just when he's about to start a new adventure—an adventure we once planned together."

"Oh, Sally," Katie said, sadness welling within her.

Sally shook her head. "Don't you worry, darlin'. Nicholas has Don now. He's a wonderful guy. He'll take good care of my boy and I just know they'll be happy in that big old house. And wasn't it just sweet that they named it after me?"

"Yes," Katie agreed without hesitation. "I think the name is perfect for their inn."

And it was.

Katie arrived back at Victoria Square just minutes before she needed to open Artisans Alley, and saw Nona Fiske rolling out her parking signs once again. She jogged over to The Quiet Quilter, her anger building with each slap of her sneakered feet on the tarmac.

"Nona! What are you doing?"

Nona looked up, but instead of looking embarrassed, she merely kept moving the heavy sign until it stood only feet from the entrance to Afternoon Tea.

Katie halted mere feet from her, panting for breath. "I thought we agreed on Wednesday night that you wouldn't be putting these signs out again."

"You agreed. Not me," Nona said, and pivoted, heading for the back of her shop, where the other signs had been stowed.

"This is a direct violation of the charter. You've been warned."

Nona turned, planted her feet on the asphalt and her hands on her hips. "What are you going to do, throw me out of the Merchants Association?"

"That's an option."

"Well, then, do it!" she said with a sneer.

"Very well, but I hope you understand what you're giving up."

"Not a thing as far as I can see."

"Do you remember how much snow we had last winter? If I'm not mistaken, over one hundred and fifty inches. If you leave the Association, you'll be giving up snowplowing and will have to contract to have the snow removed from in front of your shop."

Nona's mouth twitched, but she said nothing.

"And this lamppost," Katie said, indicating the one that hung near the front of Nona's store. "You'll have to replace the bulb yourself when it blows." It happened to be the bulb that seemed to short out most often, and Nona would badger Katie until the job was done.

"The other merchants will not carry brochures for your store," she added.

Nona was frowning now.

"And you'll no longer be included in the publicity for Victoria Square or for any of the special events we hold throughout the year, including the Dickens Festival."

Nona's eyes widened at that. One of the biggest perks of the Association was the publicity, where all members were mentioned. It was the most expensive part of their yearly budget, and Katie waited to see if Nona would capitulate.

"Are you sure you really want to leave the Association over something as silly as these parking signs?" Katie asked.

Nona's gaze had fallen. There had to be a way Katie could talk her out of her decision without Nona taking a massive hit to her pride. "Won't you tell me the real reason you've been putting these signs out?" Katie asked softly.

Nona's mouth trembled, and suddenly she

burst into tears. She hung her head and covered her face with her hands. Katie wasn't sure what to do. The woman had already called her a bitch and made it clear she wanted nothing to do with her, but Katie felt compelled to do something. She moved closer.

"Nona, please tell me what's wrong."

"It's been a year. A year!" she shrieked. Her face had gone an ugly shade of puce.

"A year since what?" Katie asked, confused.

"Since Ezra started hanging around with that tramp Mary Everett. He dumped me for her!"

"But what's that got to do with Vonne and Francine Barnett? They didn't do anything to you."

"It's this stinking tea shop," she said, waving a hand at the offending building. "Mary owned it. Every time I drive into Victoria Square, I see it. Every time I look out of my shop windows or door, I see it, and I'm reminded of my shame and how that brazen hussy ruined my life."

"Mary hasn't shown her face on Victoria Square for almost nine months," Katie said reasonably.

"That doesn't matter. If it wasn't for this shop, I'd still have my Ezra. He'd still be alive."

"But aggravating the Barnetts isn't going to change what happened. Nothing will bring Ezra back. Nothing," Katie said quietly.

Nona wrapped her arms around herself and cried even harder. "Don't you think I know that?"

Katie took a chance and wrapped her arms around the distraught woman and was surprised when she didn't pull away. "Nona, is this the first time you've cried for Ezra?"

Nona shook her head. "No, but I haven't cried for a long, long time."

And it sounded like it was long overdue.

"Everyone mourns in their own way. I don't think you've completely dealt with your feelings of loss."

"You certainly got over the death of your husband fast," Nona accused.

"No, I haven't." A day didn't go by without Katie thinking of Chad and wondering what would have happened had circumstances been different.

"You've got a boyfriend. I've seen his car parked outside your place at all hours of the day and night," Nona said.

"He owns the building," Katie reminded her. "He comes in early to make the dough for his cinnamon buns and he stays open late with his pizza business."

"And sometimes the car is there twenty-four hours a day," Nona accused.

"Sometimes," Katie admitted. *And not nearly often enough.*

Nona's sobs were beginning to slow. She pulled away and found a tissue in her skirt pocket, wiped her eyes, and blew her nose.

"Mary Everett has been punished enough.

And nothing you do to aggravate the new owners of the building will change what happened last year. Nothing."

Nona sniffed. "I suppose you're right."

"You're a valued member of the Merchants Association. You've been with us since the beginning. You helped draft our charter. We rely on you," Katie said. Okay, she was pouring it on a little thick, but she figured Nona wanted—and more important, needed—to hear it.

"Yes, you are right," she said, and wiped the back of her hand across her eyes.

"Now, let me help you put these signs away," Katie offered, and was surprised when Nona offered no resistance. She grabbed the nearest one and started rolling it toward the back of the quilt shop, while Nona did the same with the other. And Katie was pretty sure there'd be no more violations of the Merchants Association parking policy from that day forward.

Katie arrived outside Artisans Alley at seven fifty-eight—just two minutes to spare before some of the vendors would expect to be let in to tend to their booths. She saw Godfrey's car parked in the lot, although she didn't see him hanging around the door waiting to be let in. And unfortunately Ida and her entourage were already ensconced for the day.

As she approached the building's side entrance,

the women raised their placards and began to once again chant, "Unfair, unfair, unfair."

Katie held up both hands, waving them to help make her point. "Ladies, ladies—would you mind? Ida and I need to talk. Privately."

The women looked to Ida, who pursed her lips and shrugged. Grumbling, the three women moved toward the Alley's main entrance, but not far enough that they couldn't hear the ensuing conversation.

"Ida," Katie began, "we can't go on like this. You need to find something else to fill your hours," she added with authority.

"I don't *have* anything else to do," Ida said, her voice breaking. "My sister is gone, my home is gone. I've got nothing left except my job here at Artisans Alley."

"That's not true," Katie said, throwing a glance at the other women. "You've obviously made new friends at your new home at the assisted living center. They came here to support you with your protest, didn't they?"

Ida shrugged, and stared at the ground.

"I admit, the job of tag supervisor is necessary here at the Alley, but you have far more talent than you're giving yourself credit for." Okay, that was probably a lie, but Katie was on a roll and she needed a resolution to this impossible situation. "Have you ever thought about volunteering your time with a worthy organization?"

"No," Ida said emphatically.

"Why not?"

"Because only losers do volunteer work."

"Why on earth would you say that?"

Ida shrugged again. "Somebody told me that once."

"Well, they were wrong. Volunteering is one of the best, most generous things a person can do with her life."

Ida looked up at Katie. "Do you volunteer?"

"Not right now, but I have in the past—and when my circumstances change and I don't have to be at Artisans Alley seven days a week, I'll do it again for some worthy cause."

"They don't pay you to volunteer, do they?" Ida inquired.

"No. That's why they call it volunteering."

Ida frowned, her gaze fixed on the asphalt.

"Would you at least *think* about volunteering to help people not as fortunate as you?"

"I'm pretty unfortunate myself," Ida said with a bit of a pout.

"I don't see how. You've got your health. You've got a car. You drive. You can go anywhere you want. But there are a lot of senior citizens who can't get out. They aren't well, or they don't have the means to buy food to feed themselves."

"Old people are hungry?" Ida asked, sounding surprised.

Katie nodded. "They need friends, and they need food. Wouldn't you like to meet new people and become their friends?"

Ida shrugged. "Maybe."

"You could deliver meals to people several days a week. You could chat with them for a few minutes and make their days brighter. You could make sure they were okay, and if they need help, you could make sure they got it."

"It's important work?" Ida asked.

Katie nodded. "Very important work. Much more important and interesting than working in the tag room here at Artisans Alley."

"I suppose," Ida said.

"I can give you the telephone number of the Meals on Wheels coordinator. I'm sure she'd love to hear from you."

"I'm not promising anything," Ida declared.

"I won't ask you to. All I ask is that you consider making a difference in your own and other people's lives. If it isn't Meals on Wheels, there are plenty of other organizations that could use the talents of a woman like you."

Ida frowned, but her eyes gave away her interest. "Do you really think so?"

"I know so."

Ida looked over at her friends, who stood in a cluster, their arms crossed over their pastel shell tops, their expressions sour and unforgiving.

"Now, why don't you and your friends go back

to the center and talk this over. Maybe they'd like to volunteer as well."

"Does Meals on Wheels need more than just one person to help?" Ida asked.

"They sure do."

"I guess maybe we could all help. I'll have to think about it and talk with them."

"You do that. And if you decide you do want to volunteer, we'll talk about you coming back to the Alley and putting your lace back on the shelf in one of the big display cases."

"Could I come in every day and work on my tags, too?"

Katie shook her head. "That wouldn't be fair to you. You really only have to work one day a month."

"Only one day?" Ida cried.

"It isn't fair to make you work more than what you're required."

"But Rose and Vance and Edie do."

"You're right. I guess I could make an exception for you, too."

"I could come in on Sundays," Ida offered.

"We'll talk about that *after* you decide what you want to do about volunteering. Does that sound acceptable?"

Ida didn't look very happy about the situation, but she finally nodded.

"Very well. I'll wait for your call," Katie said. Sheesh—she sounded like an old schoolmarm.

"I could *come in* and tell you, and then maybe I could work on the tags."

"No, I'll wait for you to call," Katie reiterated. No way did she want Ida to slip back into her old routine.

"Oh, all right," Ida acquiesced.

"Fine. I've got the number written down in my office. I'll go get it and be right back."

Ida nodded and wandered over to talk to her friends while Katie unlocked the door to the building and made her way to her office. She grabbed the paper with the telephone number she'd written down the day before and turned to leave. As she reentered the vendors' lounge, she found Godfrey Foster standing in front of the opened fridge. "You're here early."

Godfrey started. "Are you trying to scare me to death?"

"I hope you're not going to swipe anything else from the fridge," Katie admonished.

"Don't worry. The Peterson family not only put me up for the night, but they gave me dinner and breakfast. I was just going to pour myself a glass of water. A person gets thirsty when they sweat as much as I do." He was already damp around the edges, she noted. He took out the water bottle, poured himself a mug full of water, and replaced the jug, closing the door.

"When did you say the renovations at your house would be finished?" Katie asked.

"Hopefully by Saturday. I can't wait to sleep in my own bed again." He chugged the water.

"Have you apologized to the other vendors yet?"

Godfrey shook his head, and stuck the mug on the back of the counter, no doubt hoping someone else would wash it and put it away. "I haven't had a chance to talk to anybody. But I did buy a six-pack of pop for Gwen Hardy."

"I'm sure she'll be happy to hear that. She'll be at the potluck tomorrow night. You are planning on attending, right?"

"If my wife lets me," he said, hanging his head like a beaten dog.

"Rose is counting on you to bring the napkins," Katie reminded him.

"I've got them in my car. Maybe I'd better give them to her this morning in case I can't make it to the party."

"Very well." He was about to walk away. "Ahem," Katie said. He looked at her, confused. She pointed to the mug he'd left on the counter. "You used it, you wash it," she reminded him.

Again, Godfrey hung his head, duly chastised. Really, hadn't anyone (his wife, his mother?) ever taught the man common courtesy?

As Godfrey turned to the sink, Katie headed back outside to give Ida the telephone number. When she returned, she turned on all the lights in the Alley and made her way to her office. She sat down at her desk and pondered the day so far, grateful she might have solved the parking problem, and hoping she'd managed to talk Ida into taking the Meals on Wheels volunteer job. But it was something else that niggled at the back of her brain—her breakfast with Sally.

Katie picked up a pen and began to doodle on a piece of scrap paper, tracing circles over and over again. What exactly had Sally meant when she'd said she had no regrets? Had she lived a less-than-exemplary life before she'd taken Nick under her wing? Had she done something others might think was wrong, but in her present state of health, with time running out, figured she had nothing to lose?

Like murder?

Katie shook herself. What was she thinking? Sally Casey was a lovely woman who was counting the days until she died. How could Katie even think such a thing?

And yet . . . what was it she'd said about her darling Nicholas? That he wasn't always happy. That he'd contemplated suicide after being disowned by his parents. That he'd come out to a mentor he thought he could trust and it had been disastrous.

What—just what—if Nick had come out to his industrial arts teacher? Say Dennis had no clue the teen was gay until Nick admitted it, and then Dennis had taken to picking on him mercilessly?

Seth had taken steps to keep the other boys in the class from doing the same, but he couldn't protect Nick from a teacher who took delight in verbally bullying his students.

Sally could handle guns. Seth had said that at one time she had run the skeet range at the McKinlay Mill Country Club. A Magnum had quite a kick, but what if she knew how to handle it? How accurate did one have to be to blow someone's head off with such a powerful weapon?

Katie shook her head and tossed the pen aside. There's no way Sally would have killed Dennis. No way.

And yet . . . She knew that Nick would be living and working next door to Wood U. Nobody on the Square had known that Dennis had sold the business, intending to retire to Florida. Could the thought of Dennis tormenting Nick have driven her to take care of the problem once and for all? To take out the man who had humiliated and teased the boy she had come to think of as her own?

Sally had known her way around the Square. She patronized some of the shops—even buying Nick a gift basket at Gilda's Gourmet Baskets earlier that week. Or had she gone to Gilda's with the real intent on finding out more about the murder investigation? Gilda wasn't a blabber-mouth, but the murder was sensational and she wouldn't mind talking about it if a customer asked questions—especially if she thought she could make a better sale.

The curious had asked Katie about Ezra Hilton's death the year before. The more grisly-minded had even inspected the place where the poor man had lain at the bottom of the stairs leading to the balcony that looked over Artisans Alley's main sales floor.

Sally had no regrets.

Could she really have killed Dennis Wheeler?

But what if the body found in Wood U was really Jerry Murphy? Would Sally have known he wasn't the store's owner? And yet, what would Jerry be doing at the store anyway?

No, the body found in Wood U had to be Dennis. It was maddening that the crime lab was so backed up it could take months for a DNA identification. What was Abby supposed to do in the meantime? They weren't about to release a body they couldn't identify. And how was she going to pay for a funeral anyway?

And yet . . . if Dennis was dead, who emptied the Wheelers' bank account?

It suddenly occurred to Katie that Abby might not have told her the truth—about anything. She didn't owe Katie any explanations. Did everyone on the Square know that she and Davenport had talked during his previous murder investigations? Could Abby have allowed Katie to come into her home in order to use her to feed information to Detective Davenport?

But that didn't make sense either. Abby had known that Davenport had already been replaced as the case investigator. Did she just assume Katie would run to Hamilton and repeat everything she'd been told?

Katie felt her face grow hot, and it wasn't because of the temperature.

Had Abby played her for a fool?

Wait a minute, wait a minute. You're making an awful lot of assumptions, the voice inside Katie warned. She had no way of knowing if Sally had killed Dennis, or that Abby killed him either. And just because Jerry Murphy had disappeared didn't mean he was even involved with the death at Wood U.

Still, despite all the conflicting ideas floating through her mind, it all made sense in some kind of convoluted way.

Now, who was she going to tell her theory to first? Her new friend Ray or her trusted attorney and surrogate big brother Seth?

There was a cherry pie with Seth's name on it just sitting there in her apartment refrigerator. The decision was made. Now, to wait out the day until she could talk to Seth, and hope she wouldn't go completely crazy.

Twenty-two

No matter what task she attempted to start that day, Katie could not stop thinking about Dennis Wheeler and Jerry Murphy. How could two men she barely knew occupy so much of her mental resources?

Hot and restless, she tossed her pen down on her desk and stood up to look out the window that overlooked the back parking lot. The late afternoon sun continued to beat down, the heat shimmering off the tarmac. Here it was only mid-July, but the heat wave that wouldn't quit had made the summer already seem eons long. She knew she'd regret that thought come November, when the skies would be perpetually gray and the temperatures in the thirties.

Maybe Dennis had had the right idea to leave the area for warmer climes. What was keeping her here in McKinlay Mill? Her job? She could sell Artisans Alley. It wasn't one hundred percent solvent, but plenty of businesses were sold with the hopes they'd turn more profitable under new management.

A year ago she'd felt alone and empty. Now she had friends—people who cared about her. People who looked to her as a leader, as a mentor, and as an accomplished businesswoman—even if she did mostly dress in jeans and Artisans Alley T-shirts.

And, of course, one of the biggest draws for staying in McKinlay Mill: Andy. A year ago she hadn't thought she'd ever find love again. Theirs was a rather lopsided relationship, thanks to their respective work hours, but even that had worked out for the best. When they spent time together, every second counted.

The thought of Andy made her smile. She'd hang out at the pizzeria after her dinner with Seth. If he was shorthanded, she'd jump in and help make pizzas, too. She liked working beside him and soaking up the camaraderie that prevailed among Andy and his teenaged workforce.

She shook her head and was about to sit again when she heard noise in the vendors' lounge.

"Katie! Katie!" came an agitated voice. Could that be Ida Mitchell? Someone who either showed no emotion at all or boiling anger? Katie glanced at her watch. It was nearly five. She'd thought she'd seen the last of Ida—for that day, at least. The woman was supposed to call—not show up once again.

Katie moved to stand in her doorway. Ida stood in front of the fridge, her clenched fists beating the air in an excited manner. "What's wrong?" she asked, growing concerned. Was Ida about to have a seizure?

"I got it! I got it!"

"Got what?" Katie asked.

"A job delivering food for Meals on Wheels! I start on Monday."

"That's wonderful," Katie said. "Why don't you sit down and tell me all about it?"

Ida pulled out a chair and sat down, but she still couldn't seem to stop fidgeting. "I'm so excited. This is just like having a real job. The girls and I went in to interview this morning and they let all of us volunteer."

"I'm so pleased to hear that," Katie said, and breathed a sigh of relief. No more Ida on a daily basis. Now to negotiate her new work schedule.

"We're going to make a real difference in people's lives," Ida went on to say, and Katie felt instantly ashamed. This was big news for Ida, and who knew how many new friends she would make and how many people would benefit from her—and her friends'—volunteer efforts.

"I'm very proud of you, Ida."

Ida positively beamed. After all, she probably hadn't heard many compliments during her life. Again, Katie felt ashamed.

"Would you like to talk about coming back to Artisans Alley?"

"Yes, but not today. After delivering meals all week, I may not have the time or energy to work in the tag room anymore," Ida said seriously.

Katie nodded. "I understand completely. Still, I hope you'll come to the potluck tomorrow night."

"Oh, I wouldn't miss that."

"Bring your friends if you'd like," Katie added.

Ida rose from her chair. "I will. Thank you, Katie." Ida looked apprehensive for a few moments, and then lunged at Katie, giving her a stiff and awkward hug. Katie found herself patting Ida's back.

Ida pulled back, all business once again. "I have to go. The girls and I are going shopping to find outfits that match. We want them to look like uniforms, because they'll make us look important."

Katie laughed. "I couldn't agree more."

"See you tomorrow night," Ida said with a wave, and exited the vendors' lounge.

Well, one problem solved.

Katie was about to give the store closing warning when the phone rang. She grabbed it.

"Katie? It's Ray Davenport."

"Detective, I was wondering when I'd hear from you next."

"I was wondering if you had anything new to tell me. Anything you want checked out. I'll only officially be a member of the Sheriff's Office for another fifteen minutes."

"Well, I—" Katie started, but then thought better of it.

"This isn't the time for reticence. If you've got something to say, say it now."

"I've been going over everything we know—over and over it, in fact—and some things are starting to make a lot of sense. To me at least."

"You're blathering," Davenport accused. "What is it you aren't telling me?"

"Okay, I've got some harebrained ideas I'm trying to make sense of before I share them with you."

"Harebrained or not, it never stopped you before," he said.

"Yeah, but I don't want to accuse someone of murder and then have egg on my face if I've got it all wrong."

"So you've actually got someone in mind?" he asked mildly. He probably had one of the people she was thinking about in mind as the killer, too.

"Two someones in mind," she admitted.

"You think the killer had an accomplice?" Davenport asked.

"I think the Sheriff's Office has two murders on their hands, done by two separate people. And I don't think one murderer has a clue about the other either."

"When do you think you'd like to share this information with me?"

"I want to talk to someone who knows both the people I suspect, get some feedback, and then we'll talk. Probably tomorrow."

"Tomorrow's going to be a busy day. And in less than just about twelve minutes, I can't officially act on whatever it is you might say that could lead to capturing a murderer."

"Or two," Katie added.

"Or two," Davenport grumbled.

"But surely you could talk to your former deputies and share whatever information you gather. They'd listen to you, wouldn't they?"

"In a perfect world. Sadly, we're not living in that fantasyland." He cleared his throat. "Whatever you do, don't act on anything you *think* you know."

"Ray, would I do that?"

"Yes."

"I would not. I don't want to get killed."

"Then repeat it like a mantra, will you?"

Katie sighed. "Whatever you say." She heard someone in the background call Davenport's name.

"I gotta go. See you tomorrow," he said, and broke the connection.

Katie frowned and set down the receiver. Poor Davenport. He hadn't gotten to solve his last case. He was leaving his job of over thirty years with one last murder unsolved. It had to be frustrating for him—just like it felt for her.

She'd invested too much time thinking about it. It was time to get on with her own life. And she had somewhere to be in just over an hour. But she had a feeling thoughts of murder would follow her, niggling at her brain until this case was finally solved—no matter how long it took.

Twenty-three

Katie swallowed down a pang of envy as she stood on Seth's front porch, one arm clutching a brown paper bag with two bottles of wine, the other balancing the cherry pie. She wasn't sure what they'd be cooking, so she'd brought both red and white wines. She used her elbow to press the doorbell.

Seth had inherited the house from his adoptive parents and had done an extensive renovation in the past five years. From the outside, it looked like an old farmhouse. Inside it was a showplace. He'd decorated with an eclectic palette of contemporary and antique pieces. The building Katie lived in was probably just as old, but much smaller, and with none of the finery. And it wasn't hers. Andy gave her a break on the rent, but she wasn't building equity. Heck, at the slave wages she paid herself, she never would be able to afford a modest bungalow, let alone a Victorian beauty like—*wince*—Sassy Sally's.

She elbowed the bell again and Seth obligingly opened the door.

"I was beginning to think you weren't home," she said, and handed him the bag.

"Sorry, I was in the kitchen getting things

ready." He looked inside the sack. "The red will go perfect with the steaks I'm going to grill."

"I thought we were going to cook together," she said, entering his foyer, which was lovely and cool—a pleasant change from the heat and humidity outside. "Afraid to take a chance on me?"

"Not at all. You can help me make the salad. And it looks like you brought dessert."

"It's a made-from-scratch cherry pie."

"Hey, it's my favorite. And I've got some ice cream to go with it."

"Vanilla?"

"You do know me," he admitted. "Now we can have pie à la mode."

They passed through to the kitchen, which always made Katie's tongue hang out in envy. Her aunt Lizzie's kitchen had been serviceable, but small. Since her aunt had died, Katie had always lived in apartments and never had enough room to store all her various baking pans and other equipment. Seth's kitchen was nearly the size of her apartment over the pizza shop. Granite countertops, stainless steel appliances, and what seemed like miles of counter space, with an island big enough to moor a cruise ship.

She sighed. "I just—"

"Love my kitchen. I know. You say that every time you visit," Seth said with a smile. He'd set out a head of romaine lettuce, some tomatoes, celery, and a red onion, as well as a large crystal bowl. "Everything's washed. We just need to put it together. Why don't we do that now and then we can sit back and share a glass of wine."

"Fine with me," she said, setting the pie on the counter. "Just let me wash my hands." In a minute, she joined Seth at the island, where he handed her a paring knife from the block before them.

"How are things at your law office?" Katie asked, and picked up a stalk of celery.

"Not bad. Nothing like the excitement that goes on at Artisans Alley or on Victoria Square. Although I *can* say I know a lot of what goes on behind the scenes around McKinlay Mill."

"Like who bought Wood U?" she suggested.

"Like who bought Wood U," he agreed. "And yet I can't talk about it, even to friends like you."

"I understand."

"No, I don't think you do. Sometimes clients confess things I'd really rather not hear. They ask for my advice. I have to give it, *and* I have to keep my mouth shut about it."

"Especially if what they tell you is illegal?"

He shrugged. "It's a slippery slope."

"Could whatever you know be relevant to the death at Wood U?" she asked.

"No."

Who in McKinlay Mill—possibly someone right on Victoria Square—could have told Seth something in confidence? Dennis? His killer? Someone Katie hadn't even suspected of the killing? Had Jerry Murphy ever contacted Seth?

It was circular thinking. Far better to concentrate on making the salad . . . among other things. "If it makes you feel any better, I forgive you," she said.

"For what?"

"Not telling me who bought Wood U and the Webster mansion." She sighed. "And I think I'm a step closer to closure on The English Ivy Inn."

"Don't take this the wrong way, but I'm glad to hear that. You've tortured yourself over it for far too long."

"I've been vacillating about fixing the air-conditioning in Artisans Alley. It costs so much money and I'm desperate to get out of debt. But today one of my vendors took a nosedive because of the heat. Vance found her in her booth passed out. What if she'd fallen? What if she'd broken a bone or, worse, fractured her skull?"

"I take it that didn't happen."

"No, but it could have."

"And how have you solved the problem?"

Katie sighed. "I'm selling everything I collected for The English Ivy Inn to your friend Nick."

Seth let out a long breath. "I never told him you had the stuff."

"I'm sorry to say for a moment there I thought you might have, but I suppose it must have been one of the other merchants who spilled the beans."

Seth shook his head and continued to tear the lettuce.

"Nick offered me an outrageous amount of money and I told him to get back to me tomorrow when he'd gotten over his initial glee. You should have seen him—like a kid with a new bike on Christmas morning."

"You're a good person, Katie."

She shook her head. "I just want fair market value."

Seth smiled. "You're still a good person."

Katie reached for another stalk of celery and started chopping once again. She had a lot to get off her chest, and she wanted to do it in an orderly manner. "Nick told me how you kept Dennis Wheeler from picking on him when you were both in high school."

"Someone needed to. The problem with a bullying teacher is they teach their students that it's okay to pick on their targeted victim. I wasn't going to let that happen to Nick."

"You're a good person, too," Katie said and laughed. But her smile soon waned. "I'm sorry to say Dennis continued to pick on students for the rest of his career. Including Andy, and just recently one of the boys who works in his shop."

"The kid who was arrested for arson?" Seth guessed.

Katie nodded. "Abby Wheeler told me that Dennis's father used to ridicule him. Maybe he associated that behavior with love, although she also said he never wanted to have children."

"Smart move on his part. Children often emulate what they learned from their parents, be it bad behavior, crappy parenting, or repeating the patterns of domestic abuse. Abby came to see me a couple of weeks ago."

"Oh?" Katie asked.

"I can't tell you what we talked about, but I'm sure you can probably guess."

"Let's see . . . her bullying husband just retired from his day job. That would mean he was going to be underfoot twenty-four/seven. And maybe that didn't appeal to the lady?"

"I won't tell," Seth said, and ripped another piece of lettuce.

"I visited Abby the other day at her house. Talk about weird. She had the AC set so low I wouldn't have been surprised to see my breath vaporize."

"It's been hot—but not that hot," Seth said.

Katie shrugged. "She said she gets hot flashes."

Seth laughed. "Of course, maybe she's got a body in the basement and she's trying to keep it from rotting."

Katie stopped chopping and caught Seth's gaze. "Ya think?"

"I'm joking," he said.

"I'm not. One of the very first things Detective Davenport asked me was about the state of the Wheelers' marriage. I didn't think there was anything wrong with it because I really didn't know either of them. And while Abby was terribly upset the night of the fire, she seemed to have gotten over it by the time I spoke to her again on Wednesday."

"Gotten over it? I don't think so. Maybe gotten used to the idea," Seth suggested.

Katie shook her head.

"The outside of the house was messy. The yard hadn't been tended to, paint peeled around the doorway. But the inside was immaculate. Like she'd spent a lot of time scrubbing."

"Maybe she was bored. Maybe she needed to work out her anxiety by cleaning. When my mother got out the silver polish, Dad and I knew it was time to vanish—at least for a few hours. That's how I ended up taking up golf."

"Oh, come on now. Isn't it a prerequisite for being a lawyer?" Katie said, but she wasn't finished with speculating about Abby Wheeler. "What if Abby had something she had to clean up? Say bloodstains from a very messy death. Say a death caused by a shot from a Magnum handgun."

"And just who did she kill? The Sheriff's Office hasn't established who died at Wood U."

"I've got two likely candidates."

"Her husband, and who else?"

"The Big Brown delivery guy. And now he's suddenly retired—via e-mail. If that doesn't sound suspicious, I don't know what does."

"It's unorthodox, but not impossible," Seth said.

* "And get this, he reserved two Amtrak tickets for Monday that were never used. Tickets for Florida."

"And that's significant because?" Seth asked.

"What if he and Abby were going to take that trip together? And what if something came up that interrupted their plans? Something like a jealous husband."

"Okay, now you're getting my attention."

"I'm guessing Abby came to talk to you about representing her in a divorce case."

"I don't handle divorces."

"But I'll bet you know plenty of other attorneys who do."

"I'll take the fifth on that one—or at least, part of that hypothesis."

"Aha!" Katie said with delight.

"What else do you have on the woman?"

Katie's amusement faded. "Nothing, I'm afraid, but don't you think it makes sense?"

"No, I don't."

But Katie wasn't listening. "I wonder if I should visit her again. By now the corpse has got to be stinking pretty badly—air-conditioning or not."

"You're not going to visit her. If you really believe in this demented theory of yours, call Detective Davenport."

"He's off the case. And for good reason, as you well know."

"Well, then, whoever has taken over for him."

"And is he likely to listen to me? He doesn't know me."

"Call Detective Davenport. If you don't, I will," he threatened.

"He'd blow me off, too. Even if we have sort of been working together on this one."

"If you've been working together, then he's not going to blow you off. And if Abby did kill Dennis—or her supposed lover, and why would she do that anyway?—it wouldn't be wise or safe for you to confront her."

"I wouldn't confront her. I just want to go into her house and take the sniff test."

"I forbid you to do that."

"You can't forbid me to do anything."

"Oh yes I can. When I signed on to be your surrogate big brother, I took the role seriously."

Katie glared at him.

"I'll tell Andy," he said with menace.

"That's a low blow—pulling the boyfriend card."

"You know as well as I do he wouldn't let you talk to Abby Wheeler either. And about what? A couple of guesses about her supposed bad marriage and a man who may or may not have been her lover."

"Gilda said Jerry Murphy was a terrible flirt. Don't you think a woman with a rotten husband might be susceptible to the guy's charm?"

"Maybe. But you don't know if they were even acquainted."

"Everybody on the Square knew Jerry."

"Did you?"

"Enough to say hello," she admitted. "And there's more. Ray told me that Jerry's car was found submerged in the Erie Canal. The plates were missing. They had to identify it by the VIN number."

"So now you're on a first-name basis with Detective Davenport?"

"If he's going to be a member of the Merchants Association, it makes sense."

"I guess. Was there a body behind the wheel of Murphy's car?"

"Not that Ray mentioned. He didn't say they were going to drag the canal, so I'm assuming someone dumped it there. And why couldn't that person be Abby Wheeler?"

"It could have been the Easter Bunny for all you know."

"Don't you see, everything fits."

"No, it doesn't. You're taking a lot of unrelated circumstances and trying to cram them together to make a finished jigsaw puzzle."

"Was I wrong about who killed Ezra Hilton?"

"No. But you could've been killed—and someone else was shot. And you didn't even confront that killer—who came after you."

Katie shrugged.

"What have you got to lose by calling Davenport? What's the rush? Do you think Abby's going to skip town? The murder happened seven days ago and she's still right here in the village. She either thinks she got away with it, or she thinks she has something to gain by staying."

"And what would that be?"

"The appearance of innocence."

Katie looked down at Seth's hands, which had mangled the lettuce. "I'll bet you're good in court."

"You don't want to find out," he said with the hint of an edge to his voice.

Katie rescued the lettuce and inspected it for anything edible. There wasn't much. She tossed the good stuff into the bowl. "Jerry Murphy is only one of the probable victims."

"That's right, you haven't mentioned Dennis Wheeler."

"Yes, and while it's possible Abby killed him, too . . . I think there's another just as viable suspect. And you aren't going to like my theory."

"Oh?" Seth said, and picked up the onion to slice it.

"I had a long talk with Sally Casey this morning

at the diner. She told me how Nick's parents abandoned him when they found out he was gay. And that when he came out to someone he thought of as a mentor, that mentor turned against him."

Seth let out a long breath, his expression turned to despair. "You got it. Nick did talk to Wheeler about it. The guys used to tease him because Wheeler gave him special treatment since he took to the subject better than anyone else. Nick thought of Wheeler as a mentor, but he turned on the poor kid when Nick admitted he like guys better than girls."

"Poor Nick."

"Don't tell me you think Nick might have killed Wheeler, because there's just no way."

"Actually, I think Sally did it."

Seth dropped the knife. "Tell me you're kidding."

Katie shook her head. "She told me she's dying. She told me she'd do anything for Nick. She knew he'd see Wood U from the inn on a daily basis. She didn't know it had been sold. What if she thought the sight of that store—and knowing that Dennis would be there every day—might be psychologically detrimental to Nick? Someone who felt suicidal after coming out to the bully who then picked on him mercilessly."

Seth stared at the counter as though it weren't there.

Katie went on. "You told me yourself she can

handle guns. I admit, a Magnum is pretty heavy, but maybe that's why she chose to use it. She wanted to obliterate the man who'd caused her darling Nicholas so much pain, and make sure—with one shot—that he'd never harm anyone else again."

Seth still said nothing, his expression blank.

"Sally knew that even if she did get caught, the consequences were nil. She's dying anyway. She wouldn't spend years in prison. And the most compelling thing she told me was that she has no regrets. None."

Finally Seth heaved a big sigh. He opened his mouth to say something, and then shut it and frowned.

"How well do you know Sally?" Katie asked, hoping she hadn't just lost a friend by explaining her theory.

"Pretty well."

"*Is* she capable of murder?"

"I don't know. But you're right about one thing, she *would* do just about anything she could to protect Nick."

"And that might—just might—include murder?" Katie asked.

Seth finally looked up, his gaze piercing. "I don't think you should say anything about this to anyone, least of all your new friend Detective Davenport."

"That's the thing . . . I like Sally. A lot. I

understand the fierce devotion she feels toward Nick, and I don't get the sense that she has ever done anything like this in her life."

"You've got that right. She's the kindest woman I've ever known."

"I won't say anything to Ray about it, and just hope I can live with myself for keeping such a terrible secret."

"You don't know if it's the truth. You have no proof. You're just taking a wild guess."

"And what if Sally comes to you to confess her sin of murder so that she can die with an easier conscience? What would you do?"

"I hope I never have to face that situation. What about your other theory?"

"I suppose I could call Ray. Just to get his feedback."

Seth pointed to the wall phone across the kitchen. "Be my guest."

Katie crossed the room, lifted the receiver, and punched in Davenport's number, which she'd by now memorized. It went straight to voice mail. Well, what had she expected? He was probably having dinner with his daughters. "Ray, it's Katie Bonner. I've got an idea on who killed Jerry Murphy and why. Give me a call if you want to talk about it. You can catch me via my cell phone." She hung up.

"Why didn't you just tell him you suspect Abby?" Seth asked.

"And let him get the jump on having her arrested? Uh-uh."

"Unless she makes a full confession, the cops will have to do more than just suspect she's involved. They need proof before they can arrest her. They need evidence the DA can convict her on, and hearsay—from you—isn't going to cut it."

"You're probably right. But I've got a stake in this. Jerry served all of Victoria Square. As head of the Merchants Association, I feel I need to find out what happened to him," she said.

Seth shook his head. "You, my love, are certifiable."

"Maybe," she conceded. "Now, let's hurry up and get those steaks on the grill. Ray might call at any minute, and I might have to leave."

"What for?"

"To talk to him. He might want to go and confront Abby."

Seth shook his head. "He's been removed from the case. He can't confront her."

"Then I suppose it'll be up to Detective Hamilton," she grumbled. "But Ray said the guy moves at glacial speed. Abby could take off—be long gone—before he gets around to catching her."

"If—and that's a pretty damn big if—she's guilty of anything other than being a grieving widow. Now, can we finish this salad and go sit with a nice soothing glass of wine? I don't know about you, but after this conversation, I need it."

"Great. We'll drink to me solving at least one of these cases."

He shook his head. "Oh no we won't. We'll drink to anything but that."

"Spoilsport."

"Spoiled brat," Seth countered.

Katie squinted at him. "You know, you *are* starting to sound like my big brother."

Davenport did not call. At least, not while Katie was at Seth's house. Maybe he'd gone out to dinner with his girls to celebrate his last day of work. Or maybe his workmates—those who might be on duty during his party—had taken him out for a drink to toast his retirement.

Katie returned to her apartment, changed clothes, and went back down the stairs to hang out with Andy and his boys at the pizzeria.

"Hey, Katie," Keith called from his station at the ovens. During the summer, he seemed to work just about every night. But then he was saving up for college.

"I thought you might need a hand tonight," Katie said when Andy got off the phone from taking an order.

"We're swamped. If you could take the orders, it would save me from peeling off my gloves every time the phone rings."

"Be glad to," she said, and stationed herself next to the wall phone, which promptly rang. She grabbed the pencil that hung from a string and jotted down the order on the pad that was attached to the wall. She hung up, ripped off the top sheet, and handed it to Andy, who gave her a smile.

"We work like a well-oiled machine."

"Better than a clunky one that breaks down," she said and laughed.

"How did your dinner with Seth go?" he asked, and handed off a finished pizza to Keith before starting another.

"Great. We had some very interesting conversations . . . about murder."

"I don't think I want to hear about it," Andy said with a frown.

"Don't worry, this isn't the place to discuss it," she said, eyeing Keith, who seemed more interested in the radio that blasted from the back of the shop. "Maybe we can share a couple of beers after you close."

"Do you really want to stay up that late the night before your big party?"

"Party?" she asked, confused. And then she remembered. "Oh, yeah. The potluck tomorrow night. Pooh—I forgot all about it."

"Is that wishful thinking?"

"Oh, no. I love parties, they're lots of fun—and who doesn't love to pig out on all the food, especially the Christmas cookies and other holiday fare. I think it's a great idea. I hope you can at least slip away for ten or twenty minutes tomorrow."

"I can't promise anything. You know Saturday night is my busiest of the week, but I will bring, or at least send over, that bowl of pasta salad I promised Rose."

"I could come over and cover for you," she offered.

"Then who would I hang out with? It's you I want to be with—no offense to your friends and the other merchants on the Square."

She smiled.

He smiled back. "I was going to wait until Monday to tell you, but I figured I better tell you in case you freaked out about me trespassing in your apartment."

"Trespassing?" she asked, confused.

"Yeah, I had a guy come over from Reed Electric this afternoon to give me a quote on upgrading the circuit box in your apartment."

"Oh, Andy," Katie said, "you didn't have to do that." Of course it was a lie. She'd been *dying* for him to do just that.

"You've been such a help here at the shop this week. And if I'm honest, anytime I've been shorthanded. I don't know why I made such a fuss about doing the upgrade for all this time. It was really selfish of me. I hope you'll forgive me."

"You're a businessman. I know what that means. But that doesn't mean I won't take you up on your generous offer," she said, lunging forward and planting a big wet kiss on his lips.

He looked embarrassed, especially since Keith made smooching noises once again, but continued anyway. "I scheduled the work to be done on Monday. And tomorrow morning I'll head over to Home Depot and get you a window air conditioner for your bedroom, too."

"Oh, Andy, thank you." Then again, he'd already committed to staying over on Monday. Was he looking out for his own comfort? And would a nice cool bedroom mean he might do the same more often? The idea appealed to Katie.

The phone rang again and Katie grabbed it. "Angelo's."

"Yes, I want a small cheese, pepperoni, and mushroom pizza for pickup. How long will that take?"

"Twenty minutes," Katie answered, jotting down the order, and noting the number on caller ID. "And who's this for?"

"Abby." The connection ended.

Katie stared at the order blank before her. Abby? Abby Wheeler? The voice *had* sounded familiar. She hung up the phone, tore off the sheet, and handed it to Andy.

He glanced at the paper. "Hmm. She usually has them delivered," he said with a shrug, and put the paper down. Grabbing another round of dough, he started on the pizza.

"Does she call often?"

"Once the Ezra Hilton do-not-patronize-Angelo's curse was taken off my business, the Wheelers were one of my best customers."

And Abby didn't want the pizza delivered. Well, she had said she was broke. Did broke people often order pizzas? Of course, she had ordered a small pizza, but then she was only going to eat it by herself anyway.

Seth had told Katie not to seek Abby out, but now she was going to show up practically on her doorstep. She didn't have to do more than say hello, but she wanted to do so much more than that. How would that scenario go? "Hello, Abby. Were you having an affair with Jerry Murphy? Did you kill him? And if so, why?"

The phone rang again. Katie grabbed it. "Angelo's."

"Hi, I just called a couple of minutes ago for a pizza. I'd like it delivered instead of pickup. Will that be okay?"

"For Abby?" Katie asked, lowering her voice.

"Uh, yes."

"And the address?" Abby gave it. No doubt about it—it was the Wheelers' address.

"Will I have to wait a lot longer?"

"We'll try to get it to you ASAP, ma'am," Katie said, still using her fake voice. She hung up the phone. Andy had been listening, and looked at her with an odd expression.

"What was that all about?"

Katie gave a fake cough. "Frog in my throat. I think I need a sip of water or something."

Andy shrugged and went back to work, but the wheels in Katie's mind had already begun to spin. Seth had warned her not to visit Abby, but the perfect opportunity had just presented itself. It was fate. She was *meant* to deliver that pizza. That said, she had no intension of accusing Abby of anything. But she wondered if she could get inside the house for another quick look around. She'd only seen the entryway and living room. She was sure there was a lot more to see that might help her prove her case to Ray Davenport. And yet she wasn't about to try anything stupid. If Abby was a killer, she might just come after Katie, and tipping her off that she suspected her of murder could be not only criminally stupid, but deadly dangerous, as well.

Now she had to kill at least eighteen minutes until the pizza would be ready for delivery, and hope that Andy's delivery boy was busy so that she could volunteer to take the pizza over to Abby's house. She was glad she hadn't shared her suspicions with Andy, because then he'd be sure to veto such a suggestion.

Katie kept her eye on the clock as she continued to take the orders. Tony, another of Andy's charges, arrived back at the shop when Abby's pizza still had five more minutes left in the oven.

Andy had a pile of pizzas already waiting in one of the bulky insulated delivery bags. "If you wait another five minutes, you can take this one over to Walker Street."

"Why don't you go, Tony? I can deliver Abby Wheeler's pizza," Katie said, hoping she sounded innocent.

"Yeah, if these pies get cold, my tips go down the toilet," Tony said. "And that Wheeler woman is notoriously cheap," he added. "She's stiffed me the last two times I made a delivery."

"I'm not expecting a tip either," Katie told Andy. "I just want to make sure she's okay after all she's been through this week. The poor woman."

Andy didn't look entirely convinced, but he handed off the boxes to Tony anyway. "Okay. Take off."

Katie took another two orders before Keith took Abby's pizza from the oven. "Here you go," he said.

"Do I need an insulated bag?" Katie asked.

"Only if you intend to dawdle. I want you back here ASAP," Andy said.

"This is only a volunteer position," Katie reminded him as she took possession of the pizza.

"Yeah, but you have a propensity for getting

into trouble. Please get back here in a hurry so I don't have to worry about you."

"Will do," she said and headed for the door, just in case he changed his mind about letting her go.

Now the burning question was . . . what was she going to say to Abby Wheeler?

Twenty-four

It took less than two minutes for Katie to drive through the darkened streets of McKinlay Mill to Cooper's Race, where Abby Wheeler lived. As she turned into the road, she noticed a familiar car and slowed. It belonged to Ray Davenport. She figured he must be staking out the Wheelers' house. Had he come to the same conclusion as she had that Abby had killed either Jerry Murphy or her husband?

Katie stopped and looked inside the aging sedan, but it was empty. Maybe he'd gone in on foot to peek inside her windows. It wasn't standard police procedure, but he was now officially retired, so maybe he figured he no longer had to do things by the book. She pressed the accelerator and decided she'd keep an eye out for him when she got to the house.

Katie parked at the curb and got out of her car, grabbing the still hot pizza. The darkness had swallowed some of the day's heat, but not the humidity, and she felt clammy, fighting the urge to peel her damp clothes away from her skin.

The front steps were awash in light from the colonial-style fixture at the side of the door, and Katie mounted the concrete steps. She looked to her left and right, but didn't see Davenport lurking around the yard. "Ray? Are you out there?" she called in a harsh whisper. She waited long seconds for a reply, but none came.

Giving up, Katie pressed the doorbell and heard Westminster chimes sound somewhere within the house. In seconds, the door opened, but stopped short because of the chain. Abby peeked through the gap. "Katie. What are you doing here?"

"Delivery," she said and held up the pizza box for Abby to see. "Andy Rust is shorthanded tonight, so I said I'd be happy to make a few deliveries for him. As long as I'm here, do you have a few minutes to talk?" Katie asked. Already she could feel the cold dry air seeping out of the house.

Abby looked behind her, bit her lip, and considered the request. Finally, she unhooked the chain and opened the door. Katie stepped inside. This time Abby didn't usher her into the house, but stood her ground in the entryway.

"Please wait here while I go get the money," Abby said firmly.

Katie nodded, but as soon as Abby went

through the living room to the nether regions of the house, Katie stepped farther inside, looked around, and then tiptoed into the living room. She wrinkled her nose at a sour smell. Had Abby neglected to take the garbage out for a while?

Abby soon returned from what looked like the entrance to the dining room with a ten-dollar bill in hand. Her eyes narrowed, her expression darkening as she approached Katie. "I asked you to stay in the doorway," she said, and handed Katie the money. "I hope you can make change."

Katie handed her the pizza box and dug into her pockets for change. She counted it out in Abby's hand. "Everyone at the Merchants Association is worried about you. We know this whole situation is terribly upsetting for you, and we really want you to know that you have a circle of friends who are there for you." Oh, brother. That was pouring it on thick.

"I'm flattered, but I don't feel I can show my face on Victoria Square. Look at me, thanks to Dennis, I'm forced to hide out in my own home."

Katie wrinkled her nose and sniffed. What *was* that sour odor she smelled? She had an idea, and she didn't like it. Not one bit. She knew she should get out of there—now—especially if Abby was capable of murder, but how else was she going to draw her out? And where the heck was Davenport?

"Maybe what you need is a vacation. To get away from McKinlay Mill for a few days or weeks."

"I've thought of that," Abby admitted. "But I don't have the money—thanks to *Dennis,*" she said with bitterness. "He ruined everything!"

"How so?"

Abby shook her head. "I already told you about him and his selfish ways."

"You mean because you two never had children?"

"There were more important considerations," Abby muttered.

"But it *was* a bone of contention between you."

"Yes."

"Did you ever consult an attorney about a divorce?"

"What business is that of yours?" Abby asked curtly.

"I did . . . when my late husband invested all our savings in Artisans Alley."

"Yeah, we've all heard about that—time and time again." Abby muttered that last under her breath. "Look, I'm really hungry and would like to eat my dinner—if you wouldn't mind." She nodded toward the door.

Katie backed up a step, but didn't move to leave. "Have you spoken to anyone from the Sheriff's Office lately?"

"I went down to their headquarters just yesterday."

"Did they have any news to share?"

Abby shook her head.

"Just out of curiosity, when is garbage day in your neighborhood?"

"It was today. Why?"

"What company do you use?"

"Why do you care?"

"I'm just wondering if you might've thrown out something that could be of value to the police in their investigation."

"Such as?" Abby demanded. My, she was getting a little testy.

"Oh, I don't know. Maybe one of Dennis's shirts. Like the one that was found at Artisans Alley."

"What is it you're accusing me of doing? Lying to the sheriff's detectives?"

"It wasn't Dennis who was hiding in Artisans Alley. It was one of my vendors. It was his shirt Detective Hamilton showed you."

Abby said nothing, but her hands clutched the pizza box tighter. "I'm running out of patience, and I'd like you to leave."

"Yes, of course," Katie said, and backed toward the door. "Don't forget, if you need anything from the Merchants Association—"

Abby practically pushed her out the door, slamming it in Katie's face.

Okay, that didn't go well, Katie thought as she went down the sidewalk, heading for her car.

She got in and started the engine. She put the car in gear, but looked back at the Wheelers' house. Abby was watching her through the crack in the living room curtains. Katie pressed the accelerator and headed down the street.

She pulled around the corner and parked the car, taking the keys from the ignition, not sure what her next move should be. One thing was for sure, Abby was hiding something. A smelly something. And she was antsy about something, too. And yet . . . she'd ordered a pizza. That didn't make sense.

Katie fumbled under her seat for the big flashlight she kept in case of emergencies, found it, and got out of her car. Her first priority was to find Davenport.

Cooper's Race had no streetlights, so at least Abby wouldn't see her skulking around the neighborhood. She stopped at Davenport's car, flashing the light inside. A half-filled cup of coffee sat in the holder. She opened the door and reached inside to pick it up. The McDonald's cup was no longer warm. He'd left it there some time ago. She replaced the cup in the holder and shut the car door. Where the heck could he be?

She looked down the street toward the Wheelers' house, and frowned. He had to be lurking around the house somewhere. Maybe in the backyard. Katie hefted her flashlight. It would make a pretty good weapon, if need be.

Did she really think she needed a weapon?

Call 911, the voice inside her taunted.

And say what? That Abby Wheeler has a body in her house stinking up the joint? Yeah, they'd take me really seriously with that one.

And what if Abby *did* have a body in the basement? Maybe it wasn't hot flashes that were the reason behind her keeping the air-conditioning set at such a low level, but to keep the house cold enough to keep the body from quickly decomposing during the prolonged heat wave.

You are really stupid if you don't call 911 right now, the voice taunted, but Katie forged ahead, keeping to the shadows as she approached the Wheeler house once again.

She had to have killed Jerry Murphy. But why? They were supposed to be running away together that week. What could have caused her to kill her (supposed) lover when what she wanted (another guess on Katie's part)—to leave Dennis—was at hand?

Davenport had said Murphy had bought train tickets to Florida. But what if he'd bought round-trip instead of one-way tickets? What if all he wanted was a fling and she'd wanted more?

He had a good job he enjoyed, a budding business restoring old cars. Running away with his married lover just didn't seem to be a logical step—especially for a man who liked to flirt with women. Was Abby just one entry on his dance card? Had he been seeing others as well as her?

All supposition, the voice said.

One thing was certain: Ray Davenport was hanging around somewhere near, watching the situation.

But what if he wasn't? What if he'd made it inside the house to talk to Abby and something unforeseen had happened? She'd (possibly) already killed one person. Would Davenport have been so desperate to collar one last felon that he disregarded his own advice to let the Sheriff's Office handle it?

What if Abby had killed him, too?

Katie hefted her flashlight and slunk behind a tree in the yard next to the Wheeler home. Where would Abby be right now? Sitting alone at her dining room table, scarfing down pizza? That was a good bet. Where would she have put a stinking body? In the basement? That was the coldest part of a house during the summer months, especially if air-conditioning was in use. Katie decided to poke around the foundation and hope she didn't run into spiders, crickets, and slugs.

Scurrying across the driveway, she saw that Abby's car was parked close to the house. More cover. She sidled past it and hunkered down to the window well. Damn. Glass blocks filled the rectangle where a window should have been. They let light in, but kept nosy people—and presumably would-be burglars—out. She turned on her flashlight and got exactly the results she expected—the light was reflected back at her. She doused the light and sat back on her haunches. If all the windows had been filled with the blocks, she was skunked.

She duckwalked around the side of the house to the next break in the concrete block foundation and found a real window. She turned her flashlight back on and placed it directly on the glass. The funnel of light shone on the basement floor, but there wasn't anything to see. She moved it back and forth, and several stacked cartons came into view. Not much help.

She moved along the back of the house to another window, maneuvered her flashlight to touch the glass, as sticky filaments of spiderwebs clung to her hands. She tried not to think about the probable occupant of the web and trained her flashlight on the glass.

She squinted to make sense of the sight. Mounds of what look like sheets and towels along a long cylinder of some type. Cylinder or body?

Katie swallowed down the bile that threatened to rise up her throat. It was all well and good to think there might be a body in that basement, but the realization that there really could be one sickened her.

And then she noticed the foot sticking out at an odd angle. She carefully moved the flashlight across the glass, but from that angle, couldn't see much beyond it . . . except what looked like the bottom step from the stairwell that led back to the home's main level.

Did that foot belong to Ray Davenport?

Katie stood, seized with indecision.

And then the backyard was flooded with light, blinding her.

Within seconds, a voice called out, "Don't move, or I'll blow your head off."

Twenty-five

Abby Wheeler stood at the corner of the house, arms extended, clutching a mammoth gun—her late husband's Magnum.

Katie raised her hands in submission, still clasping the flashlight in her right. "Are you really going to shoot me, Abby—in all this light? I'll bet your neighbors can dial nine-one-one just as fast as I can."

Katie's phone rang.

Abby stood there, staring at her.

Katie stared back.

The phone continued to ring.

"I'll bet it's Andy. I told him I'd deliver your pizza and be right back. If I don't answer this call, he'll probably call nine-one-one."

The gun wavered ever-so-slightly.

"Face it, Abby. You're done."

The phone kept ringing.

"I could still blow you away, you nosy bitch."

Katie sighed. Why did nasty people always call *her* a bitch?

"You could, but that would just make your jail sentence that much longer."

"You think I'd ever get parole after killing that bastard husband of mine?"

The phone abruptly stopped chirping. It must have rolled over into voice mail.

Katie blinked, stunned by Abby's last words. "Dennis? But I thought you killed Jerry."

"Why would I want to do that? I actually loved him."

"Then whose body did they find in Wood U?"

"It was Jerry," she said bitterly. "Dennis was going to do the deed. He texted Jerry and told him I wanted to meet him at the shop. Told him where the key was hidden. Jerry let himself inside, but Dennis got there late—and found someone had already killed him."

Oh dear God. Did Sally Casey even know what Dennis looked like? Had she mistaken Jerry for Dennis and killed him without proof of identity?

"Did Dennis know about the trip you and Jerry were taking to Florida?"

Abby sniffed and the heavy gun again wavered in her grasp. "He laughed. He said he'd taken steps to make sure I couldn't touch any of the money in our joint accounts. He'd moved it to other banks. He'd canceled all my credit cards and burned my driver's license. I had nothing— no money or access to it, and no way to prove my identity without a lot of hassle."

"But he made one big mistake, didn't he?"

Abby laughed, but it sounded more like a sob. "He put the gun down. I picked it up and I shot him."

"Was that before or after Gilda called to tell you about the fire?"

"Before. Maybe a minute before."

"So you really didn't have to act when you arrived at the Square last Saturday night. You knew your lover was dead—and you'd just killed your husband."

"I still haven't figured out why anyone would want to kill Jerry. Maybe another jealous husband—I never figured he was the monogamous type."

The faint sounds of a siren cut through the night.

Katie could see light behind the drapes of the neighbor's house. Movement told her that someone was watching the spectacle. *Thank you for dialing 911,* she thought.

"I'd say we're about to get company any minute now," Katie said calmly.

"I'll have them arrest you for trespassing." She glanced over her shoulder to look at the lighted window next door. "My neighbor will back me up."

"And how will you explain the bodies in the basement?"

"Bodies?" Abby asked innocently.

"There's someone lying at the bottom step of

your basement stairs. I presume it's Detective Davenport."

Abby's face twisted into a scowl.

The sirens got a whole lot louder.

"Give it up, Abby. It's all over."

"Never, bitch," she said, and pulled the trigger.

Katie dove to her right as the big gun's recoil knocked Abby off her feet. Katie scrambled in the dew-soaked grass as Abby fired again. Katie kept moving until she was out of the bright light, but smacked into a wooden fence. She scrambled to climb it, but found it was higher than her outstretched hands could reach. She couldn't find the top to pull herself up.

The gun fired again, taking out a big chunk of the fence to her right. Katie darted left. This side of the yard was hemmed in by chain link fence, and a good deal shorter. She leapt it like a fleeing gazelle.

"Put your hands up!" a male voice ordered and Katie instinctively pivoted.

Abby whirled, drawing the gun up to fire.

An explosion of sound erupted, but not from Abby's gun. She was thrown backward, smashing into the wet ground, her pretty peach sweatshirt awash in scarlet.

Twenty-six

"Will you stop complaining?" Katie grated as she walked alongside the gurney, trying to stay in step with the EMTs.

"I've got a broken foot, I've got a concussion! Don't you think I have a right to complain?" Davenport asked, and winced as the gurney bounced on the uneven driveway.

Katie sighed. "You wouldn't have gotten hurt if you'd called me in for backup."

"You?" he accused. "I was crazy to come over here on my own. I should've done what I always told you to do. I should've minded my own business."

"But you didn't. And Abby Wheeler pushed you down a flight of stairs. Just how did that happen, by the way?"

"It's embarrassing. I said I noticed the smell in her house, and she said she thought there was a dead rat in the basement. She opened the cellar door, I looked down, and she gave me a shove. It all happened rather fast."

"And while you were out of it . . . well, you know the rest."

"Yeah. Now my suspect's dead, and a fine deputy has got to live with the guilt for the rest of his life."

"She could've killed you, too. She tried to kill me. I was just lucky she couldn't see in the dark. And I'm grateful that Andy and Abby's neighbors both called nine-one-one."

They approached the ambulance, and the EMTs halted.

Davenport made a grab for Katie's hand. "Could you call my girls? I don't want some unfeeling cop to tell them what happened and that I'm in the hospital. It'll scare them half to death, especially after what happened with their mother last year."

Davenport's wife had died as the result of a car accident. Had one of the girls fielded that call, too?

"I'd be glad to," she assured him. He gave her the number and she programmed it into her cell phone.

"And ask for Sophie. She's the levelheaded one," Davenport added.

"And what will we do about your party tomorrow night?" Katie asked.

"You don't think a broken foot is going to keep me from my retirement party, do you? Not a chance!"

"All right. Then I'll see you tomorrow night. Call—or have Sophie call—if you need any-thing," Katie said sincerely.

Davenport nodded and sank back against the gurney's pillow, grunting as the EMTs loaded him into the back of the ambulance. Katie watched as they slammed the back door. She stepped back, wrapping her arms around herself to ward off the damp chill that had settled.

She glanced toward one of the patrol cars. Deputy Schuler leaned against the trunk, his face pale in the blazing light of the headlights from another cruiser. She'd heard him tell his superiors that he'd never before fired his service revolver during the ten years he'd been a deputy. He was terribly upset, but Katie had no qualms about telling Detective Hamilton what she'd seen, and that Schuler had acted in self-defense. Abby Wheeler would have shot Schuler dead where he stood if he hadn't fired first, but that knowledge didn't help the man now. He was a nice guy. As Davenport had intimated, the events of this night would no doubt haunt him forever.

Detective Hamilton suddenly loomed before her, shaking his big, heavy head. "Mrs. Bonner," he began with what sounded like profound disappointment. "It seems you still haven't learned to stay out of the Sheriff Office's business."

"Are you holding me personally responsible for the death of Jerry Murphy, the assault on Detective Davenport, and the death of Abby Wheeler?"

"Of course not. But you could have been hurt or killed. If you'd simply called my office, some of this might have been avoided."

"If I hadn't shown up when I did, I'm sure Ray Davenport would be just as dead as Dennis Wheeler."

"Be that as it may," he said sternly, "in the future I don't expect to have to warn you again that civilians should always call the Sheriff's Office and let us handle whatever crimes you wish to report."

Yeah, yeah, yeah, and be tolerated—or worse ignored. She'd gone that route before, too.

She glanced back at Deputy Schuler. "Will he ever return to duty?"

"With your testimony, I'm sure he'll be exonerated. In the meantime, he'll be restricted to desk duty."

"I'm sorry Abby's dead. I'm even sorrier that Deputy Schuler was put in the terrible position of defending himself from her. The only thing I'm glad about is that it's over."

"Over?" Hamilton said. "Are you forgetting the body that was found at Wood U?"

No, she hadn't. And she wasn't sure what she was going to do about her theory of who actually fired a gun the previous Saturday. One thing she was going to do was to keep her mouth shut about her suspicions about Sally Casey. At least . . . for now.

Hamilton seemed to have finished his little speech and wandered off to talk to the other deputies. The ambulance took off and Katie opened her cell phone once again, hitting the button for the number Davenport had just given her. It rang three or four times before being picked up. "Hello?"

"Is this Sophie?"

"Yes," the young woman said warily.

"Your dad asked me to give you a call . . ." Katie began.

Twenty-seven

Two brightly lit and fully decorated Christmas trees flanked Artisans Alley's main entrance, while Bing Crosby wished everyone a "Merry Christmas and a Happy New Year" from the building's public address system. Everywhere Katie looked, someone was laughing or smiling or spreading good cheer. The weather seemed to have broken, but it was thundershowers that had driven the party inside—not snow.

Katie examined one of the long tables laden with holiday food. As Rose had mentioned, she'd made tent cards with the names of all the dishes and who had contributed them. Edie Silver had brought her famous cheesy potatoes. Andy's pasta salad sat next to it. There were a variety of dips sitting on ice, accompanied by bite-sized veggies, chips, and crackers, and on another paper plate sat a pile of saltines, which apparently had been Ida Mitchell's contribution to the feast. Alongside that was a tent card for the stack of white napkins that Godfrey had supplied.

"It sure feels like Christmas in July," Vance said from beside a long table filled with holiday food and drink. He hoisted a paper cup filled with Gilda's champagne punch. "Or at least it will next week when the new air-conditioning system is up and running."

"I envy you for having so much faith that everything will fall into place and they won't be stymied at every turn," Katie said. To be on the safe side, she anticipated the final bill to be a good twenty-five percent over the estimate she'd been given. That was just the way things went when any kind of repair was needed at the one-hundred-plus-year-old building.

"Aw, come on, Katie—don't go looking for trouble. This is a celebration, and goodness knows we have a lot to celebrate here at Artisans Alley," Vance said.

"You are so right," Katie said, and let him pour her a cup of punch, too. "Just knowing Ida has found a new vocation and won't be in my hair on a daily basis is enough to send me into fits of the giggles."

"I'm only sorry you had to part with all the stuff you've been collecting for your English Ivy Inn."

"In a way, they'll all get to be there anyway, and

hopefully in rooms that look the way I'd planned for all along. They just won't belong to me anymore."

"But you are getting what you want. Beautiful things decorating a beautiful home. It's like it was meant to be . . . sort of," he finished lamely.

Katie's smile was wistful. "I guess you're right."

"Sorry to eavesdrop," Rose said, joining them at the punch bowl. "But there's lots more than that to celebrate. The Alley's intruder has been exposed. Shame on Godfrey for scaring us all half to death."

"And taking our food and pop out of the fridge," Gwen Hardy said, coming up from behind them.

"I got my Tupperware back," Vance said, "and that pleased Janey."

The celebration in the empty storefront was also in full swing by the time Katie tore herself away from the Christmas cheer to visit Ray Davenport's retirement party. Although as she'd anticipated, the parties seemed to have overlapped. The last time she'd looked, she'd seen Detective Hamilton munching Christmas cookies.

Sophie Davenport had set up large fans that roared in the background, while big band music blared from a large boom box at the back of the room. It was standing room only, with festive crepe streamers, and several easels filled with pictures chronicling Detective Davenport's career.

Katie moseyed on up to a refreshment table and sampled one of the stuffed mushrooms from a platter of hors d'oeuvres. She felt a tug on her sleeve and looked down. Davenport sat in a wheelchair with his elevated left foot encased in a fiberglass cast. Other than that, he didn't look too worse for wear, although the ear-to-ear grin he sported was a little unsettling.

"The kids made all the food," he said, nearly shouting to be heard over the music and the buzz of voices.

"My goodness, they're certainly hard workers."

"Sophie's been accepted at the Culinary Institute of America. She starts this fall."

Katie savored the flavor of the mushroom's stuffing. "Are you even sure she needs to go? This is to die for."

Davenport positively beamed. "She takes after her mom. Rachel was a whiz in the kitchen. She'd be so proud," he said wistfully.

"As you must be. But it looks like the apple didn't fall far from the tree," she said, gazing over at the beautiful inlaid wooden jewelry boxes and other objects that were displayed on the stands that had been empty the last time Katie had passed the storefront.

She helped herself to another mushroom and glanced through the shop's big display window.

She could see Nick pushing Sally in a transport chair. She was dressed in a gaudy green-and-red Christmas sweater, with red jingle bells hanging from her pierced ears, and a fuzzy red-and-white Santa hat.

"If you'll excuse me," Katie told Davenport, then grabbed a napkin to wipe her fingers and headed out the door.

Elbowing her way through the crowd, Katie soon caught up with Nick and Sally. "I'm so glad you could come," she said, but immediately noted Sally's sallow complexion. Her fingers clutched the arms of the chair and she looked distinctly ill. "You look festive," she said, trying to make her voice sound cheerful.

"I figured I probably wouldn't make it until Christmas and this would be my last chance to wear such a silly outfit."

"I didn't think we should come," Nick said. He hadn't dressed up for the occasion, looking somber in his jeans and a dark green golf shirt. "Sally hasn't felt well since this morning, and—"

"Nicholas, don't you go spreading gloom and doom at Katie's lovely party."

"Is Don here?" Katie asked.

Nick shook his head. He looked like he was about to cry.

"Nicholas, would you be a dear and steer this chair over to that corner over there. I'd like to have a private chat with Katie."

"Aunt Sally," he began, but she held up a hand that made him immediately go silent, and he did as she asked. He turned away, and Seth appeared from nowhere, shoving a beer bottle into his hand. Katie figured he probably needed it. She pulled up a chair. She had a feeling she knew what the topic of this discussion would be.

"Sally, I think you should know that I—"

"Oh, darlin', you don't have to say a word. I had a feeling you'd figured it out," Sally patted Katie's hand and sighed heavily. "What gave me away?"

"Seth told me you used to run the skeet range at the country club. I figured you were probably familiar with and felt comfortable handling guns." Katie shrugged. "But most of all, you love your nephew as if he were your own son. You couldn't stand the thought of him being hurt. And when you found out that Wheeler would be Nick's neighbor—that there was a chance he'd have to face him almost on a daily basis—you knew you had to do something. You knew Nick never would."

"And then earlier this week I found out that the bastard had sold the shop. That he would be out of there before Sassy Sally's ever opened." Sally sighed. "I really did mess things up. But you know, somewhere in my own mind, I still felt like I'd done the right thing." She took a shuddering breath. "Nicholas was not the only student that man publicly humiliated. He never physically abused my darling boy, but his words left lasting scars on him and on many other young men. Thank goodness Nicholas had such a friend as Seth Landers, and Don has been the best thing that ever happened to him."

Voicing the words seemed to have taken a lot out of Sally.

"Wheeler was never punished for what he did. I had to make sure that he would never wound a young boy ever again. Except . . . I learned this morning that it wasn't Wheeler who was in the shop. I'd never met the man, you see. I didn't know what he looked like. The man I confronted told me over and over again that he wasn't Dennis Wheeler, but I figured he was just scared yellah. Turns out, he had a right to be. Oh, Katie, I killed an innocent man. What am I gonna do now?"

Katie looked toward the shop and Davenport's party. She could see Hamilton nodding his big head as he listened to someone speaking. Didn't the man ever smile? But, considering his job, maybe he had little to smile about.

"The lead detective in the case is right over there in that room. Would you like to speak to him?"

"No, but . . . I'll never rest in peace with this terrible secret. I'm just so ashamed. I never wanted Nicholas to think badly of me, and now I've committed the absolute worst crime. I deserve to die. And I have a feeling, it won't be long now."

"Oh, Sally—" Katie began, but once again Sally raised her hand to put an end to the conversation.

"You better go get that detective. Is there somewhere we can go to talk? I don't want this whole gang of people listening to my confession."

"Yes. You can go inside Artisans Alley. The vendors' lounge is far away from the party. You'll have plenty of privacy."

"Then go get that detective so I can get this off my chest," Sally said in a tone that would suffer no defiance.

Katie got up and again threaded her way through the partygoers. She found Hamilton, pointed Sally out, and quickly told him what he no doubt was very happy to hear. He excused himself, and she watched as he, Seth, Nick, and Sally made their way into Artisans Alley, shutting the door behind them.

The holiday music sounded crass, and Katie felt anything but merry.

Davenport was suddenly at Katie's elbow, and handed her a glass of champagne. "Let's party like it's 1999," he said and laughed.

"I didn't know you were a Prince fan."

"I'm not. I've got kids who've listened to the radio since they were babies. Unfortunately, I know all their songs, as well as my own."

"I propose a toast," she said, raising her glass. "To the success of Wood U."

"I'll drink to that," Davenport said, and took a swig.

"And here's hoping your foot heals fast, too," she said and tipped her glass in his direction yet another time.

Davenport drained his glass, and then eyed her critically. "Was there something you wanted to tell me?"

"Yes, but not right now. Right now, let's celebrate. Let's party like it's 1999."

And so they did.

Katie's No-Bake Recipes

PUBLISHER'S NOTE: The recipes contained in this book are to be followed exactly as written. The publisher is not responsible for your specific health or allergy needs that may require medical supervision. The publisher is not responsible for any adverse reactions to the recipes contained in this book.

Peanut Butter Buckeyes

1 jar (18 ounces) creamy peanut butter
½ cup butter, softened
1 pound confectioners' sugar
1 tablespoon vanilla
12 ounces semisweet chocolate chips
2 tablespoons vegetable shortening

Cream the peanut butter and butter. Add the sugar and vanilla and mix well. Form into 1-inch balls and refrigerate. Melt the chocolate chips and shortening in a double boiler or in the microwave. Dip the peanut butter balls into the chocolate with a toothpick until they are about ¾ of the way covered. Place the chocolate side down on waxed paper. Let them set at room temperature or refrigerate.

MAKES ABOUT 5 DOZEN PIECES.

Raspberry Supreme

1 package (3 ounces) raspberry (or your favorite flavored) gelatin
½ cup boiling water
1 cup crushed ice, drained of excess water
fresh or frozen raspberries (or other favorite fruit)

Chill dessert dishes or sherbet or parfait glasses in the refrigerator. Put the gelatin in a blender; add the boiling water. Cover the blender and blend until the gelatin is dissolved. Keep the blender running and slowly add the crushed ice. Blend for about 1 minute, or until the container feels cool. Place several fresh raspberries in chilled dessert dishes or sherbet glasses, pour the gelatin mixture over the raspberries, then garnish with a few fresh raspberries and, if desired, a sprig of fresh mint.

SERVES 4.

Peppermint Patties

3¾ cups confectioners' sugar
3 tablespoons butter, softened
2–3 teaspoons peppermint extract
½ teaspoon vanilla extract
¼ cup evaporated milk
2 cups (12 ounces) semisweet chocolate chips
2 tablespoons shortening

In a large bowl, combine the first four ingredients. Add the evaporated milk and mix well. Roll into 1-inch balls and place on a waxed-paper-lined baking sheet. Flatten the balls with a glass to ¼ inch. Cover and freeze for 30 minutes. In a heavy saucepan or microwave, melt the chocolate chips and shortening; stir until smooth. Dip the patties, allowing the excess to drip off. Place the patties on the waxed paper. Let them stand until set.

MAKES 5 DOZEN PATTIES.

Center Point Large Print
600 Brooks Road / PO Box 1
Thorndike ME 04986-0001 USA

(207) 568-3717

US & Canada:
1 800 929-9108
www.centerpointlargeprint.com